GUN BARREL PLANETS

PLANET SALVATION
THE BEGINNING

BY
PHILLIP TUCKER

www.philliptucker.com.au

ACKNOWLEDGEMENT

To my family and friends. As long as a man has both, he is truly blessed. Thanks to all of you for your support. A special thanks to Steve and Diane, who helped turn an ordinary book, into something special.

COPYRIGHT © PHILLIP TUCKER 2012

CONTENTS

PLANET SALVATION THE BEGINNING

THE YEAR 2052

Simon looked around in awe at the naval graveyard, which surrounded him. The size and difference in age and design of the vessels amazed him, as he stood up to his knees in mud on a small hilltop. Beside him on its side, lay a once mighty warship. Its decks now covered with barnacles from its time on the ocean floor.

"She's a dreadnought class battleship from the First World War." His grandfather Mike called out, as he slowly came up the hill to stand beside him, breathing heavily.

"That makes her roughly about one hundred and fifty years old if she went down between 1910 and 1920," Simon replied, writing down Mike's opinion of her type and age. He would later add this information to his own notes on the ship, along with a brief description to go with his photos.

"Are you enjoying yourself?" Mike asked seriously, watching Simon record every detail of the ship, before looking towards the next one.

"I've never been happier Grandad. Thanks for inviting me." Simon smiled as he studied the remains of a large oil tanker. It lay dejectedly in two pieces, like a thrown away toy. Its back had been broken many years ago when it came to rest on the rear of the battleship that Simon had just catalogued.

"Well just remember son, the shield is only good for another three days, so let's get back to work. And use the hovercycle, walking in this mud takes too long." Mike suggested, as he slowly moved off.

"Hey, you're walking!"

"I'm the boss. When you're the boss, you can take it easy. And call me Mike; you're too old to call me grandad." Mike chuckled, as he walked casually down the hill. Simon watched him until he disappeared from view, feeling heartfelt pride that Mike was his grandfather. Mike Hayes was a legend amongst the people from Earth. He was a real hero to them, even though he never talked about his part in saving the human race.

Taking his advice, Simon walked over and hopped onto his hovercycle, setting the height for twenty metres and letting the machine rise slowly while taking in the view. From this height, he could see the southern end of the shield. As he watched, he saw the slightly opaque coloured shield shimmer, as some unfortunate sea creature impacted with it on the outside. The barrier stretched for ten kilometres from the centre of the dome, making it twenty kilometres across and Simon marvelled at the power and technology that held it in place.

As with many discoveries it had come out of the war, though unlike most, it was purely for defence. During the last war on Earth, it was believed to have saved millions of lives when the holocaust had occurred in what was called the Third World War. Like most wars, religion was at its core. At first, it was a collection of civil disturbances as militant groups tried to implement their beliefs. As it spread over the continents becoming more violent, more and more countries and their military became involved. In the end, it engulfed the world, as battlefields extended over the entire planet.

One side, thinking it was about to be defeated, launched its nuclear arsenal. The other side, seeing it coming, launched as well. Some missiles got through, although, the great majority were destroyed by anti-missiles in the upper atmosphere. Mike at the time had been working on protective shields for defence for the UN. When the poisoning of the atmosphere took place, he broadcasted his discovery to friends and foes alike. This enabled mankind to survive, under the domes of pure energy his shields projected.

The war that had been fought so fanatically was soon forgotten. All of mankind's energy and manpower was now used to try and eradicate the fatal levels of radiation, which were spreading across the globe. Simon knew he'd been born twenty years after that war and that his grandparents and parents had all taken part in perfecting the shield technology. It was that technology, which now held back the ocean that surrounded him.

Simon's parents, Susan and Andy had carried on his grandfather's work. They created shields to protect the huge vessels that travelled through the portals, joining one planet to another. Unfortunately, they'd both disappeared when he was just a baby, navigating an unknown portal. The shield shimmered again, making Simon focus on it. This time it was a much greater impact than the first, indicating a larger creature. 'Maybe a whale or a shark after the first creature' Simon concluded.

Forgetting the past knowing that thinking about it wouldn't help; he got back to the job at hand. His assignment, like the twenty other students Mike had brought along, was to categorise the ships lying on the ocean floor. It was purely for historical reference, to try and work out how the Portal worked and how these ships had passed through it, to arrive predominantly intact, on another planet. Simon's grandfather was a marine biologist and historian. He was also the first person to discover the portal.

At the War's end, the earth had been devastated by radiation. The two hundred million people left had lost all hope, slowly starving to death. Plant life had ceased to grow in the toxic environment and the only thing preventing complete annihilation of the human race, were the shields. They protected about five percent of the planet's land surface and needed huge amounts of power to maintain their integrity. The problem was, the fuel needed to power the shields was almost exhausted.

Mike, with Simon's parents' help, had built a submarine fitted with shields. It was used to recover power units from ships lost during the war. While searching for a lost supply ship, with precious long life uranium fuel rods aboard, Mike's sub, had entered the Atlantic. Searching along the American coast, they had entered an area called the Bermuda triangle. Encountering a fierce storm they had dived to a depth of over a thousand metres, hoping to pass underneath it.

Here his vessel encountered an area of unimaginable tidal riffs. Fortunately, the shield was already deployed, shielding the submarine, as it was sucked into what appeared to be a deep gorge. To everyone's surprise, a sudden calm settled over their vessel, as the sub reached a depth of two thousand metres. At this extreme depth there should have been a tremendous build-up of pressure, Mike noticed it remained amazingly stable. Watching the front nose camera, several crewmembers saw a faint light coming from the bottom of the gorge.

Fascinated, Mike proceeded further into the gorge, trying to find the light's source. It was observed that no matter how deep they went, the outside pressure remained constant. Intrigued they continued to dive when without warning, the sub's navigational equipment failed. With the ship blinded, Mike alarmed, ordered the ship to turn round. Despite every effort to turn the ship, the sub continued on towards the light, in the end approaching the ocean's surface.

Mike like everyone else was convinced they'd already turned and hadn't noticed it. Laughing at their own stupidity they surfaced, to work out their position, as their navigational instruments were still malfunctioning. Looking through the periscope and checking the deck sensors, they discovered a clear sky, devoid of radiation or pollution. As the crew hesitantly stumbled onto the deck wondering what was going on, the navigator, gasping, pointed to the sky. All stood frozen, as they stared at the star-filled sky and more importantly the two moons.

Taking as many readings as possible, the crew worked tirelessly to understand what had occurred. In the end, they decided to reverse their journey, by re-entering the gorge. With great relief, they emerged from the gorge back on Earth. They hoped the scientist at home could explain what had occurred?

Their discovery at first was greeted with scepticism, as when another submarine returned to the gorge, they found nothing. Mike, sure he was right set up an array of instruments to monitor the gorge. It was found that only twice a year for approximately one month, the anomaly, now known as the portal, became active. It took another two years, to discover the other planets, linked from this main planet Mike had discovered. The portal they found worked like an old time revolver.

Six planets were connected to the main planet called Salvation, named by the people of Earth. The six planets were named New America, New Russia, New Europe, New Asia, Southern Ocean and of course Earth. Twice a year for a month the pathway, for want of a better term, would connect to one of these planets. The open portal gave twenty days of safe passage, as either side of these days the tidal forces were too strong to navigate. Hundreds of thousands of brave men and women, desperate to escape the dying planet, earth, lost their lives finding this out, although it allowed mankind to survive.

Over the next twenty years, millions of people passed through the portal, waiting on Salvation, till the portal swung to a planet of their choosing. This allowed them to settle and start a new life, leaving behind the destruction on earth. Salvation was a planet almost entirely covered by water, with only ten percent of land being above sea level. Mike had been given a UN charter to oversee the resettlement and was instrumental in setting up the accommodation on Salvation.

Even though for many years the accommodation was basic, it helped the settlers survived until they moved on to their permanent home planets. As time passed, it was decided that the United Nations Parliament for the six planets, would be constructed on Salvation. It was hoped that by being based on the Portal system's main planet, that it could help govern mankind's future, keeping the peace.

Utilising new clean technologies, food once again became plentiful. Each planet sent what food they could spare, back to earth, through the portal. This helped those still there to survive, and improve their environment. With fewer people, the drain on resources dropped, allowing the use of clean energy to help maintain the shields and gradually repair the damaged atmosphere.

Mike, his wife and Simon's parents, helped to feed the settlers as they waited on Salvation, by starting a fishing industry. At first, it was small only feeding immigrants. Salvation's endless oceans presented a unique opportunity and as time passed the fishing industry grew in size. This helped relieve Earth's situation. Over time a trading system between the six planets, based on Salvation's vast fishing industry, came into being. The migration continued, until with improved condition on Earth, it slowed to a trickle as those left, opted to stay.

After the loss of his son and daughter-in-law, then the death of his wife soon after, Mike retired. Though still on call now and then by the UN, he remained on Salvation, continuing his fascination with the ocean. This had led to many scientific expeditions, like the one Simon was now on.

Moving slowly around the tanker, carefully taking photos from different angles, Simon added them to his notes on the description and length of the vessel. Comparing it to a list of lost ships from earth, he recognised one, which matched, before moving onto the next ship. Mike believed most of these ships had been caught in the opening and closing of the portal. It had sucked them and their unfortunate crews through to this graveyard, where they'd come to rest. It was Simon concluded, the only logical answer, though it didn't explain everything.

South of this location there was another graveyard with the remains of other ships made of alloys not common on earth. Not much was known of these ships as only skeletal remains had been found. Where they'd come from, no one was certain. Their size dwarfed the vessels from Earth. Simon had theorised that there once could have been an indigenous population on this planet. Of course proving it was another matter. In his spare time, which was rare on this expedition, he'd walked around the scattered remains of the ghost ships.

There was something not quite right about these ships, though he couldn't work out what it was. Chances were they had come through the portal like the ships from earth, ending up on the bottom of the ocean. The only thing was they were all cone-shaped, indicating they were all submarines or something similar. Why had only subs been pulled through the portal? If he was right and there had been a population here, could they have discovered the portals and been using them? He knew in time he could solve the mystery; he just didn't have enough evidence at the moment.

Seeing the artificial light start to wane, meaning it was approaching 4 o'clock in the afternoon Simon decided to call it a day. Packing up his equipment, he mounted his hovercycle, heading off. Their sub sat on the bottom, directly in the centre of the shield, projecting the shield out evenly throughout the dome, this made it easy to locate. Of course, it wouldn't have been too hard to find anyway. Jet black and four hundred metres in length, it was typical of the mass-produced transport submarines used to bring people from earth.

Unfortunately, at the moment, all vessels in use were nuclear powered. This type of power generation was universally disliked after the War, but it was needed to supply the massive power requirements, for both the shield and the ship's every day running. When Simon had first come aboard and studied the shield output, he'd noticed an incredible wastage of power by the type of program in use. Going to his computer he had rewritten the program, making sure his new system worked before he told his grandfather.

Mike after studying Simon's new idea had been impressed and made the changes, reducing the power output from maximum to a medium level. Simon had received a well done in return. His thoughts were interrupted as approaching the sub he saw several other hovercycles lining up to enter.

Taking his turn, he entered the ship's hover bay, securing his cycle. Signing aboard in the logbook, he then entered the decontamination block, where everyone had to rinse off the salt water and mud before entering the sub's accommodation area. Going to his room he then had a much-needed hot shower.

Rubbing his chin he realised another shave was overdue, it would be his second that week. It had always amazed him how slow his facial hair grew, as all his friends by now were shaving regularly. 'Late bloomer' Mike had told Simon when he asked him about it.

"Don't worry son. Someday you'll curse having to shave every day, I can assure you." Mike laughed, playfully digging Simon in the ribs.

Examining himself in the mirror Simon was happy to see hair on his chest and thighs if not on his chin. His body, which had always been whippet thin, had muscled up over the last year, giving him an athletic look. At some dances he had attended, he found the opposite sex seemed to like his appearance. Deep down he worried that his family's fame was more the reason for their interest. Changing into his boat clothes, knowing that worrying wouldn't help his chin hair grow, he went to the galley for something to eat.

As Simon entered the galley, he felt the unease, as the group of young students gathered there, watching him while he served himself a meal. It always made him feel alienated the way everyone looked at him. He figured that because of his parents and grandfather, he should somehow be moving mountains or discovering something brilliant. 'Must be a disappointment to see me working in the mud with the rest of them', Simon thought, as he gathered his meal.

Sitting at a vacant table, Simon chewed his food, while silently reading his notes from the day's work. Tonight he knew Mike would be leading another study group on the ship graveyard, and he wanted to be ready. Deep in thought, he didn't notice a young woman take the seat across from him.

"You could try saying hello!" The girl suggested, making him look up.

"I'm sorry I didn't see you." Simon stammered out, tongue-tied looking at her shyly.

"Now that didn't hurt did it?" The young woman replied smiling, looking at Simon, studying him.

"Is there a problem, do I come up to expectations?"

"I was about to tell you, that you've got sauce all over your chin, bighead." The girl replied, moving to another table. Looking around at the others watching, Simon embarrassed got up from his seat and approached the girl.

"I'm sorry it's just that no one really talks to me."

"There's a shock, look what happens when someone does!" She retorted, as slowly a grin spread across her face.

"My name's Simon,"

"Mine's Katherine, but my friends call me Kate. And you've still got sauce on your face."

Sitting down, wiping his chin, Simon asked where she was from and what she was doing here, as his eyes inadvertently studied her well-crafted body. She told him that she was from the first planet discovered called New America, being settled mostly by Americans. She admitted happily that she had competed against more than a thousand other senior students on her world to get on this expedition. This made Simon concentrate on what she was saying and not her body.

"That's amazing I didn't think the test was such a big deal," Simon answered honestly, as Kate looked at him.

"That's your problem, Simon. Everyone here earned their place in the team competing against the best on their home planets. You're here because the test we do is measured against your marks and as yet, no one's got even close." Kate was astonished that he didn't know.

"I thought the test paper to come on this trip, was just my grandad's way of making it hard for me," Simon answered. He remembered how Mike had put the exam in front of him at dinner one night. He'd told him to fill it out if he wanted to go on the expedition.

"Don't you go to University?" Kate asked puzzled?

"Well sometimes, though I've mostly been homeschooled by my grandfather."

"Bloody hell, everyone here is jealous of your marks, and you didn't even know." Kate laughed, explaining how Mike's test paper had become the standard paper for anyone who wanted to join scientific expeditions on Salvation.

"I thought no one talked to me because of my parent's fame," Simon said honestly, liking the way Kate's face lit up when she got excited.

"No, they think if they say something you'll think they're juvenile."

"That's stupid I would respect anyone's opinion on this expedition," Simon assured her, as others within hearing, wandered over to discuss things they had seen.

Simon came of age that night, as the group pulled their chairs into one large table to discuss the day's events, letting their own ideas bounce back and forwards, no longer worried at what others might think. By the time they'd stopped discussing their ideas, they noticed Mike in the doorway. Realising they were all late for the debriefing, they all stood, preparing to move to the conference room. Signalling for them all to sit back down and relax, Mike got himself a cup of coffee.

"We can do the debriefing here." He suggested, settling down to listen.

The conversation tonight was more spirited than any other Mike had seen out of this group so far. The reason he knew was that Simon, at last, was interacting with them, causing ideas to flow freely. Most had come to the same conclusion as Mike, that the portal opening and closing was a natural occurrence. One young man from New Russia had a different slant. He believed the portal was too coordinated to be natural. He'd studied the openings and closings, and believed there was some kind of power surge triggering the portal's operation. He also believed, that at one time there may have been more planets in the system thus explaining the unknown ships.

"Then who built it and why?" Simon asked intrigued by this new train of thought.

"I don't know. Maybe humans in the past had reached a peak in science where they had built it and moved through the portal to another universe." Ivan suggested, not as confident as before.

"What if there's more than one portal system?" Simon asked the group, thinking Ivan might be onto something.

"Well let's all think about it tomorrow, now you all need sleep so you can work in the morning." Mike chuckled, as the group groaning broke up.

Lying in bed, Simon thought about Ivan's concept, wondering if this was what might have happened to his parents, so long ago. Could they have travelled to another planet through the portal and then had the portal lock that planet out? It could mean they were still alive. There was also the young woman tonight named Kate, she too filled his dreams, for different reasons.

THE SECRET

Waking in the morning, his mind teeming with ideas, Simon hurried out ten minutes early to find Mike. He was not in his cabin, so leaving his questions for later, he decided to get on with his assignment. Entering the hovercycle bay, he found Mike there waiting for him.

"Sleep okay?" Mike asked Simon, an unreadable look on his face.

"I kept thinking about what Ivan said. Do you think it's what could have happened to mum and dad?"

"I'm not sure Simon. It might explain their disappearance if they entered a totally new system. No one really knows what happened, so let's concentrate on today. I've got something to show you." Mike whispered, signalling Simon to follow him. Going to the north at high speed, Simon noticed Mike checking behind them consistently, as he headed for a mass of twisted metal to their front. Circling the rusted steel, Mike set his cycle down followed closely by Simon.

"Leave the cycles here we'll walk for a while," Mike said softly, looking around secretively as they approached the twisted remains of an ancient shipwreck, one of the mystery ships. Entering the rusted mud covered hull, Mike climbed deeper into the bowels of the ship. Coming to a barnacle-covered tunnel, which was once a hallway, Mike pulled out two torches from his backpack handing one to him. Simon gathered by the torches that he'd been here before.

"Be careful and watch your step!" Mike warned as they descended a new ladder. Entering a vast cavern, which once had been inside the original hull, they continued.

"What's going on Mike?" Simon asked wondering about the ladder, as Mike pulled up, signalling to Simon to take a break.

"On my last expedition, I discovered an energy reading coming from this ship. When I came down here, I deducted the reading was under this ship, not in it."

"Why the secrecy?" Simon asked softly, looking around as well.

"I'm worried about something that's all, I'll tell you later. For now, this is our secret." Getting a nod of acceptance from Simon, the two of them moved on. Climbing down several more improvised ladders, they, at last, came to the bottom of the external hull. It was clear Mike had cut through what was left of the hull with a laser on a previous trip. Cleaning away the mud, Simon stared at a glass-like surface, showing a control room of some sorts inside.

The consoles were of a type Simon had never seen before; some seemed to work by projecting multiple screens above the user's workstation, giving a 3D effect to the information being displayed. Simon knew that they were light years ahead of the system used by the Human race at the moment that was for sure. So engrossed was Simon on the control, it took him a while to concentrate on the glass surface they were on. He saw that it had two layers, the outer one pulsing.

"My God, it's one of our shields!" Simon shouted, shocked to his core by finding one under a ship that had been here for hundreds, if not thousands of years.

"No, but it's similar," Mike replied, a small smile on his lips.

"But how is that possible?" Simon babbled, his mind trying to fathom out this development.

"I'm not sure but the technology and power signature, are significantly different to ours."

"Could it have something to do with my parents' sub's disappearance?'

"I know they disappeared in this area that's all. They communicated with our base that they had found something important about the portals, that's all I know. This vessel, if it is a vessel, was buried long before your parents venture here. If there is a connection, I can assure you I'll find out what it is." Placing his hand on Simon's shoulder, Mike comforted him, as they both stood there silently, pondering what this control room meant.

What are you going to do with it?" Simon asked, breaking the silence, his eyes never leaving the shield.

"We'll finish the expedition, then allow some time to go pass. When it's safe, we'll come back here and salvage this thing. For now, it must remain our secret." Mike whispered as they headed up the stairs dismantling the ladders as they went. Coming out of the huge rusted vessel, Mike buried the ladders in the mud, totally covering them. He then silently checked the area, making sure they weren't being watched. Seeing no one, they moved off to complete their work, recording and photographing the ships on the bottom of the ocean.

Arriving back at the sub, Simon found Kate and several other students cleaning off their hovercycles, before getting out of their protective suits and boots.

"How'd you go?" Kate asked Simon, as they walked to the decontamination area, dressed only in their tee shirts and underwear. Simon's eyes kept wandering to Kate's body, as he tried to concentrate on answering.

"Good, I managed to complete several areas on the grid," Simon replied happily trying not to look at the outline of her breast, as they stood face to face.

"Did Mike go with you?"

"Yeah, he wanted to discuss how I was going and keep an eye on me as well I suppose," Simon answered, his heart hammering in his chest.

"Which sector did you work in?" Kate shot back, as Simon hesitated, seeing her in a different light. He wondered if she was deliberately using her body to confuse him.

"The one I was assigned. Why are you so interested?"

"No reason. Just wanted to know what you two were up to that's all." She smiled, turning away and entering the female side of the block. Simon watched her go; intrigued by the sway of her body and the interrogation she'd given him. Maybe 'I'm just getting jumping' he thought, but the questioning somehow worried him.

Clean and changed, Simon met the other students for dinner, repeating the nights, as they went over today's discoveries, preparing for tonight's study group.

"Simon, can you report to the Captain's cabin!" Crackled over the intercom, interrupting Ivan's analysis of an old wreck he'd found. Simon excusing himself left.

"Sorry to disturb you, Simon. I thought we should have a talk." Mike said as he closed the cabin's door locking it.

"What's the problem?" Simon asked looking at the door, as at home they never locked doors.

"Everything here is not as it seems son!" Mike murmured as they both sat down. Mike without another word turned on a wall monitor. The recording, showed Kate talking to Simon outside the decontamination block before she entered.

"What's going on? Why are you watching the crew and me?"

"Keep watching Simon, I'll explain in a minute." Mike raised his hand stopping any more questions, as Simon watched the screen. Seeing himself entering the male rinse area; he saw Kate reappear moments later, watching the door he'd entered. He was just about to say something when Mathew, another student from New America, appeared on the screen.

"Did you find out what they're up to and where they went?" Mathew asked Kate, grabbing her by the arm. Moving away from him, breaking his grip, Kate answered.

"He said he was just working with Mike in the survey area and don't touch me again."

"Do you believe him?" Mathew asked, ignoring her protest.

"No. Simon and his grandfather are up to something?" Kate said softly to Mathew, watching the hallway.

"Get closer to him. Sleep with him if you have to, but find out what they're up to!" Mathew ordered her, storming off. Kate stood there looking downcast for several seconds, before moving away. Simon was just about to comment when Ivan appeared around the corner on the screen, he had apparently been listening, as the video feed ended. Silence settled on Mike's cabin as they both sat quietly thinking about the video.

"I thought this nonsense was behind us Mike, now everyone had a separate planet of their choosing."

"You can't change human nature, even though in the last war America and Russia were on the same side, there has never been much love lost between them," Mike replied he was upset that even after the near destruction of mankind, man still hadn't learned.

"Is this why you're keeping the object from the others?" Simon asked quietly, understanding his grandfather's concern.

"Yes, son. The technology we might find on that vessel could give one planet the edge over the others. We can't allow any planet to dominate the other worlds."

"But Salvation controls the portal to all planets and the UN is based here!" Simon pointed out.

"Yes it is, but its forces are mostly for policing the portals, and none of their ships are armed with heavy weapons. We didn't think it would be necessary." Mike felt a fool for never contemplating that old rivalries, might resurface.

"Do you think they know about the ship?"

"They might have a suspicion that I was onto something by returning to the same location. Mind you, I only overlapped a small area to include the ancient ship."

"Or someone saw the power reading on the ship's instruments on the last expedition?"

"You could be right son; the crew is made up of UN personnel recruited from the six planets. There could have been a spy on board?" Mike answered before shaking himself and standing up, grinning. "We're getting as bad as the rest of them. When we come back, it will be with our own crew, we'll worry about the others then." Mike put it behind him.

"What will I do about Kate and the others?"

"They're most probably only doing what they think is right for their planets. Just be careful Simon and let's see how close Kate gets!" Mike chuckled as Simon blushed, making his grandfather burst into laughter.

Walking back to the galley, Simon's mind whirled at having Kate closer. She was a stunning looking girl and smart, but also it appeared untrustworthy. Simon who would be eighteen next month had to admit he'd had little or no experience with the opposite sex. Except for the odd quick kiss or a quick grope at dances he had attended occasionally, he'd never really had the time to seduce a woman. He was up on biology and reproduction from school, and Mike's father and son talks had helped.

The problem was, he sadly lacked experience having been too busy studying. Sitting there apprehensively he wondered how he might perform, getting more nervous by the minute. In the end, he walked back to his room, having a cold shower, trying to calm his rising tension.

During the group meeting that night, Kate had sat right next to Simon, the proximity causing his skin to tingle. He had to admit he liked what he was feeling. The meeting, as usual, was intense, with a great deal of time spent on Ivan's theory of the portals being man-made. Simon contributed to the general discussion, but Kate's presence became a constant distraction as he tried to concentrate on the subject. After the group broke up for the night, Kate walked quietly beside Simon, back to his cabin.

Stopping at his doorway, a silence developed between them until Simon leaned forward, kissing her on the lips. At first, they kissed hesitantly, then more aggressively. Simon's hands glided over Kate's firm curves, his body was physically closer than he could be with another person and his desire to meld with her spiralled out of control. Suddenly to his surprise, Kate broke away, trying to catch her breath.

"I can't do this Simon." She cried, tears in her eyes as she ran off down the passageway, leaving Simon staring after her.

'Was I that bad at kissing?' Simon asked himself disappointedly. Opening his door, wondering if his heart would ever stop hammering, he turned in for the night. Laying alone in the dark, Simon wondered what drove Kate to abandon that moment. Unable to sleep he spent most of the night thinking about her and that kiss.

ABANDONED

The next day was the final day of cataloguing the graveyard. Everyone was warned to be back before 1500 hrs, as the shield would start to collapse at around 1600hrs. Being slightly behind in his assignment, Simon headed out early, hoping to achieve all his objectives before they had to leave the area. Completing his work ahead of time, he was just about to start back, when he saw a hovercycle coming from the north. That was the area where Mike had discovered the shielded craft. Having a couple of hours to spare, Simon drove at speed towards the ancient ship.

Arriving at the wreck, he stopped his cycle and cautiously looked around. Hidden beside a pile of barnacle-covered metal, Simon spotted a hovercycle. Descending slowly, Simon turned off his cycle, leaving it next to the other cycle. Following a set of footprints in the mud, Simon entered the same hole that Mike had shown him yesterday.

Cautiously moving further into the ship, he came to the barnacle lined tunnel. Pausing at the entrance, hearing nothing, he warily moved inside into the darkness, where he was struck from behind. Falling into the dried mud, Simon saw a pair of feet stop in front of him before he blacked out.

Coming to, Simon tried to get to his feet. Dizzy, he collapsed back into the wet mud, his head pounding. Trying to orientate himself he got into the sitting position wondering what had happened. The cold water trickling around his feet, not only revived him; it sent a warning to his slowly recovering brain. 'The Shield is coming down!' it screamed. Forcing himself to his feet, Simon staggered back through the vessel, as seawater rushed in; flowing into the area he'd just left.

Running unsteadily through the ankle deep water, he reached his cycle. Quickly mounting he activated the machine, 'nothing happened'. Splashing water on his face he looked at the console seeing someone had removed the control circuit from the main board.

"Shit" Simon screamed as he sat looking at the cycle, wondering why he had sworn. It hadn't improved his predicament, but he had to admit he felt better. Pulling the side panels off the cycle revealed the circuitry boards and the hydrogen power cells. These cells powered the air cushions allowing up and down hovering, and forward propulsion. Grabbing a small tool kit from his pocket, Simon modified the wiring to allow at least the hover mode to function, as the water reached his waist.

Setting it for roughly the same height their sub would rise to when the shield came down, Simon mounted the cycle as he joined the wires together. Rocketing up to the designated height Simon was nearly thrown from the cycle as it shuddered to a backbreaking halt, at the preset height.

"Well that worked, what do I do now?" Simon said out loud, as below him water slowly rose up the side of the ships returning them to their graves. Finally coming up with an idea, Simon reached back behind his seat and unscrewed the refill section of the hydrogen cells. Letting the pressurised hydrogen escape from the back, would propel him forward, so this gave him propulsion. It had two potential side effects.

One, the hydrogen might explode, on the hover section of the engine. Two, he would quickly run out of fuel. Having no choice, he opened it. With a loud whoosh, the bike shot forward, as Simon used his body position to steer the cycle towards the submarine's location. Trying to calculate the fuel remaining, Simon rocketed forward, barely in control of the flying bomb.

"Shit I'm going to miss!" Simon screamed in frustration, as the sub rapidly came into view ahead and to the right of his course. "What do I do now?" Simon groaned as water started to lap against the underside of his cycle. Coming parallel to the sub he realised there was only one thing to do, as he awkwardly jumped from his cycle, tumbling into the cold seawater. Coming to the surface, spitting out a mouthful of water and coughing up the rest, Simon swam frantically towards the sub.

To his relief, he found that because the water was approaching the narrower top of the shield, it was less turbulent, allowing him to swim freely. The two hundred metres to the sub took nearly twenty minutes to swim as Simon exhausted grabbed hold of the side of the sub. Holding on breathing heavily, another problem arose. How did he get inside?

The hovercycle entrance was on the underside of the sub in a large bay area. As it was now submerged below the waterline, it would be locked up tight. The only alternative Simon could think of was to use one of the escape hatches on the top deck. These were used when a vessel was in trouble, and a small rescue submersible could dock onto one of the hatches, allowing an airtight seal. This could then be used, to gain access through an airlock, to the sub. Simon, of course, didn't have a submersible, so he had to get there before the rapidly rising water.

Scrambling up the side, cutting himself several times on his legs and hands on barnacles, Simon rushed the last twenty metres reaching the hatch as water started running down the deck towards him. Unscrewing the hatch, Simon jumped down into the airlock, pulling the external hatch closed behind him, just as water gushed in behind. Twisting the handle frantically, Simon managed to stop the seawater flowing in through the hatch. Collapsing onto the bottom of the chamber thoroughly exhausted and waist deep in seawater, he starting to get the shakes his adrenalin rush, faded.

After several minutes, his breathing returned to normal, and the shaking stopped; he knew he'd made it. Feeling better, he used a small pump installed in the airlock, to empty the seawater out, before cautiously opening the internal door. Making sure no one saw him; he climbed out and quickly closed the hatch. Reaching his cabin without being seen he took off his wet clothing changing, before bandaging his legs and arms. Presentable, he then walked to the shower block, showering. Finished, he hurried to his grandfather's cabin.

Entering in a rush, he swiftly locked the door. Mike surprised and worried by Simon's swift entry, tried to calm him down enough to hear his story. In shock, Simon blurted out what had happened, going from nervousness to anger then back again, as Mike sat quietly hearing him out, thinking about what to do.

"I can't believe no one noticed I was missing!" Simon exclaimed tears in his eyes, wondering why Mike hadn't checked that he had returned.

"You weren't missing son!" Mike answered, getting up and pacing back and forth across the cabin before explaining. "When the shield started to weaken, I checked the computer logs, confirming that all personnel were on board. You like everyone else had returned and signed on. Obviously whoever hit you had no intention of letting you survive." Mike admitted sounding more than a little scared, at the near loss of his only grandchild.

"What do we do now?" Simon asked, trying to come to grips with the idea that they had a murderer on board.

"Nothing, we act like everything is normal. We'll see who reacts when you walk into the galley." Mike suggested, changing the screen to show the galley area. That night at dinnertime, Simon walked in and helped himself to some stew, being as casual as possible, sitting down and eating. He said hello to the gathering of students. Observing no unusual reactions to his presence, Simon retired early, complaining of a headache.

Kate and several others were not present, and Simon secretly hoped that she wasn't involved in this mess. The rest of the night passed without incident, and the following day the sub sailed back to its base in New Vancouver, without further incident.

NEW VANCOUVER

Making landfall, the students disembarked, heading for their individual compounds here at the UN's main port. Because the opening of the portal for every planet happened twice a year for twenty days, all planets kept a permanent base here on Salvation. Salvation's capital, Geneva was ten miles inland, though all accommodation was located next to the sea, at New Vancouver. Each compound covered more than ten square miles, and each had a port facility, making them all, a country unto themselves. The planet's compounds, sat in the order that the portal opened.

Earth was first, followed by New America. Next was New Russia, then New Asia, followed by New Europe and finally the Southern Ocean planet. The Southern planet was made up of all the people who for different reasons wanted a fresh start, devoid of Earth's political systems. They still maintained a navy but were neutral, having nothing to do with the other planets. Because all the portals came out below the sea level on each planet, underwater maritime travel was the main means of transport.

Mike's place, where Simon lived, was on the coast south of New Vancouver. He'd purchased the land to set up his commercial fishing industry based around a large harbour located there. Bordering the harbour, he'd set up a small town where Mike, his family and a large group of friends and employees lived peacefully. Most like Mike didn't want to live in the hustle and bustle of the city to their north, preferring the less hectic lifestyle of their small harbour.

On land, transport was based on a squat version of the hovercycle. It could travel over cleared flat land and needed no roads, leaving no environmental footprint. It was much larger, allowing for 4 occupants to sit comfortably out of the weather. Driving it was similar to an old Earth car, Mike had told him, though for some reason different planets had the steering on different sides. When Simon pointed out how silly this was, suggesting making one model would be more cost effective Mike had just laughed.

"Good luck with that one son. Vehicles have always been considered special to different countries on Earth. Changing which side they steered on, would be unacceptable to even the most easy-going planets." His grandfather pointed out, leaving Simon mystified.

The trip home was mostly made in silence. Mike was absorbed in planning the coming expedition. Simon, on the other hand, sat quietly reliving his near-death experience, at the ancient wreck. It was in the past now, but for some reason, he kept having flashbacks. Arriving at their home, both men went inside unpacking their gear, each working through their own problems. Simon finished, went for a quiet walk down to the harbour to clear his head.

Reaching the water's edge and feeling better, he sat down, watching children fishing from a small jetty. Their laughter and chatting reminded him of carefree times from his childhood He too had fished many times from this wharf over the years with Mike and his friends enjoying their companionship. To his left was a small-protected inlet, containing a collection of sailing ships.

Most had been brought from Earth in the hulls of submarines. Unlike Earth, sailing hadn't really caught on here, as with only a small landmass, the sea's swells could be massive, making sailing out at sea risky. Further out in the harbour at anchor were several large ships of the fishing fleet. They were surface ships not submarines like most of the Gun barrel planets ships.

Looking across the bay, he could see the Salvation docks, where the ships had been purpose built. Dwarfing the shipyards were the massive fish canning factories. These Mike had slowly built up over the years, providing the much-needed food requirements of Earth. Except for those two facilities, the skyline around the bay was only lined with houses and trees. There was a small shopping centre and hotel, halfway around the bay from where Simon stood.

Keeping a natural balance, they'd been constructed behind a vast forest to conceal their outline. Power stations and the Water and Sewage pumping systems were all underground leaving the landscape clean. Mike had been instrumental in convincing the UN to make all factories and fishing fleets on Salvation run on hydrogen, to cut down on pollution. Mankind had finally learnt to preserve his environment.

Even the newest passenger and transport submarines ran on hydrogen, although military vessels were all still nuclear. Simon and many other scientists wanted to change this by working on reducing the power required for shields and weapons. They'd had some success, but not enough to convince the military to give up a reliable power source.

In the past when he felt depressed, coming down to the jetty had lifted his spirits. He enjoyed watching the busy harbour and its people who had travelled here from Earth, to give themselves a second chance at life. Now as he sat watching the harbour, his happiness at being back deserted him, leaving him confused. His near death experience being left to drown made him doubt if mankind's vision of everlasting peace would succeed.

Someone had tried to kill him for no reason. He had no idea who it was, and that was what riled him. Whoever it was, had without hesitation left him to drown, then covered it up by signing him in. He was troubled by the possibility that he may still be perceived as a threat and be at risk of another attempt on his life. Since that night he'd had several vivid dreams of being trapped having failed to make it into the sub. The dreams left him bathed in sweat shaking like a leaf in the wind. He thought about telling Mike of his fears but had instead kept it to himself, not wanting to worry him as well.

Looking out to sea feeling disheartened, he snapped out of his speculation as a sub breached the surface, steaming towards him. Getting up, he watched as the sub manoeuvred through the moored vessels steering towards the jetty. What surprised him was its size. It was small compared to the submarines in use these days. As it came closer, Simon realised that it was similar to the one Mike had commanded when he first found the portal. Nosing into the dock, he saw a name written on its bow. 'Penelope' it read. That was Simon's grandmother's name, which meant it was Mike's first submarine, transferred through the portal from Earth. The walk home was a jumble of confused thoughts, as he speculated on the presence of the sub.

At dinner that night Simon mentioned the sub, wondering what it's presence meant.

"After your trouble on the expedition, I brought the trip forward, we leave in two days."

"Is that your sub from Earth, that you found the portal with?"

"Yes, the Penelope a fine sub though a lot smaller than the subs today. Its advantage is that it needs only a small crew."

"Why'd you name it after grandmother?"

"It was a different time than Simon, we use to name our ships for luck, not just give them numbers like today," Mike replied chuckling.

"Why don't we do that now?"

"We lost so many ships passing through the portals that it became bad luck I'm afraid," Mike answered as they both thought about Simon's parents.

"Well, I'm glad you named this one after grandmother. It makes it more family somehow."

"Yes, it does." Mike smiled. "Anyway be ready to leave at a moment's notice. I've rounded up a crew made up of trusted friends this time. As soon as they all arrive, we'll set sail." Mike's excitement was contagious, as they both hurried off to prepare.

Over the next two days, Simon helped prepare the sub. Mike had assigned him another problem to solve, how to lift the object from the bottom. It took him most of that time to just come up with an idea, let alone a solution. On the second night, as they moved onboard, Mike broached the subject, asking what he had come up with.

"Did you think of anything?" Simon asked.

"Maybe, but let's hear yours first."

"I thought we could use a small sonic charge to clear away the ancient wreck, then by getting our submarine right next to the object, we enclose it in our shield. Then it's just a matter of carrying it back to port resting on the shield's inside wall." Simon said distantly as he visualised the task.

"That is brilliant son, I never thought of using the shield to carry it!"

"What was your plan?"

"I couldn't think of anything. Mind you, I knew you'd come up with something." Mike replied, chuckling at the look on Simon's face.

"Do you trust my judgement that much?"

"Of course I do Simon. When you came on the expedition, I already knew you had brains. The day you came to me and casually told me about the power loss on the reactor, I knew you had inherited your father's ability to solve problems. I'd been working on the power problem for over four months, and you saw it straight away, that's a rare gift."

"It just seemed a better way of doing it."

"Well, just keep it up son; we need more of those types of solutions if we're going to pull this little trip off," Mike replied, giving Simon a pat on the shoulder, before sending him off to load more equipment.

THE SALVAGE MISSION

Having worked all night preparing the submersible for departure, Simon slept until 10:00am. Waking, focusing, he stared sleepily around in his small cabin. Touching the wall beside his bed and feeling the slight vibration passing through the hull, Simon guessed that the sub was underway. Grabbing his towel and toothbrush, Simon slowly walked down the passageway to the shower block. There were no private showers or rooms on this sub; everyone had to share, unlike the expedition's colossal submarine.

Wandering back to his cabin, Simon found someone else's gear had been stacked on the spare bunk. Simon at first had thought he'd got lucky having a cabin to himself, this meant he had even less space to work in. Dressing quickly, wondering whom his bunkmate would be, Simon headed to Mike's cabin. Being the Captain allowed Mike one special perk, he didn't have to share his room.

Simon thought he'd be able to study the problem of lifting the object from the bottom here, without interruptions from his new companion. Tapping on the door, Simon waited before he heard Mike yell come in.

"How are you settling in?" Mike asked a grin on his face.

"Okay I suppose, but I noticed someone's bags on the spare bunk, it's going to make it hard to study."

"I bet it will!" Mike replied chuckling.

"What's so funny?"

"You'll see in a while. In the meantime what's up?"

"With sharing the cabin, I wonder if I could work on my salvaging plan here."

"Good idea, I only sleep here anyway. Most of the time, I'll be at the command centre, using my computer there. Just leave room for me to sleep okay?" Mike replied, before leaving.

The salvage operation was a lot more complicated to work out than Simon first thought. To be safe, wanting no mistakes, he would calculate the lifts requirements then have the computer check them over twice, to see if they were correct.

Unfortunately, this computer was an older type and couldn't communicate verbally. It only had typing keys, which made the whole operation slow. Looking at the time monitor on the computer, Simon noticed it was nearly 6 in the evening.

His stomach becoming aware of the time grumbled, reminding Simon he hadn't eaten all day. Packing up, he quickly walked back to his cabin hoping to meet his roomy, praying he didn't snore. Finding no one, he headed for the galley.

Grabbing a tray, he piled on what appeared to be stew, before looking for a seat in the crowded little room. Most of the people here were friends or workmates of Mike and well known to Simon, so he said hello to the group, as he sat down. Most asked how he was enjoying the small sub smiling secretly, some chuckling. Simon not understanding wondered what they were getting at. Chewing his food slowly Simon's mind drifted back to his salvage plan as he slowly went over it again in his head.

"Are you going to say hello this time?" A familiar voice said pleasantly, as Simon looked up and started choking on his food.

"Kate, what are you doing here?" Simon replied, clearing his throat and swallowing the food from his mouth, as the people around him laughed.

"Couldn't let you have all the fun," Kate said smiling at Simon's reaction, as the room full of smiling people watched Simon's discomfort at Kate's appearance.

"I thought you went home?"

"That's not how the portals work my friend. I've got two more months to go before my home planet's portal opens, and the compound isn't much fun!" Kate replied smiling, watching Simon's reaction closely, after her embarrassing moment with him outside his room on the sub.

"How'd you get on board?"

"I told Mike if he didn't let me go, I'd tell my superiors about the thing on the ocean floor," Kate answered mischievously.

"How did you know?" Simon shouted angrily.

The room went silent at Simon's outburst. Kate stood frozen unable to comprehend the sudden outburst of anger.

"What's wrong Simon, why are you so upset?" Kate softly asked she could see he was having trouble breathing.

"Someone tried to kill me on the last expedition. They left me to die near the object." Simon sobbed, sounding close to breaking. Looking around the room, Simon had trouble catching his breath, as sweat cascaded down his face. Staggering to his feet, he inadvertently upended his food tray, sending it crashing to the floor. Completely confused, he rushed from the room as the noise of the people behind him erupted, all wanting answers.

With Simon's departure, all eyes turned to Kate. Most were upset, demanding to know what was going on. Murder was something these people only remembered from their past on Earth. Salvation was not without crime, though people rarely died as a result of crime. Someone deliberately trying to kill another person hadn't occurred for years. Many of the people gathered in the galley felt a sense of foreboding with the mission, as if something sinister awaited them. John Brendan, the sub's second in command, raised his hands, silencing the crew, signalling for Kate to reply.

"I don't know what to tell you, its news to me," Kate answered defensively, knowing the high regard Mike and Simon were held in by these people.

"Might be best if everyone sits down and I'll explain," Mike suggested as he entered the room, having heard Simon's outburst from the opposite doorway. After an hour Mike had filled them all in on what he knew had happened to Simon and the object.

"Wouldn't it be better not to touch this unknown machine?" One of the crew asked, getting support from many others.

"If only we could my friends, but Kate knows about it and you can bet others do as well." Mike pointed out.

"Can you add anything Kate?" John asked he'd been watching Kate closely.

"I don't know if the other worlds know. Mine knows something is down there, I was told to try and find out, although I wasn't involved in any part of hurting Simon!" Kate declared her voice shaking with emotion.

"I know you wouldn't Kate," Mike said patting her on the shoulder before continuing. "I'm sorry friends that I kept the attack on Simon from you. But salvaging the object now is critical, we can't let any of the planets advance their technology far beyond the others. We all know from the past what happens when one race thinks its superior to another!" Mike reminded them.

"We're all with you Mike you know that. Someone trying to murder Simon has shocked all of us. I think we should take precautions in case the threat still exists, we may all be in danger." John put forward.

"Okay from now on we'll run with shields on. It will slow us down a bit, though we'll be a lot safer and I hate to say it, I'll activate our weapon systems." Mike replied sadly. With an agreement from the crew, the meeting broke up.

Simon sat on his bed his hands shaking. The release of his pent-up emotions, from post-traumatic shock, had rolled over him, leaving him exhausted. He'd convinced himself that the incident was behind him; tonight's events demonstrated this was not the case. When Kate had joked about the object, it was as if someone had grabbed his lungs stopping him from breathing. He made a complete fool of himself, running from the galley as if a demon was after him. He'd totally lost it.

Looking down at his hands he saw the shaking had stopped. Getting to his feet, he changed out of his sweat-drenched clothes, before lying back down. A tap at the door made him pull himself together, as he told whoever it was to enter.

"How are you going son?" Mike asked as he and Kate entered the cabin, both sitting down on the spare bed.

"I think I'm okay now, I just don't know what happened. One minute I was okay, the next I lost it."

"You been through a lot son, I should have known it would catch up with you."

"I didn't know about the attack Simon, all I knew is something was on the bottom," Kate said honestly, her eyes misty as she tried not to cry.

"Let's forget about it shall we and I'm sorry for accusing you." Simon smiled, feeling better.

"Anyway we're safe on this sub, so let's gets some sleep, tomorrows another day," Mike reassured him, getting up to leave.

"I didn't get to find out who's sharing this cabin!"

"That's me!" Kate giggled, as Mike roared with laughter at the look on Simon's face, before leaving. Several thoughts went through Simon's head as he sat there silently working through this new revelation.

"But you're a young woman!"

"Have you only just noticed? That aside, this is the last bunk in this little vessel, so we'll just have to manage."

"What about getting changed?"

"We'll hang a sheet across the middle of the room; it will give us some privacy," Kate informed him, a small smile on her lips. Grabbing one of the spare blankets from a storage cupboard, she connected it to hooks on the walls, there for that very purpose. The room grew deadly quiet as the two of them settled in for the night. Turning off the light Simon lay there in the dark listening to the rustling of clothing, his imagination running wild.

"Good night Kate," Simon said nervously his voice-cracking coming out as a croak.

"Good night Simon," Kate replied her voice tantalising him, as he settled down for a long lonely night.

Knocking on Mike's door and getting no answer, Simon entered. After a quick stretch, he got down to work, calculating the energy needed to lift the object. With his new bunkmate making his sleep restless, to say the least, he looked forward to concentrating on this project. His idea of carrying the object inside the shield proved more difficult than he first thought as he ran through his calculation double checking his answers.

The grumbling of his stomach made him look up from the computer.

It was way past lunchtime he realised having been hard at it for over four hours. Simon deciding on a quick snack got up to leave, to see Mike standing at the door, with two plates full of food.

"Thought you'd be here, so I brought you something to eat," Mike smiled, looking over Simon's shoulder at the screen.

"I should've thought to bring a computer from home, this one's a dinosaur compared to the new self-educating models."

"That computer might be twenty years old, but it designed the shields we have now son. I wouldn't say it was useless!" Mike answered. He knew computer technology hadn't changed that much since the war.

"I suppose you're right, but it's not communicating with me, makes it slower for me to check information," Simon replied checking his calculations, while he ate his meal.

"How'd you sleep?" Mike asked neutrally changing the subject.

"Okay, although your surprise was a bit of a shock."

"Yes, it was worth it, to see your face son." Mike chuckled.

"It should be okay with the screen in place, it gives us both some privacy, even though it's a little cramped." Simon knew space was a premium on a sub.

"Well if it doesn't work out, you could move in here, but space is tight here as well."

"We'll see how we go, but I've got to admit, at least she doesn't snore like you do," Simon replied grinning, as Mike hurled a pillow at his head.

THE SECRETS OUT

Three nights on, while everyone slept, the sub arrived at its destination above the ancient ship. Mike, who was on watch, studied the vessel on the radar screen, comparing it to the image from their last visit. His eyes grew wide, focusing on the differences. Grabbing his microphone, he pushed Simon's cabin number and called him. Simon hearing the phone squawk, jumped from his bed in his underwear as Kate in similar dress grabbed the phone as well. Simon being slightly closer reached it first, picking it up and answering.

"Simon here, what's the problem?" He asked, knowing he was being rung for a reason. As he waited for Mike to answer, he focused on Kate standing in the half-light beside him, taking in her dress. She was wearing a thin silk-like shirt, which barely covered her thighs. Simon realised that she wore nothing underneath it. He, in turn, became aware that except for his small jockey shorts he was naked as well.

"Can you come up to the bridge immediately?" Mike's voice echoed through the phone, as Simon stood staring at Kate, as she stared back at him. "Did you hear me, Simon?"

"Yes, I'll be right there." He stammered out. Replacing the phone, he continued to stare at Kate. 'All I have to do is pull her to me' Simon told himself, wanting her, as he felt the start of arousal. This broke his concentration. Coming out of his trance, he moved behind the screen.

"Mike wants me on the bridge, do you want to come?" Both reached for their clothing.

"Okay," Kate replied softly, dressing quickly.

Hurrying forward to the bridge, Simon tried to clear his head, but Kate kept appearing in his mind. 'Why did she just stand there looking at him, instead of covering herself?' He knew he wanted her, but did she want him? Calming himself, he knew the movement had passed as they reached the bridge. Entering the control room or bridge, as the navy call it, Simon went immediately over to Mike, who showed him the readings.

"That can't be right, can it?" Kate said to Simon, looking at the picture a puzzled look on her face.

"What is it, Kate!" Simon asked.

"It just looks like someone has already blown it up!" Kate job was to help with the demolition.

"You're right Kate. At first, I thought it might have been caused when we dropped the shield the last time. Someone's beaten us to it!" Mike sounding worried.

"But the energy reading is still there!" Simon informed him, as they watched the power readings on the outside sensor array, trying to make sense of it.

"I don't understand, if they went to the trouble of clearing away the ship on top, why didn't they remove the object?" Mike asked, talking more to himself, than the others.

"Take a look at the radar image 500 metres to the north, is that wreckage new?" Kate asked.

"You're right again Kate. It's huge; I'd say a submarine and far bigger than this one." Mike replied, lost in thought staring at the screen.

"It would appear others know the location of the object and one of them was sunk trying to reach it," Simon admitted, studying the radar image of the submarine.

"But what happened?" Kate replied nervously.

"I'm not sure Kate, best we wait until morning, then we'll be able to see a lot better," Mike replied as they all returned to their beds to ponder what had happened.

The next morning bright and early, the whole crew of eighty gathered at the bridge or in the hallways leading to it, to find out what was going on. Going over the radar images and comparing them to the camera screen picture of the wreckage, Mike and Simon came to the same conclusion.

"It would appear she was hit by a powerful laser blast!" Mike informed them, as the crew silently and with a great deal of unease, took in this information.

"Surely she would've had her shields up" Simon replied studying the live pictures.

"I'm not sure either son, but I suggest we deploy our shield to enclose the wreckage and the object, that way we may find out what happened here," Mike ordered. As the crew broke up, going to their stations. Kate remained with Simon studying the screen. Amazed she watched the ocean water being forced back by the expanding shield, as it slowly spread across the ocean floor.

"It's amazing to watch how these shields work!" Kate said, working out the water pressure that shield was holding back.

"Yes its certainly impressive, Mike told me when they first used to do this, the shield was deployed, and then the water had to be pumped out using a pipe under the shield" Simon replied distantly, still watching the wreckage.

"It must have taken ages to do that," Kate said before catching her breath. "No!" She screamed, her face going as white as chalk, as she stared at the monitor. Simon seeing her reaction looked as well. At first, he couldn't see what had upset her, but as the water receded, a clear shot of the sub's bow showed the American flag.

"I'm sorry Kate!"

"I don't understand, what were they doing here?" Kate asked her voice full of grief.

"They must have come for the object?" Mike replied, coming up beside them.

"How did this happen? I know my people, they would've been careful. I can't believe someone got that close without them deploying their shields." Kate moaned.

"Kate I've studied the wreckage and compared it to wartime photos. It's my guess that the laser was fired inside the shield!" Mike explained.

"Do you think they had a saboteur on board?" Simon replied thinking it a remote possibility, as the ship was from their home planet.

"We won't know until we get aboard her, with luck the computer memory can be salvaged. That will be where we start." Mike suggested as the crew prepared to disembark.

Once the shield was in place, Simon, Mike and Kate boarded their hovercycles and followed five other crewmembers to the sub wreckage. Entering through a huge hole in the side, a feeling of horror gripped everyone, as they went deeper into the destroyed sub. Simon upon boarding started for the bridge section, accompanied by Kate. Unlike other transport subs, this one although the same design had not been built for moving cargo or people. This was a military ship, carrying massive firepower and several hundred soldiers, by the bunks and cabins they'd passed.

"What was a warship doing here on Salvation, Kate?" Simon asked as he stopped to rest, wondering if she would tell him.

"Simon every planet has naval forces here on Salvation, no one trusts anybody!" Kate answered distantly as she looked about, wondering why there were no bodies surely sea creatures weren't that swift or hungry.

"I thought everyone was happy, now they had their own planets."

"Look, Simon, you live here linked to Earth and the other five planets, while our world has only access to this planet twice a year. Salvation is the key to the portal system; we're just worried one of the other planets might try to take control here, stopping us from having access." Kate said honestly.

"But the UN controls this planet, why not just support it!" Simon asked not understanding the situation.

"The UN is made up of the six planets, plus Salvation; they hardly agree on anything and do even less," Kate replied angrily, as Simon studying Kate seeing a flaw in his friend.

"As long as your planets' leaders think that way, it will continue!"

"You're dead right, Simon!" Mike answered coming up behind them silently and startling them both.

"You two live in a dream world, you've no idea how isolated the planets feel cut off from Earth!" Kate replied her anger still there.

"Look around you Kate; do you think the crew of this ship are happier now with your government's decision?" Mike asked sternly, as he went past them leaving Kate and Simon standing there.

"We're just trying to protect ourselves!" Kate said defensively.

"We'll talk about it later, let's get moving," Simon replied as they followed Mike. Another ten minutes of climbing over debris they arrived in the command centre. Silt had already started to cover the instrument panels. After digging through the bridge area, Simon managed to find the hard drive of the computer system and quickly dismantled it.

"Where is everyone, I thought there'd be bodies?" Kate suddenly said, making both Mike and Simon turn around.

"My God you're right Kate, I never even thought about that. I'm too used to visiting ships that have been on the ocean floor for decades." Mike replied.

"Best we leave people; we don't know what type of weapon was used. Maybe it annihilates the human body for all we know." Simon said trying to work out a reason for the lack of bodies.

"I noticed scrape marks on the way in. At first, I thought it was just loose equipment, maybe something made of metal removed the bodies." Mike theorised.

"But for what reason?" Simon asked.

Arriving back at their sub, Simon went straight to the command centre, where he tried to interface the backup hard drive taken from the wrecked submarine. Kate left them 'needing time to think' she said, returning to her cabin. Mike making sure everyone was clear, collapsed the shield over the doomed submarine returning it to the ship's graveyard that surrounded it, while leaving the area around the object clear of the water. That afternoon Mike held a service for the crew of the American submarine, saying a few words before returning to the task at hand.

While Simon analysed the sub's recordings, Mike went ahead with preparations to lift the object. He and the crew carefully cleared away all leftover debris from around it, while on the bridge; they recorded all information they could on the object. Mike pushed everyone to get the job done, wanting to be away from here as soon as possible. Having entered the data from the American ship onto his computer, Simon studied the logs, entered into the ship's computer. He found that the Americans had tried to lift the object by cables run from their vessel, outside their shield, using divers.

It appeared that during the lifting was when the attack had occurred and the logs gave no hint of any warning to the enemy's presence. Finding no concrete information from the electronic sensors, Simon decided to study the camera monitoring recording system. From watching these, Simon deduced that everything was going as planned; the crew in the bridge area seemed excited and happy, till the tape suddenly stopped.

Checking the outside cameras, Simon watched the bow camera at the exact time the tape stopped. He saw a sudden flash on the screen before it went dead. Checking the others one at a time, Simon saw the same flash, but not its origin. Finally, he came to the last two cameras. These were not being used for surveillance; they'd been set up to record the lifting of the object. It showed two divers with an American flag in the background, watching the cables start to take up the slack on the object. One gave the victory sign to the camera, as behind them the object changed colour.

Both divers must have been warned by their sub as they both simultaneously turned around facing the object. The object seemed to explode outward as Simon's monitor went blank. Playing it several times sweat started to break on his face, as Simon checked the last camera. This one was some distance from the object, showing the sub hovering above the object the American flag on its bow clear to see.

Mesmerised, Simon watched the divers turn as the object changed colour and a beam of light exploded against the American sub cutting through her hull, before she exploded, the monitor again going dead as the recording stopped.

"My God." Simon mouthed as his mind clouded with fear, as he became aware of what had occurred and what it meant. His train of thought was interrupted, by Mike's voice in the background. It announced over the ship's intercom that they were about to attempt the deployment of the shield around the object. Springing from his chair, Simon raced across the control room from his monitor, grabbing the intercom, from the wall.

"Mike! Stop the lift! Get everyone away from the object immediately!" He screamed into the microphone, as those around him stared at his wild behaviour.

"Okay Simon settled down, we've stopped and are moving back to the sub. What's the problem?" Mike asked surprised by Simon's outburst.

"The other sub was destroyed by the object," Simon said calmly, still breathing heavily as silence followed his statement.

"Everyone back on board! John if you can hear me, once we're all on board drop the shield, and move us away, then redeploy the shield." Mike ordered fear in his voice.

"I hear you, Mike. Just make sure you're all on board." John replied giving Simon a well-done pat on the shoulder, before sitting at the Captain's control console.

Simon sat in the control room as Mike and John, plus anyone else who could see the monitor studied the image of the salvage attempt.

"You're right Simon, there is no doubt the beam came from the object," Mike admitted, shocked and confused.

"How is that possible, I thought shields didn't allow lasers to pass through?" John asked.

"I never heard anyone say it could be done, but we just saw it." Mike pointed out, lost in thought.

"The question is what we do now?" Simon asked his eyes drawn to the object, as it sat peacefully on the ocean floor.

"I'm for leaving, there's been too much death already from this thing," John suggested as many of the crew around them nodded their agreement.

"As much as I'd like to agree, we can't leave that thing sitting on the bottom waiting for someone to find a way to move it." Mike pointed out, scared that someone might find a way of penetrating the objects defences.

"Maybe we can study it from a distance using the hover scooters to take just a few of us close!" Simon put forward, intrigued by the object, wanting to know what secrets it held.

"I think that's all we can do at the moment, but if after a week we're no closer I think we should leave," Mike suggested feeling the fear of the people around him.

"Fair enough, we know the last expedition was safe at a distance, so we give Mike and Simon a week and then go," John replied neutrally as the meeting broke up. Getting back to his cabin Simon found Kate lying on her bed still in her work clothes. He told her about what had occurred and having only one week to study the object.

"We should leave now Simon, no good will come of this."

"We can't just give up, what happens if someone else tries?" Simon said worried about her.

"I'd better go change," Kate responded, walking out the door, ending the discussion.

Donning his pressure suit, Simon joined Mike in the hovercycle launch bay, under the sub's belly. Pressurising the room, the bottom of the subs launch area opened up, as Mike and Simon lowered their hovercycles into the cold dark blue waters. The object was half a kilometre to their west, and as Simon grew accustomed to being underwater. Mike smiling pointed the way, and they started off. It was about eight in the morning on the surface, about three hundred metres above them, but with the clarity of the water, it was just light enough to see.

Approaching the shield Mike called for Simon to slow down as he descended, parking right next to the shield of the object. Getting off his cycle, Mike walked up to the shield and to Simon's amazement, hit it with a hammer he'd brought with him.

"What did you do that for?" Simon shouted into his radio.

"I just wanted to be sure you'd be safe near this thing," Mike replied with a smile, signalling Simon to come down.

"Well, at least we know it doesn't react to outside force, so what made it destroy the sub?" Simon asked as he ran his hands over the surface. "Maybe it sensed they were trying to move it?"

"You're saying the shields alive?" Mike said with a grin on his face.

"Maybe not the shield, but something here is aware of our presence," Simon answered feeling he was being watched, as Mike chuckled.

"Maybe it's just your imagination?" Mike replied, as he too looked around. Moving with great care, they connected several different electronic devices to the shield wall. These were to monitor for any frequencies or radiation, emitted by the object. They hope this might give them a better idea of how its shield worked. Finished, Simon decided to walk around the entire shield area, seeing if he could find a clue to its origin.

Running his hands along the surface of the shield, Simon marvelled at the power necessary to maintain this barrier, for the period it had been here on the bottom of an ocean. So lost in thought was he, that at first, he didn't notice he was going downhill until the mud reached his waist. Stopping he retraced his steps heading back up to knee level when it suddenly hit him, he was walking on steps.

"Mike can you hear me!" Simon asked his voice filled with excitement.

"Hold your horse's son, what's up?"

"Have we got something for clearing away the mud?" Simon asked excitedly.

"Yeah, we've got some pumps why?"

"I think I've found some steps!" Simon informed him.

"Is your oxygen okay Simon, check the gauge immediately?" Mike ordered sternly.

"Look it's okay Mike, my oxygen's fine, come over here and bring your cycle," Simon replied calmer this time. Moments later Mike's hovercycle landed next to Simon. Jumping off he came straight over and looked at Simon's gauges.

"I'm not crazy Mike, come here and walk along the shield wall." Mike reluctantly complied.

"I can't believe it, but you're right son. The grounds too smooth and the steps are too even, I'll call John, and get him to organise a pump to be brought here." Mike chuckled, infected by Simon's excitement. The pump took over two hours to set up and another two to lay the sediment pipes. These would allow the mud to be released at a distance to keep their visibility intact. After an hour of sucking up the mud, Simon and Mike had cleared twenty steps down the side of the shield. Low on oxygen, and having trouble seeing, they decided to take a break.

Returning to their sub, they found John and half the crew waiting for them, eager to find out what was going on.

"Are you sure they're steps, Mike? It could be just a natural rock formation." One of the scientists on board suggested.

"I don't think so, but we'll soon know, and this time we'll set up a camera so you can all watch," Mike answered.

"If you two are right, it means at one stage this area was above sea level. We're pretty deep here, so what does that tell us about this planet?" Kate asked neutrally trying to work it out.

"You're right Kate, it's a mystery. We won't know what's going on until we find where these stairs lead. So we'd better get back." Mike suggested, ending any more discussion, as they refitted their new pressure suits.

Travelling back to the object, Simon was surprised to see Kate following on a cycle, and as they landed, she took over the operation of the pump, while Mike and Simon slowly worked the sucking nozzle over the ground area. It took most of the day, but by nightfall at least thirty steps had been uncovered. They headed down under the shield, stopping at of all things a smooth rock wall. The three of them stood there studying, what they presumed to be a door. Mike glancing up noticed the shield had changed colour above where they stood.

"Let's come back in the morning?" Mike suggested, his eyes never leaving the shield, as Kate looked up and saw the colour change.

"It knows we're here!" Kate replied her voice sounding scared, as Simon looked up and saw it as well.

"Let's move away, maybe it has some type of defence system watching the approaches," Simon whispered

"You could be right Simon, now I know why the other sub was destroyed, this isn't a ship enclosed, it's a base," Mike said quietly ushering them away.

Back on board the sub, Mike and the others showered and then met in the galley with the rest of the crew. Mike explained how the American sub when it had laid its cables around the dome must have set off a self-defence system in the base making it defend itself.

"What's a base doing on the bottom of the ocean?" someone asked.

"Like Kate said earlier, maybe this was once dry land, and some massive environmental change caused this world to flood." Mike put forward.

"That's hard to believe considering this planet has only a small percentage of land mass. Where did the extra water come from?" Their navigator Kevin Johnson said softly from the back.

"My God! It's the portal, that's where the water came from!" Simon exclaimed, realising whoever had built this system may have opened the portals onto planets with massive oceans. After twenty minutes of explaining his idea of what had happened, the room turned quiet as everyone tried to take in this theory.

"I thought the portal was a natural link?" John replied, wondering what happened to the builders.

"So did I, but a student from New Russia on the last expedition thought the portals were too precise to be a natural occurrence. I for one now believe him." Simon answered, sure he was right.

"Well, hopefully, we'll find out tomorrow, for now, let's get some sleep," Mike suggested, as everyone slowly wandered off to bed.

The next morning found Simon and Kate up early, checking their air tanks and preparing their dive suits. They were just about to put them on when Mike stopped them.

"Simon I think we're going about this the wrong way," Mike explained, having had all night to think about it.

"In what way Mike?" Simon replied keen to go.

"Look if your theory is right about this planet being flooded, then the colour change in the shield the other day as we approached, could be because we're surrounded by water. The defence system might register that as hostile if you think the people who built this base, breathed oxygen." Mike said confidently.

"That could explain why it acted so violently when the other sub tried to move it surrounded by water. And why on the last expedition we could approach the shield without a problem, as the shield was in place." Simon replied, a slight smile on his lips thinking Mike was spot on.

"So you two think it feels safer when it detects a breathable environment?" Kate said standing behind them in awe of these two men. They talked about theory so far away from their reality that it left her feeling very dumb.

"Let's face it, Kate, if someone did build this base and the portals, you've got to admit they're light years ahead of us," Mike replied grinning.

"Maybe we should leave it alone then" Kate appeared worried.

"It's too late now Kate. With the loss of their sub, the American planet and all the other planets for that matter are going to want to know what's inside. Who knows what could happen then?" Simon replied a little fear in his voice.

"Okay, let's forget the diving gear, I'll have John deploy the shield like we did on the expedition, it will take a couple of days to clear the water, but I think it will be safer," Mike said before heading off to the bridge.

THE MEETING

After waiting two days for the shield to expand, Simon excitedly moved towards the object. Reaching the spot where the steps started, he found no sign of them, as the mud had refilled the area. Unlike before, when they had used a suction pump to clean away the mud, this time it had to be shovelled out of the way making Simon in the lead, sweat profusely.

"Need a hand?" Mike asked from behind him seeing Simon's shirt was drenched in sweat.

"No thanks. There's not enough room for you down here with me anyway." Simon answered reaching the bottom step and banging the shovel against the shield, getting colour changes in the process.

"I don't think it likes that!" Kate said nervously from behind Mike.

"Well, it's going to have to put up with it!" Simon replied breathing heavily, as he bumped the screen again. Finally reaching the smooth rock surface, and clearing an area where the stairs ended, Simon tapped his shovel against the rock surface hearing a metallic sound.

"It's not rock Mike, it sounds like an alloy material," Simon said studying the wall.

"No indications of some way to open it?" Mike asked suspiciously wondering how to get in, as Simon again tapped around the surface with his shovel.

"No there are no marks or handles, it's dead smooth," Simon replied fascinated by it.

"Why don't you rest Simon?" Kate suggested, watching Simon breathing heavily. Taking her advice, Simon took off his gloves and passed his shovel back to Mike. Losing his balance on the step as he passed the shovel, he put his hand out to stop himself against the rock wall. Instead of touching something solid, Simon found nothing to stop his fall as he tumbled forward passing right through the wall.

Standing up slowly, Simon looked back to see Mike and Kate beating against the wall. He could see their lips moving, but no sound came from their striking the shield or yelling. Turning around Simon found himself at the start of a long hallway, which headed towards the centre of the shield.

"How did that happen?" Simon asked himself, looking again at Mike and Kate who searched the doorway frantically, trying to help him.

Putting his hand out, it passed back through the shield, scaring the hell out of Mike and Kate, as he walked out to them.

"Simon, are you okay?" Kate asked hugging him fiercely.

"I'm fine, did you see what happened?" Simon asked, liking the hug, as Mike gave him a wink before Kate pushed him away.

"You idiot you scared me half to death!" Kate barked this time.

"Any idea what happened?" Mike asked a grin on his face.

"I'm not sure, one second I was on this side, the next I was on the other."

"That's bloody unbelievable!" Mike exclaimed, coming forward hitting the shield with his hand and bouncing off, hurting his fingers inside his gloves.

"Do you think it picks up your skin?" Kate asked mystified, as Mike took his glove off and repeated hitting the shield with his hand, this time it went through, astounding him.

"Well, how the hell does it do that?" Mike asked, running his gloved hand along the shield, while his other hand passed through.

"At the moment I don't care, as long as we can pass through," Simon said walking through again and waiting for the others. On the inside Simon watched Kate and Mike take off their gloves and slowly come through to stand beside him.

"How come it didn't stop us when it detected our clothing?" Kate asked looking down the passageway as Simon led off.

"I think it detects somehow that we're human, allowing one person at a time to come through," Simon answered, as he walked further down the tunnel, triggering lights in the ceiling to come on, which made Simon stop.

"Well if it lets you in through a shield surely it can turn a light on," Mike said behind Simon chuckling, as they walked down the passageway. Coming to another blank wall, Simon was just about to put his hand out when the door slid open squeaking as it did.

"Looks like, no one's been here for quite a while!" Kate whispered, standing very close to the other two, feeling a little scared.

"Yes, you're right about that," Mike answered as he joined Simon who was staring at the room they had just entered. It was the control room they'd observed from underneath the ancient wreck. The room was filled with screens and machines, which were functioning without anyone present to supervise them.

"My God, what do you think it does?" Kate asked as Mike and Simon reverently walked around the room, gazing at each machine lovingly, as if they were hypnotised. Kate getting no answer, let them do their thing, as she too wandered around trying to work out what went on here.

Simon couldn't believe how lucky he was to be here, as he slowly walked around the room, working out how the base functioned. Sitting down at a console he took to be the main control system, Simon stared at the keys seeing the English language in use. The language aside, he found the computers used a standard binary code system like Earth's. This was something Simon found to be more than a coincidence.

"Any luck?" Mike said from behind him, as he stared over Simon's shoulder, watching what he was doing.

"Their language is English, which should make it easy to decipher. The funny thing is, their Binary code is the same too. Could they be our distant ancestors?" Simon replied, his eyes locked on the screen.

"I'm not sure what's going on son. They may have visited Earth in our past, passing on their language so they could communicate. The fact that this base has been under water for some time means they haven't used the portal for a long time.' Mike put forward. Simon was just about to ask another question when Kate out of breath ran towards them.

"I've found something I think you should look at!" Kate exclaimed, the fear in her voice making Simon stand up.

"What's wrong?" Both Mike and Simon asked at the same time. Kate trembling ran into Simon's arms her breathing coming in great gulps. It took several minutes for her to calm down enough to lead them across the room, to the far corner. Simon, on guard, moved in front of Kate as they reached the other side of the control room. Here they found an elevator, tucked away in a small foyer.

"I thought I'd find out where it went," Kate said softly, as Simon felt her hand trembling.

"You shouldn't have gone anywhere without us." Simon pointed out, worried about her.

"Well, you two were so absorbed with the equipment I thought I find out where this lift went," Kate said showing she had just been trying to help, as the three of them entered the lift.

"What's down there?" Mike asked, pressing the only button, indicating down.

"Its best you both see for yourselves," Kate answered softly, moving in behind the two of them.

As the door opened into a clean, spotless room, Simon wondered what had scared her. Looking at the floor, he saw long scratches in the tiles heading away from the lift door, towards a door opposite them.

"I think they were made by fingernails," Kate said a little shaken.

"Could've been made by some creature for all we know," Mike replied, but his voice didn't sound confident.

"Then how'd the creature write that?" Kate pointed to some faded writing on the far wall, near the other door. The message was simple, written in English; it said 'Death awaits get out.'

"It looks like it's written in blood!" Mike said more to himself than them, as he stood thinking about what this meant.

"Could some creature have broken in on this level?" Kate asked, feeling more confident.

"I'm not sure, how far did you go?" Mike asked. He was impressed she'd come down here on her own.

"This is as far as I went when I saw that message I thought it better to go get you two," Kate replied honestly.

"Good thinking. I think we'll leave coming down here until Simon works out the control room and we've got more people and weapons." Mike replied, shepherding everyone back into the lift. Kate stayed close to Simon as he held her around the waist comforting her on the way up.

As the lift door opened, Kate smiling, told Mike and Simon that she'll return to the sub. Simon at first wanted to accompany her. Kate assured him, she would be okay, pointing out, that finding out how the base worked was their major priority at the moment.

"That girl's got it all, good looks and intelligence. She'd be a great catch for someone?" Mike pointed out smiling, as he watched Kate cross the dry ocean floor to the submarine.

"I agree Mike, so stop pushing," Simon grumbled, watching her too.

After another four hours of working, Mike signalled to Simon, that it was time to leave for the day. Getting back to their sub the crew was excited about the discovery, all wanting to join the group the next day. The scratches and the message was put down to some creature, which a hunting party, armed with lasers could take care of later. After lobbying and light-hearted begging from the crew, Mike allowed the crew in groups of five to visit the base. Another five crewmembers could stay in the control room with him, to try and work out its purpose.

That night Kate and Simon after showering returned to their blanket divided room. Preparing for bed, Kate admitted to Simon that she was a little scared of what was on the bottom level.

"It's most probably nothing Kate, just some sea creature."

"Then why stop and write the message when he could have got into the lift?"

"I don't know Kate maybe he thought he had time and the creature surprised him, or he was too badly hurt already." Simon too had questions about the message. Like why did it say 'get out' instead of 'watch out'.

"I know I sound silly Simon, but I feel someone or something, is watching us in that base."

"Look when I get to the base tomorrow, the first thing I'll do is get the surveillance system, if there is one, working. That way we will all feel safer, and it might be able to tell us what's down there." Simon said light-heartedly, hoping this would reassure her.

"Thanks, Simon, but tomorrow I'll stay close to you, I feel safe with you," Kate whispered with something in her voice that made Simon feel good.

"If you still feel scared you can sleep over here?" Simon suggested, hearing Kate giggle.

"In your dreams!" Kate replied. Simon laughing hopped into bed, turning off his light. Kate still had the light, as she changed into her pyjamas. Simon lay frozen, staring at the outline of her naked body silhouette on the blanket. His heart started racing as his inner voice roared for him to go to her.

"Good night Simon," Kate whispered, her very voice arousing him, as he tried to control himself. "Are you okay?" She asked puzzled by him not answering.

"Yes, I'm alright, just thinking of something else."

"I bet you were." She sniggered, before turning off her light and going to sleep, leaving Simon staring at her outline.

The next day the whole crew was up early drawing straws for who could go first. Mike the night before had picked his five assistants to help with the control room equipment. So when Simon and Kate arrived, they found the visitors, plus the assistants, ready to go. It felt more like a day out hiking with friends, as they all arrived at the entrance. The crewmembers looked on in wonder, as the shield let only humans pass through it. Excited the scientists and engineers who made up the five assistants, poured over the alien equipment trying to work out how each piece function.

John, on his turn at visiting the base, gazed at the elevator door. He wanted to take some men and locate this creature that had, they believed, killed the unknown writer of the message. Mike seeing his look had given his permission, but only after Simon got the surveillance gear up and running.

"What do you think it is?" John asked wanting to know what he and his men would be after.

"Hard to tell could be a sea creature or something left here to guard the place for all we know," Mike answered, staring at the door.

"It'll wait, Skipper, best to go in prepared" John replied showing his qualities as a safe commander. This was one of the main reasons why Mike had picked him as his second in command.

Simon in the meantime had returned to the main control panel, absorbing himself in learning everything about the base. He scrolled through the millions of files looking for the key to its operation. He'd worked out, that a thermal reactor powered the base. It was located three miles below them, supplying unlimited power. It had been built he had deducted, for controlling the portals, although he concluded, it had a second function. That was for planetary defence, something he didn't understand.

"Why build it for defending the planet?"

"Maybe the builders had enemies," Kate replied from behind him, where she had been since they had arrived quietly watching him work.

"Oh sorry, I didn't mean to speak out loud," Simon replied surprised she was there.

"A bomb could have gone off behind you, and you wouldn't have noticed," Kate said smiling her eyes shining brightly causing Simon to smile as well.

"I'm sorry to ignore you Kate, but it's just so incredible!"

"Well, I've got a surprise for you," Kate said handing Simon a small box. Opening the box, Simon drew out a headset device similar to the latest ones that Simon used at home to talk to his computer.

"Where did you find it?" Simon asked like a kid with his first chocolate bar.

"It was in a drawer under the console."

"That's funny I thought I'd search all those drawers yesterday," Simon admitted, amazed he'd missed them.

"Maybe you're not all knowing?"

"God this will make it go a lot faster," Simon replied adjusting the headgear and slipping it his over his ear. "Computer my name is Simon, open a channel," Simon commanded like he would his computer at home.

"We have waited for you for so long!" A collection of voices flowed through his senses, as data streamed into his brain, overwhelming him with its complexity.

"Who are you?" He asked fighting through the pain as information on the base overwhelmed him.

"We are your Gods you will obey us!" The voices commanded as Simon collapsed overcome by the computer's download.

THE GODS

"Thirsty, I'm thirsty." Simon cried out as a wet rag was pressed against his lips relieving the pain he felt. Opening his eyes, blinding flashes appeared causing him to close them again in pain, before trying again as the pain slowly receded. A distant voice asked 'Are you okay Simon?' The volume of the voices increased, as the question was repeated.

"Yes, I am. What happened?" Simon said with a croaky voice, as more water was applied to his lips.

"We're not sure, you were using the headset I found when you collapsed, we thought it must have been faulty." Kate's voice said from a distance. Focusing Simon saw that he was in his bed and Kate was leaning over him in her underwear dampening his lips with a sponge.

"God you're beautiful" Simon whispered, making a small smile on his aching lips, as Kate wiping tears from her eyes pressed the intercom telling Mike, Simon was awake. Getting up, Kate grabbed her robe hastily tying it around herself, as Simon watched drinking in her beauty. A knock at the door heralded the arrival of Mike and half the crew.

"Boy you scared us all Simon, do you know what happened? Was the headset faulty?" Mike asked clearly worried and agitated.

"No, I think it just overwhelmed me. I couldn't handle the amount of data it tried to download into my brain." Simon replied, admitting it was most probably his fault.

"Well from now on everyone sticks to the keyboards, until we sort the whole system out," Mike replied, getting agreement from all in hearing range. After the crew had departed, Mike filled him in on what had been going on, until Kate suggested letting him sleep for the rest of the night. Mike taking the hint, went to leave, Simon stopped him.

"There's something else Mike?" Simon whispered, stopping Mike.

"What is it?"

"I heard multiple voices, like humans all talking to me at once," Simon replied softly, seeing Mike look at Kate. "I'm not crazy, they scared me! They said I was to obey them, that they were our Gods!" Simon explained, knowing he sounded weird.

"Look we'll talk about it in the morning son, for now, rest," Mike replied leaving.

"God he didn't believe me!" Simon said, shocked by his grandfather's reaction.

"Look, Simon, there's more than just you collapsing at the machine, you went crazy, yelling at us all, that you were our God." Kate was embarrassed for him.

"I don't remember that Kate, all I remember is the voices." Simon worried that he might be losing it. Kate lay down next to him hugging him to her.

"I believe you, Simon, there's something evil about that place, and no one can see it. They're only interested in the secret knowledge they can unlock from it." Kate informed him, her eyes distant as she thought about the message on the wall.

"Well, we'll get to the bottom of it together," Simon replied, holding her to him, as he fell back to sleep.

Waking the next day, Simon found himself alone. Still dizzy, he looked around the room getting his bearings. Seeing on the wall clock that it was near lunchtime, he slowly sat up steadying himself. Showering and shaving off a small beard he had grown, Simon walked through the half-empty ship, arriving at the galley to find it deserted. Serving himself a meal Simon sat quietly until footsteps heralded the approach of a crewmember.

"Hey sleepy head, how are you feeling?" Kate asked, smiling.

"Where is everybody?"

"They're all at the base some even stay there now!" Kate replied, unhappy with the situation.

"Why would they do that?"

"So they can learn more."

"There's nothing wrong with that Kate, it could make all our lives better," Simon said wanting to go to the base as well.

"If it's so good, what happened to the people who built it?"

"Well come with me, and we'll find out together," Simon answered, standing up and putting out his hand, which Kate smiling held firmly, as they departed.

"I don't want to lose you, Simon," Kate said nervously as they walked down the ramp from the sub.

"You won't Kate," Simon said softly squeezing her hand as they approached the base. Taking their gloves off Simon and Kate put out their hands passing through the shield. They then proceeded along the passage coming to the control room door. This door automatically opened last time they'd been here, now it refused to let them in. Simon thinking the door was jammed tried again, it wouldn't budge. From behind them, John approached.

"We can't get in for some reason?" Simon told him. John thinking they were having him on tried also.

"What's going on, I was just here?" John exclaimed. He explained, how he'd been just about to go explore downstairs with four of his men. They hoped to locate the creature, if there was one and deal with it. He'd been called back to the sub after a warning light on the heating system had come on. Luckily it was just a fault with the sensor, so he had returned.

Sitting down Simon told him what had happened with the console and the voices, wondering if something else was going on here.

"There's something else Simon, I've noticed the crewmembers who work here, are no longer comfortable on the sub. They all want to stay here permanently. I find it worrying." John said softly as if the control room would hear him. Two hours drifted by as John and Simon took turns, trying the door until, without warning, it opened.

"Must have been a glitch?" John put forward, his voice sounding unsure, as they hurried inside. Looking around the control room, Simon observed that all the people there seemed half awake as if coming out of a daze. Spotting Mike, he hurried over to him.

"What's going on Mike?" Simon asked loudly, as everyone in the control room looked towards him.

"There's nothing wrong with us, we're all working as you can see," Mike replied, but his eyes showed confusion.

"Your screen is blank Mike, what are you working on?"

"Something immensely important to the future of mankind! It's so important that we have all decided to stay here permanently!" Mike answered, raising his voice, getting support from most crewmembers, while others looked confused.

"What great discovery Mike, you can tell us?" Kate asked suddenly, as Mike's face went blank.

"It's too complicated for you to understand; only the Gods would understand it!" Mike replied as he hesitated "Why would I say that?"

"Everyone out of this base now and back to the ship" John ordered, drawing his sidearm, as the four men he had left there, slowly followed suit, realising something was wrong.

"How dare you!" Mike shouted angrily, but seeing the look in Simon and John's eyes, he left quietly with the others. Passing back through the door shield, John led the whole crew towards the sub. Simon volunteered to stay behind for a while and tidy up the equipment, which was everywhere. Kate not wanting to leave, stayed with him watching as Simon moved swiftly around the room.

"What's wrong with them Simon? Mike and the others act like you did before you collapsed."

"I'd say someone or something has been trying to influence the crew."

"Why would they do that?"

"I'm not sure, but I'll find out," Simon replied as he walked across the room to the main console.

"Don't touch it, Simon!" Kate's voice revealed how scared she felt.

"Unless I get an answer, I'm going to erase its memories!" Simon said out loud, as he began to operate the keyboard.

"Please wait Simon do not hurt us!" The same voices he had heard shouted, startling Kate who grabbed Simon's hand.

"Who are you and cut out the God talk!" Simon said as the voices talked amongst themselves before a female voice began to speak.

"It was not a lie Simon, at one stage thousands of years ago, we travelled to your world, and were indeed treated like Gods. Unfortunately, you have advanced to a stage where you now know we are just another race of people, although we are still years ahead of your people." The female voice informed them.

"That still doesn't excuse the brainwashing!" Simon replied angrily.

"We were worried that your first contact with us might have damaged you, we thought the others might decide to destroy us!" The voice said sounding afraid for the first time.

"What you've done to them, can it be reversed?" Simon asked understanding their situation now.

"Yes a small electrical charge will bring them back to normal, and for communication sake my name is Elena." The voice replied sounding more confident.

"Kate can you go outside the shield and contact the sub and tell them what happened," Simon told Kate who nodded no.

"I'm not leaving you alone here. Look what happened to you last time." Kate pointed out, hearing subdue chattering amongst the voices.

"We would not hurt Simon," Elena replied to Kate's question.

"Like you didn't hurt the others?" Kate replied anger in her voice.

"We had to stop them; they were preparing to go to the lower level," Elena answered defensively.

"We've been to the bottom level, you didn't stop us," Kate said not believing them.

"We knew you would stop when you saw the message, the brave sailor left there fifty years ago," Elena answered a touch of awe in her voice.

"What is down there Elena?" Simon asked suspiciously.

"One of our enemies, he survives while the rest of his race perished in the flood," Elena replied fear in her voice again.

"Is he like you or us?" Kate asked her voice sounding worried.

"No, he is from another world, linked from here by the portal," Elena replied still sounding scared.

"We have people on all those planets," Simon said worried for the settlers.

"No his planet is locked out. You can no longer access it." Elena answered, sounding a little more confident again.

"You mean there are more planets linked to the portal?" Simon replied excitedly.

"Yes, Simon. Though before you get excited about it, remember we are a lot more advanced than you are and we were destroyed by the enemy, who are still out there!" Elena replied hoping Simon got the message.

"How did the sailor get here?" Kate asked changing the subject.

"He was a crewman on an English nuclear submarine which came through the portal; from the planet, you call Earth in the Earth year 1995. His ship survived the portal somehow intact but still came to rest in the graveyard as you call it, with steering problems. The enemy who feeds on flesh, went to the submarine thinking they were dead to harvest the bodies but was repulsed by the men on board. They sent divers after him armed with a primitive spear-like weapon.

They followed him and entered the lower level through an entrance made by the enemy thousands of years ago when they sought to destroy us. The divers all died except one who found the elevator and came to this room. We tried to communicate with him, but he was frightened, by a machine talking. He went back down to fight his way past the creature to warn his ship. He scribbled the message after receiving fatal wounds in battle than in one last act he fired his spear-like weapon into our enemy, wounding him. " Elena said truly impressed by the sailor.

"What happened to the others?" Kate asked sadly.

"The creature flooded their ship then took their bodies to store for the future," Elena answered sadly.

"Is that what happened to the crew of the sub that tried to move this base?" Kate asked fearing the answer.

"Yes, unfortunately, it has now a large supply for the future," Elena replied.

"Why hasn't it attacked us?" Simon asked.

"Its tunnel is blocked by your shield, which is different from ours, it cannot pass through it at the moment. Unfortunately, the enemy is very resourceful, it might yet find a way to breach it." Elena replied sounding unsure.

"How did it defeat your shields, they're quite impressive?" Simon said truthfully.

"It has one weakness we didn't perceive. It will allow humans through, and our enemy can mimic any life form, while your shield though primitive, allows nothing to pass through."

"Why then hasn't it attacked you here?" Kate asked.

"The elevator will let our type of life forms in, only when they are cleared by this computer. We altered it, so it can now detect 'the enemies' different forms, something we didn't know before the attack on our Planet." Elena answered, sounding tired.

"You sound weak somehow is there a problem?" Simon asked.

"We can communicate through the console, but our bodies lay in chambers preserving us until it is safe for us to wake. It draws on our limited strength, and for safety sake, I must now rest. We will talk again in twelve Earth hours, goodbye." Elena said before silence descended over the chamber.

"Well that was interesting, but do we believe them?" Kate asked Simon, who raised his finger to his lips telling her to be quiet. Pointing to the door, Simon led Kate out of the control room and back to the sub.

Once aboard, Kate and Simon found armed guards at the entry doors stopping angry crewmen from leaving as heated arguments broke out all over the ship. Getting several stun weapons down from the rack, Simon adjusted them, to fire a low voltage charge. He then issued them to the crewmen after first stunning them as well, just to make sure. It took about an hour to electrocute the whole crew, who all appeared slightly embarrassed by their behaviour. Mike especially couldn't believe he had been brainwashed until John showed him his black eye compliments of Mike.

"God I'm so sorry John!" Mike said looking ashamed, as Simon and John burst into laughter, making him even more embarrassed. After the crew had settled down, Simon brought them up to date with his talk with the entities connected through the base's console. Going over all he'd been told and warning them of the presence of an alien, he could see worried looks around the room.

"Do you think our lasers might be effective against this creature?" John growled.

"I'm not sure, but at least our shields seem to be effective," Simon replied optimistically.

"Of course we're working on the assumption that this creature is the enemy and not these beings who tried to brainwash us!" Mike replied, angry at being deceived.

"I don't trust any of them," Kate said getting support from the majority of crewmembers.

"I think we have only one option!" Mike said before continuing. "I think the majority of the crew should depart, leaving only myself and a select few, here to study. The rest can drop the shield, and go back to port. Then in a month's time, you can return if we transmit a predetermined code." Mike suggested, wanting the majority of the crew away from here.

"What if you don't contact us?" John asked none too happy about leaving them here.

"You contact the UN and tell them everything; hopefully they'll seal off the area," Mike replied wondering if they would, as the room grew silent.

"Well, now that's sorted, who's staying?" Mike asked looking around the room.

"For a start, I want three armed guards, who know how to use the new lasers." John insisted to the quiet room, as ten of his men put their hands up. "Kevin, Bill and Jones will do,"

John said as the others moved back, not showing much disappointment. Simon looked at the three guards remembering all of them were single, he judged this was no coincidence.

"I'll stay too," Simon said softly, getting a smile from Mike who knew he would.

"And me!" Kate said nervously.

"Are you sure Kate, you were against going near the base in the first place?" Mike asked surprised.

"Someone's got to look after you two!" Kate replied grumpily making the crewmembers chuckle. Her feelings for Simon were clear to everyone there, except Simon. When no one else volunteered, Mike thought about asking some others, but a look from Simon told him they'd manage. So thanking everyone for their help, the meeting broke up leaving the volunteers to organise the transfer of equipment.

Once the supplies were dropped off at the base, Simon went about installing one of their smaller shields in the entry corridor, feeling that the creature could try to enter that way since now the entrance was visible, while before it was buried. He had another for down on the lower level, but for now, they'd rely on the lift security. Looking out of the shield, Simon stood with Kate as the sub's shield slowly collapsed, and the water rushed in to fill the area which moments before they had casually walked across.

When the shield had withdrawn entirely the sub floating above them, engaged in its engines. Moving forward gaining speed, it disappeared into the distance. Turning back to their work in setting up a living area where they could sleep and eat, Simon suddenly felt that someone was watching him. Turning around and looking out through the shield Simon saw a man size shape disappear around the side of the shield. Although it vanished, the feeling of being watched continued.

"Something wrong Simon?" Kate asked coming to stand beside him.

"No nothing just looking around that's all."

"One thing I like about you Simon, you lie badly." She smiled, moving away, unpacking more supplies.

CONFRONTATION

After a week of analysing and studying the control room, Simon and Mike had a firm grasp of how the portal worked. They now knew they could manipulate its opening and closing, to a cycle of one opening every ten days. This they believed would make travelling and trade much easier for the Gun barrel planets. By reducing the time open, they also could cut down on the tidal forces each side of the opening and closing, making the system safer for travelling.

To do this would mean adjustments to power input, which was simple, the problem was the switch room was on the lower level.

"There's no hurry to do it straight away Simon, we'd have to warn the planets before we tried anyway," Mike admitted, not wanting to venture down there.

"We can guide you." Elena's voice said happily from the console, which didn't surprise anyone because since they had moved in, the entities had been pushing for them to confront their enemy.

"Why are you so keen for us to deal with this creature?" Mike asked always suspicious of these entities.

"It would make your stay here more secure," Elena answered her voice still sounding happy.

"I don't buy it, Elena. What are you not telling us about the lower levels? Clearly, there is some urgency?" For a while, the voices bickered amongst themselves then fell silent before a male voice spoke.

"My name is Rile, and it is left to me to tell you why we need you to go to the lower level." Rile said his voice flat with no emotion, as he continued. "It appears the creature has been digging a tunnel. At first, we thought he was just trying to extend his area by breaking through into storage areas and machinery areas we have on that level. But we were wrong; he is digging towards our hibernation chamber, hoping to kill us while we sleep."

"Why didn't you tell us earlier?" Mike asked still not trusting these entities.

"You don't trust us humans; you too could enter and kill us, just as our enemy could." Rile replied trying to sound okay, but his voice quivered.

"Trust is a thing in small supply around here!" Kate said looking around the room, her eyes resting on Simon.

"Can we get to your room and the power room without going near him?" Simon asked not looking at Kate.

"No, he knows you'll try soon, he's been watching you from outside the shield." Rile told them, as they all turned around looking out into the surrounding water.

"That's what you saw when we first got here isn't it?" Kate asked Simon, knowing now he didn't want her to worry.

"Yes I saw a shadow, and I assumed it was the creature," Simon replied feeling guilty.

"You could have mentioned it to us!" Bill one of the guards said slightly angry.

"What would it have achieved other than making everyone nervous?" Simon answered. As if on cue, the creature impacted with the shield with a loud bang making everyone jump back away from the shield. It was man-sized, its entire body covered by a shiny black wetsuit. Its hands and legs appeared similar to a human, but the fingers and toes were much longer. Its head though roughly the same size as their own had two large eyes and a small nose. The one major difference in appearance, were the two rows of shark-like teeth, which gave the creature a savage look, as it stared hungrily at the six humans.

"Unfriendly looking sod isn't it?" Mike said as he walked right up to the shield next to the creature. Showing no fear, the creature moved back, before hitting the shield again. Mike taking out his laser pistol, tapped it against the shield smiling at the creature, which looked at the gesture before nodding and swimming off.

"Well, you certainly pissed him off sir!" Bill said smiling at Mike's theatrics.

"Just wanted to show him, we can be just as stupid!"

"How could it survive out there without air?" Kevin, another guard, asked.

"It was hard to see, but it had a small tube on the side of its mouth. I'd say it has some sort of air tank in its suit." Mike replied having seen it when he approached the shield.

"What are we going to do?" Kate asked.

"We're going to go down there and show this creature the door," Mike answered, going to a portable shelf and taking down a laser rifle, checking if it was fully charged.

"Do you think that's wise?" Simon asked not sure.

"Well I'm not that brave; I thought we take the other portable shield just in case." Mike grinned as they all made ready.

As the lift door silently opened onto the bottom level, the six-team members reluctantly stepped out into the unknown, spreading out in the room their eyes on the exit door across from the room marked by the blood covered writing beside it.

"If I were him, I'd be waiting just outside!" Simon suggested, sounding a little scared as he pointed his weapon at the centre of the door, the others following his lead. Kate was the only one not holding a weapon. She stood behind the others; her job was if necessary to deploy the shield if their laser weapons failed. Bill one of the guards walked forward, weapon held a lot steadier than he felt, as the door sensing movement opened automatically, revealing a pitch-dark corridor. An uneasy silence settled over the group, as the group shuffled forward joining Bill in the doorway.

"I mean you no harm!" A garbled voice spoke from the shadows, as if its mouth was full of rocks, instead of teeth. Bill surprised by the voice froze, as the others moved up beside him.

"Did you say that to the man you killed here?" Mike growled trying to get a fix on the voice.

"They attacked me after I entered their ship by mistake, I had no choice."

"Will you let us pass?" Simon asked.

"No, unfortunately, I cannot Simon." Everyone looked sideways at Simon.

"How is it you know my name?"

"I can read your lips, and I already speak your language."

"Why won't you let us pass?" Simon asked again.

"By increasing the power, you give my enemies the chance to break free of their hibernation and retake form!" There was anger in the voice.

"What do you want?" Kate asked from behind Simon.

"You are a very intelligent female. I want to return to my planet!" The group stood there silently, taking in this new information.

"Look we're not sure who to believe here, but even if we could open the portal can you get through it?" Mike asked honestly.

"I have a small craft that I have constructed with a shield. It should be possible."

"We have much to discuss, we will return to the top level and work out a solution if possible," Mike answered still watching the darkness.

"I will wait for your answer. I have nowhere else to go." The voice answered sadly, as the group backed into the lift. Arriving back at the control room, Simon rigged the console so everyone could listen. Simon went over their encounter with the creature, and its demand to return home, as the entities remained suspiciously quiet.

"Well, what's your side of the argument?" Mike asked when no one had answered.

"For all intent and purpose, this whole mess is our fault." Rile said sadly, before explaining. "Many thousands of years ago, more years than most could possibly imagine, our race 'the Roax', reached a point in our evolution, where we had conquered the Galaxy around us. Finding that their Galaxy contained only a few planets worth settling, a group of scientist sought to find a way to breach the limitation of space travel, by propulsion. Through a series of experiments, they found it was possible to bend light, filtering it through a tunnel-like structure of pure energy, thus giving birth to a system capable of reaching the furthest planets in the universe.

Sending out high-speed drone spaceships, we soon located thousands of planets worth exploring and using their known positions it was now possible to travel to them in a fraction of the time. Unfortunately, our race had become arrogant, and overconfident in their superiority. Travelling throughout the galaxy, being welcome as Gods, by the races they met, we thought ourselves invulnerable, which increased our own opinion of ourselves.

When a group of our people opened a portal to Oregarth, the homeworld of our enemy, we were warmly welcomed having no idea that the enemy's race was nearly as advanced as ourselves. The planet was devoid of animal life as the Oregarthians were in massive numbers and being meat eaters had completely stripped the planet of food. Our people found that this was how they lived, stripping a planet of life then moving on.

They had a huge fleet of spaceships, which they used to find other suitable planets with. Once they'd located a new source of food, they'd move on repeating the process. Our portals as you call them fascinated the Oregarthians. They saw it as a way for them to travel to infinite numbers of planets to continue feeding.

Of course, our people were appalled by the way the enemy lived and attempted to change them. By demonstrating our weaponry that was far more advanced than theirs, we hoped to force the enemy race to change, but it backfired. The Oregarthians, fearing we meant to destroy them, fought back. Secretly they had built an armada of submersibles, which they now used to travel through our portal to our home world. With superior numbers, they overpowered our planets' defences, and though millions were killed, they continued to pour through the portal onto this planet.

Caught by surprise we were slaughtered, and because the enemy had learned to mimic our form, it made our advanced shields useless in protecting us. In desperation fearing for the rest of the universe, we came up with the idea of opening portals to different planets with large areas of water. They found by overriding some of the safety protocols they were able to let water pass through the portal. This destroyed the enemy, who were now trapped by the massive tidal waves, which swept over this planet and onto their home planet.

When the portal to Oregarth finally closed, our race was devastated by what had occurred. With our industrial complexes underwater and our cities destroyed, it was decided to abandon this planet. Many went through the portal to distant planets to live out their lives in peace. Another group seeking revenge refurbished our fleets of space warships, which had sat idle since the discovery of the portal. They set course for Oregarth wanting payback for the invasion. A handful of volunteers fearing the enemy might return, stayed behind to man this base.

We knew at the time that Oregarthian scientists had been working on building a portal system of their own. Luckily they failed for some reason to bring one into operation. We have manned this base since then, forced in the end to enter the hibernation chambers, to extend our lives. How one of the enemies has survived amazed us. His doggedness in trying to destroy us shows how truly dangerous his race is. We should let him return to his planet, it would only be fair.

The problem is, what if they are still waiting on the other side, what if they come through again, what then?" Rile asked seeking a way out of this decision.

"Look even if they are waiting on the other side, I think it's only fair that the creature is allowed to leave. Let's face it, by the sound of it, the fault lies with both parties in this war, and it's only fair that we let him go home." Simon suggested as silence settled over the group.

"I agree with Simon, and we have our own shields as a backup, we can always block the portal if there's trouble," Mike replied; secretly glad to see the creature gone.

"How long can the portals stay open for?" Kate asked thinking about the enemy.

"We will keep it open until you return." Rile answered still sounding worried.

"We will need to deploy one of our larger submarines Mike; the power to block the portal will be immense," Simon stated, calculating in his head the power use.

"There is one other problem too." Rile said sounding a little afraid.

"What now?" Mike asked knowing with these entities you never got the full story.

"To stop interference with the portal, the shield must be deployed on the enemies' home planet side of the shield." Rile answered.

"That could be a suicide mission!" Bill exploded, his voice sounding tense, making it clear he wasn't keen on going.

"You could be right Bill, but I still think it's the right thing to do under the circumstances," Mike replied.

"We could rig the sub to run with a small volunteer crew, just enough to run the ship and defend themselves," Simon suggested, getting a scared look from Kate, who knew he would want to go.

"Or we could just kill the creature. Remember it's already killed a lot of humans." Kevin one of the other security guards pointed out.

"Yes that would be simpler, but if we fail to kill it, it will then know our weapons are useless against it, placing the whole portal system in danger when it breaks through to the entity's hibernation chamber down there." Mike pointed out, not sure if he even wanted to try to kill a creature trapped here on its own, for over a thousand years.

"How do we get a bigger submarine here without anyone knowing, or should we tell someone?" Kate asked realising decisions were being made that should have been made by their government, not just them.

"We have to contact John. The problem is for secrecy it would have to be sent from outside the shield, preferably on the surface. If we use our sub transmitter to contact the sub as we'd planned to, everyone will hear it and know where we are." Mike said looking around the room.

"And how can we possibly do that?" Kevin asked mockingly.

"I could talk again with our friend down there; maybe if I tell him what we plan, he would allow one of us out through his tunnel," Simon replied seeing a shadow move outside the shield.

"You've got to be kidding Simon, what if it decides to make you dinner!" Kate retorted her voice full of fear.

"If it kills me, it would be stuck here until John returns and lowers the shield again trapping it in its cavern. With the rest of the crew, I'm sure you would be able to destroy it. No, I think it will agree if it thinks it can trust us to honour our side of the bargain." Simon said confidently.

"You take a great risk, Simon, just to save an alien life form." Rile's voice echo from the console, making everyone turn that way, as during the whole discussion the entities hadn't added anything.

"Without compassion for others, mankind will never survive." No answer came from the console.

As before, Mike led the others out of the lift, fanning out to face the exit door from the lift room on the lower floor. Approaching the door with the blood message, it silently opened revealing darkness.

"I judge you're there?" Simon said a small smile on his lips.

"You constantly amaze me, Simon." The gravel voice sounded from the dark.

"I figured you most probably watched our conversation upstairs."

"Yes I did, even the part where Kevin thought it would be better to kill me!" Kevin looked a little embarrassed.

"Will you help me reach the surface and transmit a message?" Simon asked. Sensing the creature was somehow amused by the situation.

"Yes I will Simon, but you cannot bring a weapon, only the radio."

"You're not going without a weapon, Simon!" Kate cried out from behind him.

"He must travel inside my small ship female, I too am vulnerable!" By the tone of the creature's voice, they could tell he was making a significant sacrifice.

"Look if this is going to work, we must all trust each other," Simon exclaimed, looking around the room he received nods from everyone, including an on edge Kate. "Will I need oxygen?" Simon asked the creature, who was now visible standing in the hallway in front of him. The creature though strange in appearance, wasn't entirely hideous, as Simon had first thought. It had a humanoid shape; only its teeth seemed dangerous.

"No, I breathe air too, and my ship has a good supply. I know it sounds empty, but I guarantee you all that Simon will be safe with me." Even with the gravelly voice, Simon thought the alien sounded sincere.

"Okay, I may as well get it over with," Simon said walking forward towards the creature, leaving everything, except a radio behind him.

Wait!" Kate said running forward and grabbing Simon, before giving him a passionate kiss on the lips. "For luck," she said a little embarrassed, before returning to the others without another word.

Simon walked cautiously beside the creature, deeper into the tunnel system. Once they'd moved out of sight of the others, the alien turned on a switch hidden in the wall, illuminating the tunnels. Now he could see, he looked at his companion, marvelling at the creature's grace as it moved beside him matching his strides in a smooth fluid motion. Unlike before when the creature wore a tight wetsuit, it now wore a free-flowing gown that hung down to its ankles.

"What's your name?" Simon asked feeling more comfortable with the creature. The creature at first looked at Simon, his eyes and expression unreadable, studying him before answering.

"You amaze me, Simon, here you are walking down a dark corridor with a creature which has fed on human flesh, and you want to know my name." The creature made a strange gravelly noise that Simon took for laughter.

"You forgot intelligent in the description of yourself."

"You are correct Simon, in this situation it makes all the difference. For if anything happens to you, I will be trapped here forever, and that is something I don't want. And by the way, my name is Radon or close to it." The creature replied sounding amused.

"How did you manage to survive for so long?"

"The same way my enemy has by hibernating."

"How long does a member of your race usually live?" Simon enquired.

"About two hundred of your Earth years. You must remember though, that the time in hibernation is not living, it's lost to you.

"So you have some type of detection equipment that warns you of danger, so you can awaken if humans or objects come close?" Simon was trying to work out why it was awakened when they arrived. This made the creature stop and study him.

"You are an enigma to me, Simon." Radon replied looking at Simon closely, before continuing. "I have watched you along with the others, and even though you are primitive compared to the entities, your intellect seems to be far ahead of both our races. What were your parents like?" Radon asked as he continued to lead.

"I didn't know them. When I was young, they disappeared while navigating the portals as we called them, between planets."

"Who raised you then?"

"Mike the one who approached the glass when you first appeared."

"Ah the brave one, yes if I didn't know better, I'd have said he'd seen alien races before." Radon replied lapsing into silence, before suddenly stopping again. "Those shields you use, how did you come by them?"

"Our race invented them. Actually, Mike and his wife and my parents were the ones who invented them and then improved on them." Simon replied proudly.

"I have never seen shields like them, they are impressive!"

"The entities said they were primitive but different, that's what makes them hard for you to penetrate."

"Don't believe everything they say, Simon, your shields are far superior to ours and theirs I can assure you."

"That's why they could fire through their shield it's not their technology at all, it's their shield is just weaker?" Simon said excitedly finally solving the problem of the attack on the American planet sub.

"You are partly correct Simon. Because their shield is weaker, it can be programmed to allow the shield to weaken in a small area for a fraction of a second. This allows the laser to fire through it. But there's a problem with that answer. How did your race, which is primitive, when compared to the entities, build advanced shields, and I might add advanced lasers? From what I've seen, you still haven't caught up in other fields of technology, like your computers or submersibles."

"I don't know Radon. I only know that a war was fought on my planet, these weapons and shields appeared towards the end, stopping the conflict." Simon knew it wasn't much of an answer.

"I can hear in your voice that you speak the truth as you know it Simon, but I must think on what I have seen and heard. The answer is there I can feel it. One question though, if you can't fire a laser through your shield, how do you fire at all?" Radon asked sounding confused, as they reached the water.

"As the weapon fires, the computer simultaneously drops an area in the shield where the beam is being projected. It does the same for the sub's propulsion by allowing the propellers to be outside the shield."

"That makes your ships vulnerable?"

"Not really. In a time of conflict, the shield encases the whole sub, allowing small windows of time for propulsion when it's safe to do so." Simon explained. Radon didn't answer this time thinking about Simon's reasoning. Simon's race, despite their friendly appearance, had a firm grasp of military tactics. Their subs, though primitive, were practically invulnerable against his race's weapons. Only in superior numbers could an enemy take on these shielded ships and even then it would be costly.

Coming back to the present Radon pressed a small button on a pendant he had around his neck. The water beside them started to bubble as a small sub like vessel broke the surface. Jumping on board, Radon quickly entered signalling Simon to board as well. Climbing into the sub, Simon held tightly to the sides while Radon in the only seat activated the drive system.

A small humming sound started, as the small sub moved forward diving into the dark water. The sub followed a dark tunnel for a hundred metres before the light from the ocean's surface flitted down, growing stronger as they rose.

Breaking the surface Radon opened the top hatch letting them enjoy the sunshine, while Simon sent the pre-recorded message to John.

"Well, that was easy!" Simon smiled as Radon gave him a toothy smile in return.

"Yes that was easy Simon, the rest will prove more difficult" Radon answered as he closed the hatch, the sub diving back down into the depths. Back in the cave, Simon and Radon retraced their previous walk along the deserted tunnels.

"Well, that's done all we have to do now is wait for the sub and open the portal," Simon said looking forward to going through to Radon's world.

"Can I trust you, Simon?"

"Yes I would think so, I trusted you didn't I?"

"I told a lie about being able to travel through the portal. I thought you mightn't agree if you knew I would have to travel on board one of your ships."

"It won't be a problem Radon I'm sure Mike will agree, he's a good man," Simon replied, but he felt a little doubt that maybe they wouldn't be too happy about it.

"I sense some doubt in your voice."

"It's just you've been living off human flesh for over a thousand years, it's bound to worry the crew."

"I took only what I needed to survive Simon, I have mostly lived off sea creatures during that time."

"But there are thousands of bodies missing from those wrecks, someone took them," Simon replied watching Radon.

"Come with me, Simon." Changing direction Radon led Simon deeper underground. Coming at last to what once was a viewing platform; Simon looked down into a large cavern. There he saw a large group of what appeared to be humanoid robots standing frozen near a large metal opening through which an elevator passed.

"That is where all the bodies go Simon. Those robots collect them from the wrecks then bring them here dumping them on that elevator, to be processed and stored."

"Why would they do that?" Simon shocked, sensed he already knew the answer.

"How do you think the entities have survived down here, they are connected to these machines, which somehow keep them alive."

"They're living off humans!"

"They're surviving in hostile conditions. You have a lot to learn about the universe." Radon answered, before leading Simon back towards the elevator.

"One more question Radon. How is it you speak our language?"

"Yes, that is a good question, and if you find the answer, I'd like to hear it. In all my race's travels, the intelligent life forms we encountered, always speak the language of the great ones like we do."

"Who are the great ones?"

"Another good question. All I know is they were a race that existed millions of years ago. Other than that, I know little about them."

Standing at the lift after Radon had gone, Simon discussed his conversations with Mike, as he listened silently taking in all the information and gauging its relevance.

"Yes, it makes you see things in a new light when you see both sides survived on the flesh of humans," Mike replied, wondering how much they could trust either side.

"What about our shields and lasers being superior to theirs?" Kate asked, trying to fathom how mankind could have advanced in these two fields and not others.

"That's for another day Kate, even though I'd like to know how our friend knows about our weapons?" Mike replied.

"He probably got one from the destroyed American submarine," Simon answered, knowing Mike had made changes to their own weapons making them a lot more effective.

"What about Radon travelling on our sub, how do you think the others will take it?" Simon asked, knowing how he first reacted when seeing Radon.

"They'll put up with it, they're good people," Mike replied, but his voice betrayed a little apprehension.

"So what do we tell the entities when we get back to the control room?" Kate said not trusting any of these beings.

"As little as possible until our friend is gone, then we'll worry about it," Mike replied as they all climbed into the lift.

Radon stood in the corridor outside the lift room having listened to Simon's conversation with the others. They were not like the Roax, the other human-like race his people had been at war with. Surprisingly he found himself liking Simon. His survival here had been at best miserable, and he longed to return to his own kind. He found himself intrigued by this new race and he had to admit to being a little scared. How had they advanced so far in such a short time? Simon, he found to be an enigma, he talked to him as an equal, as he did with the entities without any guile. Yet Radon felt his warmth and friendship something his own race had trouble showing.

He had watched both Mike and Simon in the control room, using equipment supposedly more advanced than theirs, but they had easily overcome all obstacles. That's what scared him; that his own people might view Simon and his people with more fear than the entities' race. The fact that they evolved so much faster than they could, would make them in the future a more dangerous adversary, something that his people might want to deal with now.

THE OREGARTH PORTAL

John's return was, to say the least, a surprise, when his colossal sub arrived, accompanied by eight others. John's submarine took up position beside them, deploying its shield, while the eight other subs, separated into groups of two, taking up positions around the portal base. Mike viewed this development with growing unease, as he waited for the shield to push back the water, allowing travel between the base and John's sub. When the water had cleared, Mike gathered his small group and hurried to the entrance. The sound of approaching hovercycles heralded the arrival of John, who had also brought at least twenty UN troops.

"Why did you bring soldiers John?" Mike asked suspiciously, as the two groups met outside the base.

"You just don't go and borrow a giant sea-going sub, without questions being asked," John replied with a smile, as he had his troops relax, while he talked privately with Mike's group.

John explained how upon reaching their home, news of the loss of the American subs and the object had become widespread. After being summoned to the UN, John had at first been accused of having something to do with the American subs loss. In the end, he had been forced to come clean and fully explain what was going on. Amazingly the committee had fully backed what Mike and the others had done, communicating the situation to all the six planets, which had all grudgingly backed the UN's claim over the base.

"That's why the escort, each planet, sent two ships as so-called support vessels. In other words, they don't trust us." John pointed out, with a slight smile on his lips.

"There are only eight subs, there should be twelve if each planet sent two?" Kate pointed out.

"Both Earth and Southern planet have no armed subs on Salvation, so they didn't feel the need to send any," John replied.

"It mightn't be a bad idea to have this amount of firepower on hand, especially if things go wrong when we open the portal." Simon pointed out, as John looked at Mike.

"What portal opening?" John asked suspiciously.

"There's a lot to discuss, let's get to a more comfortable location" Mike suggested, as John led them towards his sub.

THE PORTAL

"I've got to tell you, Mike, I don't like the sound of this expedition, especially having an alien aboard," John exclaimed wondering if Mike and Simon were all right after being at the base. It had taken nearly two hours to bring John up to speed on the mission, and Simon had to admit it sounded pretty wild.

"And the entities in this base are okay with it?" John asked still worried.

"We're not sure, they've gone rather quiet about it. But they did agree that it was time for the alien to go." Simon replied neutrally.

"I suppose it's better than just killing him. How long have I got to get the crew ready?" John said giving in.

"Thanks, John, but this trip will be with the minimum of crew, only enough to operate the navigation and weapons," Mike informed him.

"Don't tell me you two are going and not me!" John asked angrily.

"You've got a wife and three children, John. This mission could be one way. Do you really want to risk not seeing them again?' Mike replied softly. John stood there preparing an answer, as to why he should go, but both Mike and Simon could see the conflict in his eyes.

"Look, John, someone's got to stay here at the base and deal with the entities. You know them, you know what they're like. I can't think of anyone better qualified to protect this base until we return." Mike added, cutting John off before he could answer.

"Okay, you win I'll stay, but the marines are going with you, at least the unmarried ones!' John replied forcefully. Mike knew there would be no arguing on this point.

"Fair enough, let's brief the others," Mike suggested as the men moved off, followed closely by a very solemn Kate.

It took several days to prepare the sub and select the crew. After briefing the other world's subs that were present, it was put to Mike that an equal number of submarines be sent from each planet. Furious Mike had told them angrily that the UN was already made up of joint forces, and they would be all that was going. He tried to convey that this was a peaceful mission, not an invasion.

In the end, they all grudgingly agreed, but Mike knew that none of the planets were happy with the situation. The final crew including marines came to just over a hundred far more than Mike wanted, but the minimum number John had insisted on.

"Really Mike when you think this sub was capable of carrying over ten thousand people during the evacuation of Earth, I think one hundred would be pretty bearable." Simon smiled at his grandfather's stubbornness.

"It's just if something goes wrong, I want the bare minimum of causalities," Mike replied, looking at Simon.

"Don't even try, I'm going!" Simon answered, seeing where Mike was going.

"You're my only living family Simon; it would kill me if something happened to you," Mike said softly, as Simon came forward hugging him.

"I've put a lot into planning this mission Mike, nothing's going to happen," Simon replied as Kate entered.

"And don't try that on me either," Kate, barked, having heard their discussion.

"Wouldn't dream of arguing with you girl," Mike replied submissively, as he and Simon tried not to laugh.

To prevent problems occurring between the Gun Barrel planets openings and closings, the entities decided to open a separate portal. They explained how there must be at least 100 kilometres between portals. Mike and Simon found this quite interesting; as the entities hadn't mentioned anything about distances between portals. Mike enquired why they hadn't mentioned this before, they pointed out that no one had asked. They explained that to prevent tidal rips on the surrounding oceans, the portals had to be kept apart, as the closer, they were the more unstable, they were to enter.

"I don't trust them, Simon!" Kate said nervously, after hearing of this latest revelation.

"They're behaving themselves. It's no big deal travelling the extra distance, although it would've been nice to know so we could plan beforehand. Anyway once I get back, I'll have a serious look at how the whole system works."

"If we return," Kate whispered as they boarded their sub for the journey to the new location. Sailing south for several hours, they reached the secondary portal site. At a distance, the 8 subs representing the four planets silently followed, as if expecting some form of trouble to materialise. A communications link had been established between the entities and Mike's sub, so it came as no surprise when the portal violently opened into the ocean's depth.

"Well, this is it, my friends," Mike said with a smile, ordering full power and the shields deployed as the sub leapt forward, diving towards the portal. Turbulence far greater than encountered between the Gun barrel planets battered the sub. It continued to rock violently, as it forced its way through the pressure waves, trapped inside the portal.

"Are we going to make it?" Kate squeaked out as everyone aboard grabbed hold of anything solid to prevent them being thrown to the deck.

"The shields are holding just fine. The worst should be over any minute." Mike replied happily, reassuring the crew. It took over three days to navigate the portal, and unlike Mike's prediction, the pressure waves didn't diminish, until they were through to the other side. The turbulence that had started upon entering finished as the sub cleared the portal. Approaching the surface, the crew suffering from motion sickness; slowly pulled themselves together, going to battle stations.

"That was quite a ride!" Simon smiled, looking around at the relieved crewmembers.

"Radon's planet must be a lot further out than the six planets on our portal system," Mike replied, knowing a trip to any planet through the portal took just over a day. Simon concluded that Mike thought the extra distance had caused the turbulence, he wasn't sure.

"I wonder if it was this turbulent for Radon's race?" Simon speculated.

"Maybe you should ask him?" Mike suggested.

"How is he surviving the trip anyway?" Kate asked, knowing Simon was the only one to visit him, while they'd been aboard the sub.

When Mike had agreed to let Radon travel on board, it had been conditional that he was locked away. Towards the rear of the sub, was a disused accommodation section, he was held there. He had also insisted on two guards being stationed outside his door at all times.

"I actually think he is enjoying the trip" Simon smiled. "He seemed to think our sub although an old design is quite smooth." Simon continued, as the others laughed.

"Since we're through now, wouldn't it be a friendly gesture to let him come up here to the control room," Kate suggested as everyone looked at Mike for a decision.

"Okay, bring him up, but the guards come too!" Mike insisted as Simon raced off to get him.

Radon was in his own way happy to be allowed in the control room, even though some of the crew gave him a wide berth. He couldn't believe his luck that this new race had brought him home. As he stood beside Simon, he watched the crew ready themselves, completely unaware of what could be waiting.

"Your race is truly amazing!" Radon said through a mouth full of teeth, sounding like he was crunching gravel.

"What do you mean Radon?" Kate asked.

"Your ship is at least a century behind the entities or ours, yet you brought it through a portal as if it was an everyday occurrence.'" Radon answered, getting friendly looks from a few crewmembers for his compliments.

"That's because, for over ten years, millions of humans travelled through portals from our home planet, after the war that made a living nearly impossible," Mike explained sadly.

"Still it is an amazing feat for a race just taking their first steps in exploring the galaxy." Radon replied as the crew ran through their equipment checks.

"Was your crossing this rough?" Simon asked.

"I can't remember it being that bad, but I think the distance affects the portal somehow, although I've only travelled through a portal twice." He admitted as the room grew quiet.

"Any sign of life?" Mike asked as the crew watched their sensors, waiting for the computer to interpret any information it received from the surface.

"I've got something Captain." One of the crew informed him.

"What is it?" Mike asked excitedly.

"We're being scanned by an object above the planet. Could be an early warning satellite system of some kind?" The operator replied, his eyes never leaving his panel.

"Sir, I'm picking up a lot of radio chatter to the north, a port city I'd say." Another operator informed him.

"Well they know we're here, let's head towards the port, see what a greeting we get!" Mike suggested, getting a respectful nod of approval from Radon, as he watched the crew silently. He was secretly worried; he'd expected a confrontation as soon as this sub had cleared the portal. 'Where were his people?' he asked himself, as they slowly approached the port.

THE ROAX

Adrian sat in the planetary defence room inside the Citadel, bored to death. He'd been put on guard duty here, as punishment for getting drunk during an exercise. This was nothing out of the ordinary these days, as boredom on this God forsaken planet; meant drinking hard was the only escape.

When over a thousand years ago the Oregarthians had attacked the Roax people, forcing the excavation of the planet, a fleet of warships had set sail for Oregarth. Entering hibernation chambers, the fleet had taken over two century to cross the universe. Coming out of hibernation the squadron had deployed, going to battle stations as it approached Oregarth.

After pulverising any visible structures, the fleet short of fuel had touched down next to the planet's largest ocean. They discovered that the planet was deserted and had been for quite some time. Needing time to recover from prolonged hibernation their commander decided to build a forward base on Oregarth.

Short of resources, the fleet cannibalised nearly a third of their ships, leaving their crews and families, who had travelled with them, here on the planet. In case the Oregarthians attacked; a large Citadel had been built out of the ships left behind, saving only two in case of an emergency. It made a formable base surrounded by shields, and armed with banks of laser cannons, covering every approach.

Over the next few centuries, the number of people had grown, causing the need for food and housing outside the Citadel. Villages had become towns, and towns had become a city, as the survivors spread out throughout the surrounding countryside. But the Roax never forgot why they had come here, and despite having never seen the enemy, they remained on watch.

All youth both male and female spent their time in the defence force. It was compulsory to serve five years between the ages of eighteen to twenty- three, with part-time call-ups after that period, until the age of fifty. Great strides had also been made in both agriculture and science. These advances made life bearable on Oregarth, but it wasn't home.

The Roax hungered to return to their home planet, only duty made them remain here, waiting for word of the remaining fleet. Its absence had caused a great deal of debate, as nothing had been heard from the fleet for over a hundred years. It had engaged several enemy fleets and destroyed many homeworlds of the Oregarthians by hibernating between jumps to different galaxies.

Since the last jump, no communication had been received, only silence. Adrian was amongst a growing group of people who believed that it was time to return home. Sitting at the console Adrian stared out the window beside him, watching the surf break against the outer harbour wall. He prayed that something would happen just to break the boredom.

As if the Gods had heard his words, the terrifying roar of a klaxon horn sent a wave of dust over the room. This was followed a split second later by the early warning satellite tracking system erupting into life on Adrian's console. Bolting upright, it took several seconds for Adrian to get over the shock, before recalling his basic training on the procedure.

"Must be a drill?' Adrian shouted out loud, going to the manual to find out exactly what he had to do first. The first instruction in the manual was to confirm contact before issuing an alert. Sounded like a good idea to Adrian, so after taking several deep breaths, he switched on the video link to the satellite to look at the supposed threat. What he saw was a massive vessel of unknown origin sailing straight towards his position. Fear gripped him, summoning what courage he had left; he hit the mobilisation button, putting the whole planet on alert.

Panic broke out all over Oregarth, as the entire population abandoned whatever they were doing. Racing to their prepared position, shields sprang to life all over the planet. Thousands of soldiers manned their weapons as the main command centre in the Citadel, filled with its general staff.

Commander Corban, the Roax's military commander, hurried into the command centre thunder on his face.

"What the hell is going on?" He spat out, looking around the room, wanting to know why the alert had been issued.

"We're under attack Sir!' Adrian stuttered out, as Corban's gaze locked on him, making him flinch.

"We better be son, or you'll be shining urinals for the rest of your miserable life." the Commander bellowed, Coming over to Adrian he looked at his screen. What he saw made him look again, unable to at first comprehend. "Looks like a rusted pile of garbage, where'd it come from?" Corban smiled, thinking it could be a prank.

"The instruments have confirmed, that it came through a portal Sir" Johan Kirk the second in command replied, as all in hearing turned in shock.

"That's impossible! We're the only ones who had that ability, and our device was lost in the ocean." Corban bellowed, watching the alien vessel approach the city.

"What do you want to do Sir?" Johan asked softly, knowing some action must be initiated.

"Have the satellites engage her. Let's see what they do." Corban smiled, as orders flashed around the control room.

"Do you think that's wise Sir? They might be just another race exploring the galaxy like we did. Firing on them might be considered as an act of war." Johan warned, a little surprised by his commander's course of action.

"The Oregarthians could have discovered how to make portals Johan. We can't have them regain this world because we failed to act. Open fire!" Corban yelled as multiple lasers opened up from several satellites, hundreds of miles above them.

"Direct hit Sir!" Adrian shouted from his console, as laser beams slashed from the sky, vaporising the seawater around the sub, throwing steam hundreds of metres into the air.

"Well done staff!" Corban shouted, congratulating his staff, who clapped and shouted battle cries.

"Anything left?" Johan asked softly, as Adrian sat silently watching his screen.

Adrian couldn't believe his luck at being here today. All thoughts of boredom were gone, as he realised the enormity of his part in his people's history. Sitting there, he realised the whole room and the planet's population were waiting for him to report the kill. Seeing his screen picture started to clear, he was just about to relay the good news, when his screen went white, before going blank. Looking at his dead console, he was horrified when the computer klaxon sounded for the second time that day, warning of the loss of all the satellites, which had engaged the mystery vessel.

"What the hell is going on private?" Corban bellowed at Adrian, as Johan looked at Adrian's console, the room around them became as quiet as a tomb.

"The enemy vessel has fired back destroying all our satellites" Johan answered.

"That's impossible! Those satellites have our best shields nothing can pass through!" Corban replied as sweat started to break out on his forehead.

"They're gone Sir, and the enemy ship is continuing with no visible damage." Another staff member confirmed from a secondary satellite not engaged in the attack. The room remained silent, as fear grew amongst the staff members. All knew that this antique looking ship had rendered their defences useless.

"Maybe we should evacuate the city?" Corban suggested, sounding a little shaky, as the enemy vessel appeared over the horizon heading straight towards them.

"Why don't we try and contact them? We've got nothing to lose!" Adrian said out loud, before realising it, causing everyone to turn his way.

"He's right Sir. They haven't targeted anything else. Maybe they fired, only in self-defence?" Johan suggested, giving Adrian a well-done pat on the shoulder.

"Can't hurt, but who can speak Oregarthian?" Corban asked distantly. Having no one available who knew the Oregarthian language, the communication officer started transmitting anyway, using multiple wavelengths.

A BAD BEGINNING

Mike couldn't believe his eyes when the screen went white as the laser beams hit their shields. Many of the crew were knocked off their feet as the beam vaporised the water, making the sub drop several metres.

"Any damage people?" Mike yelled as the two guards watching Radon, pushed him to the side of the room, drawing their weapons.

"Leave him alone!" Simon shouted, making the guards back off.

"Simon's right men, I don't think Radon's people are responsible," Mike said as he analysed the attack.

"Who else would it be?" Radon asked, having expected his people to attack.

"The signature of the laser beam is the same as the entities beam we have on record from the American's sub attack," Mike replied sadly.

"If the Roax are here, where are my people?" Radon asked fear and anguish in his voice.

"I don't know my friend, but I don't like being fired upon. Weapons officer, take out the satellites that fired on our ship." Mike ordered angrily, as a shudder ran through the ship, as their weapons discharged.

"Targets are destroyed, Sir." The weapons officer confirmed.

"That should get their attention!" Mike smiled, as the crew softly chuckled. The ship continued towards the port city for several minutes, before the Communications officer reported that they were being hailed. Putting it on the loudspeaker, the crew all listened as Mike grabbed a handset.

"We can hear you, why did you fire on us?' Mike asked.

"I am Commander Corban; this planet is under my control, on behalf of the Roax nation," Corban announced formally.

"Well I've got news for you commander, the Roax nation is no more. We have come from your homeworld, which we now occupy. We call it Salvation." Mike replied just as formally, as a silence ensured.

"How is that possible?" The same voice exploded through the speakers, as a smile spread across Mike's face.

"It's a long story, my friend, we'll fill you in once we berth in your port," Mike replied, which caused a long pause.

"All right then, you have our permission to enter our port, we'll discuss how you arrived here then." The voice conceded, sounded put out, as the transmission ceased.

"What do you make of that?" Mike asked the others, as they all thought about their first contact with the Roax people here.

"I think we should tread carefully," Simon suggested as Kate beside him held his hand communicating her misgivings.

Commander Corban looked around the room, trying to gauge the effect that the mysterious vessel's commander's news had on his staff. The revelation that another race now controlled the Roax home planet had shaken them. There was also the realisation that they could use the portals, something that Corban found frightening. Across the room, Corban noticed Johan deep in thought, so he decided to get his opinion on the situation.

"What do you think Deputy Commander?" Corban asked neutrally.

"I'm not sure commander. The sub captain sounds very confident, I'm not sure why, but he worries me somehow." Johan replied distantly.

"I too have a problem with these people talking to us so flippantly. It offends me that they think they are our equals." Corban growled angrily.

"Still it will be good to hear their story and find out how they withstood our attack," Johan suggested, hoping to be able to finally go home.

"Yes, that's one thing I too would like to know. As long as they have that advantage, we dare not antagonise them, and I find that unacceptable!" Corban replied as they issued orders to make arrangements to greet their new visitors.

Mike, Simon and Kate stared down from the bridge of their sub, as their vessel nosed into the dock. The Roax soldiers heavily armed looked on silently. Not knowing of their visitor's shields capabilities, two soldiers approached the shield expecting to pass through, like they could with their own. They were thrown back, shocked by the shield's power. Mike after talking to the control room, arranged for the shield to be altered, giving them a small doorway, where a passageway gangplank was installed allowing access.

Taking no chances, Mike told the marines on board to cover the entrance at all times, to make sure they had no surprises. Then with Simon and Kate, he walked up onto the dock, where Johan formally greeted them.

Getting a brief welcome and a weak apology for the attack, he asked them to accompany him to the command centre. Agreeing they were led to a heavy troop carrier like vehicle, with an open top. Jumping into the vehicle, it moved off as five other carriers fell in behind them. News of their arrival must have spread from the command centre, as people lined the road, staring at the three visitors and their large escort. Travelling to the Citadel, Simon and Kate marvelled at the Citadel's structure, built out of derelict spaceships hundreds of years ago, it still looked impressive.

"That truly is an amazing structure!" Simon admitted to the soldier accompanying them.

"Yes, it is, as are the rest of the city structures. Our forefathers had a flare for building." Adrian whispered back, knowing he was told not to talk to these new arrivals.

"You're all a long way from home, it must be strange living in another Galaxy?" Kate smiled.

"It's okay, but a great many of us would like to see our home planet."

"Well we've got plenty of room; you could always travel to your home planet with us," Simon replied softly, as Adrian sat there stunned.

Getting over it, he was about to reply, when they came to a stop, at the Citadel. Although everyone smiled politely, Simon picked up the undercurrent of tension, as the young private named Adrian introduced him to his commanding officers. Mike happy to clear the air put down their attack on his ship, as an accident, hoping this would put it behind them. After small talk and refreshments, the senior officer named Johan who had first met them asked why they had come to this planet. Simon explained how Radon had become stuck on Salvation after the war and they had decided, to return him to his people.

"You have one of our enemy's soldiers on board your ship!" Corban roared, overhearing the conversation.

"The war is over Commander Corban. Best your people learn to live with your former enemies!' Mike replied neutrally, silencing the room.

"You are wrong Sir, the war continues. At this moment our fleet searches for their hiding places. There will be no peace with an enemy that attacked our world unprovoked." Corban shouted angrily, as several soldiers' hands moved to their weapons.

"That is not true; you fired on their planet first!" Kate shouted back, causing the room to freeze. Corban looked from the visitors to his people. He saw they were shocked and confused by the young woman's statement.

"How could you possibly know that?" Corban spat out, hoping to trap Kate, thinking the Oregarthian had told them.

"Your own people left behind on your homeworld to protect the portal told us!" Mike replied flatly, as the room erupted in noise.

"You are lying!" Corban growled, his eyes drilling into Mike, who rose from his seat signalling for Simon and Kate to prepare to leave.

"Your race's arrogance led to this war when you thought to demonstrate to the Oregarthian's your superiority in weapon's technology. All you did was force them into fearing you." Mike told them, walking towards the doorway followed by Simon and Kate.

"Arrest them!" Corban yelled as soldiers barred their way, some reluctantly.

"Do you really want to go down that road Commander? We might be years behind you, but our weapons and shields are more than a match!" Mike replied dangerously.

"You forget we hold you three." Corban smiled.

"Well, I'm sure when our ship starts to take your city apart, its residents will be sure to thank you." Mike shot back. A stalemate continued for several seconds until six elderly people appeared at the door, the soldiers present snapped to attention.

"Stand down!" A grey hair woman said firmly as the soldiers around Mike withdrew.

"Elder Helgar this is a military matter," Corban informed her, not impressed by the six new arrivals.

"The emergency powers you hold at the moment are in the event of an attack by enemy forces, these people have come in peace." Another elderly gentleman pointed out.

"You are relieved, Commander. You have embarrassed our people by your stupidity, leave immediately!" The woman roared, as Corban back straight, left the room. Johan also made to go when the woman stopped him.

"Johan we have noted you cautioned Corban not to fire on the visitor's vessel, which he ignored. You acted correctly and are now in command. Cancel the alert and let the men go home." The woman ordered with a smile, as the contingent of soldiers left the room, leaving just the six elders, Johan, Mike's group and six soldiers, all privates.

"Not the best of welcomes I'm afraid?" The woman continued politely, signalling for Mike and his friends to sit.

"Corban's typical of a lot of military men I'm afraid. Our race is no different." Mike replied smiling.

"Yes, we're sorry about that. When the alert was called, the civilian authority is overruled for the sake of expediency in dealing with a threat. When we learned you'd been fired upon without warning, we decided to step in." A male of the group explained.

"We only came in peace to drop of a lone survivor of the Oregarth race on Salvation, we had no idea your race was here," Simon answered honestly.

"We believe you. My name is Ileana, and this is Rue, Benjamin, Cordia, Goren and Borack." Ileana said introducing them all. Simon, in turn, introduced Mike and Kate, as the group sat down to talk.

Adrian and the other privates who were only there as security for the elders, stood spellbound, listening in as Mike told them what had happened on the Roax's home planet in their absence. Ileana, in turn, gave them an honest account of all that had occurred since their fleet had set sail to the present day.

"So you haven't heard from the fleet for over a hundred years?" Kate asked amazed at the time gaps in space travel.

"Yes it could be they're still travelling in deep sleep, waiting to awake at their next target, but I don't know," Rue said sadly before continuing. "They reported a large enemy fleet of ships of unknown design, bearing down on them before communications ceased. They either destroyed the enemy and went after the survivors, or were destroyed; I think the second is more likely." Rue explained as the soldiers in the room gasped.

"Not a word of this leaves this room, am I understood?" Ileana ordered as the soldiers nodded their understanding.

"You're not sure though are you?" Kate asked trying to give some hope.

"Our race has an arrogant streak I'm afraid. If they'd been victorious, they'd have sent a full report of the victory. No, I think we finally met our match." Ileana concluded.

"The reason we've told no one is up until now we only had two old spaceships for use in an emergency, and they haven't left the ground in five hundred years. They can only hold 500 people each, and we've a population of about thirty thousand." Goren explained sounding worried.

"That's why your arrival is such a blessing, as we fear the enemy they encountered out there in space, might someday come here looking for us!" Cordia added her fear visible.

"We wouldn't be much help in a battle, even though our shields and weapons are far superior to yours," Mike told them.

"We don't want to fight anyone. We just want to go back through the portal with you." Ileana practically begged as the room went silent. Mike was lost for words, expecting them to ask for help defending this world, something he wouldn't have done, but this was different.

"I see no problem with taking everyone, but it will take several trips, and you realise you'll be starting from scratch and your home planet is badly flooded and occupied.

"The alternative is being wiped out my friend. I'm sure we'll manage, and anyway we can always use the portal to reach another planet, your people don't inhabit." Rue suggested, getting a nod of agreement from Mike.

"Any idea who the enemy was?" Simon asked mystified.

"No. Only that their ships were totally different from the Oregarthian's, in propulsion and shape."

"Why the interest Simon?" Mike asked intrigued.

"If they find their way here, then what's to stop them from heading to Salvation? I like to know what we're up against." Simon replied.

"Well they haven't found us yet, so let's discuss the logistics of moving our people back to our home planet," Ileana suggested as the group planned the evacuation of the Roax.

Because the Roax had been on Oregarth for half a century, each person had built up a significant amount of possessions. Everyone wanted if possible, to take everything with them, which caused a great deal of discussion. In the end, it was decided to arrange several trips and bring more submarines through the portal allowing each person to take up to a hundred kilos of belongings. The ship Mike had brought through the portal was large enough to carry several thousand but hadn't been used for human transport in a decade. With the help of several hundred Roax personnel the ship was quickly converted to transport three to four thousand people with their belongings.

The first trip was scheduled for 40 days' time, with the majority of people being women and children. Simon when not working on the ship's conversion spent his spare time with Radon searching for signs of his people.

"They're out there somewhere Radon. Don't worry, we'll find them." Simon reassured him, as they wandered aimlessly around the city. At first Radon's appearance had sent shock waves through the Roax people. As time passed, their fear had been replaced by curiosity, as people welcomed him, asking about his life and his race. After a time most people just said hello having excepted him. Adrian who had become a companion on these walks, always asked about Salvation, as he guided them through the city and the surrounding countryside.

The two operational spaceships from the first fleet landing were a source of wonder to Simon. Because the entire population was leaving through the portal, security on the ships had been abandoned, as their usefulness was no longer needed. Simon and Radon studied the ships, working out their basic design and control functions. Simon knew they hadn't been used for over a century and wanted to see if they could actually fly.

"Do you think the Roax would let me have one when they leave?" Radon asked secretively on one of their many trips to the ships.

"I don't know Radon, they might object to you having our technology, especially our weapons and shields," Adrian admitted sheepishly.

"That's no problem; I could give you one of our shields in their place," Simon suggested, getting surprised looks from Kate and Adrian.

"You can't do that Simon. Your shields are far superior to ours. It would give his people an incredible advantage over our forces." Adrian told him, worried by Simon's openness.

"This planet is thousands of light years from our planet. Do you really think that it would matter?" Simon replied not worried.

"You're a good friend Simon, but Adrian is right, even I can see that." Radon chuckled, slapping Simon on the back, as they moved on.

That night as Kate lay in her bunk in the darkness across from Simon, she thought of his comments and how innocent he really was. She felt herself blushing, thinking back to the time when they had both faced each other half naked when Mike had called for Simon on the phone. Kate knew she loved Simon and he her, but his unswerving morals of being a gentleman kept them apart.

Simon across from Kate lay on his bunk staring into the darkness where Kate lay. 'Go to her' his instincts screamed at him, but he felt she might feel threatened or frightened by his actions, so he stayed where he was frustrated.

"Simon!" Kate's voice whispered through the darkness, bringing Simon fully awake.

"Yes, Kate," Simon answered his voice cracking with the sense something was about to happen.

"You really like Radon don't you?" Kate asked, sitting up on her bunk. Simon watched her silhouette stir in the darkness. She was just visible by the light from an old clock on the wall above the entry door. Simon lay there captivated by her outline, as his imagination strained against reality, as he tried to see her actual body in the darkness.

"Are you okay Simon?"

"Yes I'm okay, I was just thinking about how to answer your question." He lied, as he slowly sat up, his legs brushing against hers. "Radon's all alone, and he's been that way for a long time, I just feel we owe it to him to help find his race," Simon answered his eyes searching the darkness, as he visualised Kate's face.

"You can't give him the spaceship Simon," Kate replied as she too felt how close they were, making her tremble.

"I could go with him."

"You can't Simon, don't even think about it!"

"It's the only way I get the use of the ship. Let's face it, when the Roax people leave here, it's useless to them anyway." Simon answered trying to win her over, as Kate moved across onto his bed hugging him.

"It's too dangerous Simon. I don't want to lose you!" Kate cried, her tears wetting through his shirt onto his chest, as he held her, stroking her hair.

"Come with me Kate, you know how I feel about you," Simon whispered into her hair, kissing her softly on her neck, as he slowly turned her head seeking her lips. After several tentative attempts, he found them, kissing her before she pulled away.

"I'm scared, Simon. We've come so far, and are so far from home, yet you want to go further." Kate moaned softly; as she pulled him to her, returning his kiss, as he pushed her down onto the bed.

"We will always be together no matter where we are Kate, but I must do this. I feel that I've been led here to help Radon find his people." Simon replied short of breath, as he pulled her nightdress over her head before quickly standing, removing his clothing.

"We'll talk about it later," Kate whispered as Simon moved above her, covering them both quickly with a blanket.

Departure day arrived, and the first load of passengers and equipment boarded the sub for the trip back to Salvation. Mike had decided to Captain the sub leaving Kate and Simon in the city until he returned. Simon had told him of his idea, at first getting a blunt, angry no. After several days of arguments, Mike gave up trying to stop him, in the end letting Simon go ahead with his idea. He did put two conditions on it, one the ship was flyable and two the Roax elders agreed to give him the ship.

Simon found the elders were none too happy about him taking the ship. Deep down they were scared the enemy who'd defeated their fleet might locate them here. He, in the end, assured them that he wouldn't set out until everyone was safely on their way to Salvation. Satisfied, they agreed, putting one extra condition on the ship's use. He would find out what happened to their fleet. Promising to at least try, he moved onto the second part of the deal with Mike, fixing the ship to fly. Simon would find this much harder.

The problem was that after several hundred years, the inside accommodation and controls systems needed either repairing or reprogramming. The shield technology and weapons platforms were the most significant problems, as they needed to be replaced. This caused some indignant looks from Adrian's friends who along with some of Mike's crew were helping repair the ship. Simon was adamant that they needed replacing. Putting on a demonstration, he fired one of Mike's new lasers straight through a Roax shield, proving their vulnerability and inferiority. After this demonstration, all division on the upgrade stopped, even though, a few of Adrian's friends seemed offended at their equipment being called inferior.

It took nearly six months for Mike to return, having had to explain to the UN assembly on Salvation, 'what the hell was going on'. After the initial explanation of the new settlers by Mike, the Roax elders had also spoken to the assembly giving their side of the story, explaining how they had come just to settle, willing to live wherever the council decided. The decision took a while as several planets' representatives had to be sent for, through the portals. After several conditions were put in place, the Roax people were allowed to stay.

Ileana and the other elders were overjoyed with their new home, travelling with Mike to visit Elena and the other Roax scientists left behind thousands of years before. With their advanced technology, they freed Elena and the others from the machine on the base, welcoming them home as lost brothers and sisters. Over half of the Roax population opted to stay on Salvation, the other half decided to start over on a planet of their own, led by Corban.

Mike had generously given the ones staying a large tract of land near his own harbour settlement, south of the capital. Promising to help them resettle when he returned, he arranged for them to be housed in the same accommodation that the people from Earth stayed in during the great migration, as it was now called.

When Mike finally returned, with three more submarines, he had bad news for Simon. The UN was against Simons little excursion into the unknown, fearing he might somehow bring the Roax's enemy through the portal. Simon was taken aback, as Mike poured them a drink each in his cabin, waiting for Simon's reaction.

"That's ridiculous!" Simon fumed, worried for his friend Radon, who had worked closely with Simon to repair one of the ships.

"Look you've still got till I return from dropping the remaining Roax people off," Mike told him. The Roax people had asked for the planet to be stripped of valuable equipment, to help in their resettling. All equipment that couldn't be removed was to be destroyed rather than left to fall into enemy hands.

"It's a waste of time Mike. Most of their equipment is old and needs work. Better to start afresh, using a mix of our technology and theirs."

"Well the UN thought since Corban's group decided to be alone that sharing everything mightn't be such a good idea." Mike chuckled, thinking how pissed Corban's group had been, at being treated as equals.

"That's a good point. He seems the type to carry a grudge about our first meeting." Simon confessed, not liking the man.

"How are the repairs going anyway?" Mike asked wanting to see how much progress Simon had achieved.

"Better than I'd thought possible," Simon replied, giving Mike a complete rundown. The repairs Simon told him were almost completed, mainly in part due to the ships being built of a special alloy unknown to Simon. It was light and practically indestructible, built by the Roax to withstand ageing. The reason why it looked so derelict, was being exposed to the planet's atmosphere something it wasn't designed for. This over the centuries had turned the original silver colour, to a rusty red.

Of course, the weapons system was another thing, needing complete redesigning, as Simon had now designed a better, and more powerful laser cannon. In the meantime, Simon hoped with his new shields, they'd be more than a match for this mysterious enemy, which had overcome the Roax ships. To save time and resources, the inside had only been outfitted for a small crew of maybe forty, making the refit a lot easier. Pouring them both a cup of coffee Mike had to admit he was impressed.

"How powerful are the new lasers?" Mike enquired having only just improved the old ones himself.

"I calculate about ten times," Simon answered as Mike blinked, surprised.

"How could you possibly do that?"

"I took the power supply system from a Roax laser which is far superior to ours and combined it with an Earth crystal which focuses the beam. I was amazed that the Roax having visited Earth hadn't taken advantage of our crystals." Simon pointed out.

Mike stood there looking at Simon, as he explained his improvements as if it was an everyday happening. He knew combining two different technologies, was near impossible, yet Simon had completed the laser system as if he was fixing a broken radio. Getting over it, Mike moved on.

"How long before she'll fly?"

"She can fly now, but there's something else I want to show you," Simon whispered, moving to the door and locking it. Mike took in the gesture and prepared himself, knowing the look Simon had. He'd seen it before when Simon had an exciting breakthrough. After the laser, Mike didn't know what to expect.

"When I was in the Roax base on earth, just for safety sake, I copied their portal design. From Radon and Adrian, I've gathered the locations of distant homeworlds of the Oregarthians. I believe with the use of one of these ships, I can travel through a portal from this planet to several of their homeworlds. By travelling this way, we can be there in a fraction of the time taken to travel there by conventional space travel." Simon suggested as Mike struggled to take in what Simon had said.

Taking a large gulp of his drink, Mike sat there studying Simon as amazement turned to fear. Simon was so much like his father and mother that it scared him. As he sat there silently listening, he came face to face with the same scenario he'd had just before Simon's parents had disappeared.

"I can't lose you, Simon, it would kill me!"

"You won't lose me, Mike. I wouldn't try something that would put Kate or the other crew in danger, you know that." Simon assured him, hugging Mike knowing what he was thinking.

"Even if it was possible, a spaceship isn't a submarine Simon. Travelling through a portal requires the planet to have water to form a bridge."

"Not necessarily. The Roax built their system for ease of travel. I believe a shielded spaceship could pass through a portal without risk. Also, by using its more powerful engines, it would cut down on travelling time." Simon explained, before showing Mike his calculations.

As time went by Mike reluctantly had to admit that Simon's planning was flawless, he also realised that he'd be going with him. Simon at first was against Mike going, knowing although safe, he couldn't give a time as to when they'd return. Mike, he realised, was essential to the Roax people settling on Salvation, as well as to the UN base there.

"If you're going son, I'm going, and that's it!" Mike growled ending further argument. "Anyway, who's going to keep an eye on Kate and you?" Mike smiled, as Simon admitting defeat, continued detailing his plan.

THE CREW OF THE KATHERINE

It took a further 6 months to strip the planet of useful equipment, while destroying the remaining technology. In this time Simon busied himself with the building of a control centre for operating the portal. Using cannibalised systems from all over the planet, Simon constructed a prototype of the Roax's base founded on their technology. Since the base was remotely controlled from the Katherine, Simon installed a new shield to protect the base.

This was in case they had visitors here, while they were travelling. Secrecy had been maintained with Simon using the cover story that the base was a tactical storage area for equipment they might need and a secure place to leave the second spaceship protected for future use. No one took much notice anyway, as their main focus was on leaving as soon as possible. While Simon busied himself with the portal, Kate handled the delicate problem of finding the crew.

After approaching several people and getting blunt nos, Kate in the end advertised for crewmembers over the local radio station hoping to get a better result. Out of the Roax still on Oregarth and the crew on Mike's subs, only thirty volunteered. Kate knew they needed at least forty at the minimum, so reluctantly she went back to asking.

In the end, the crew numbered twenty from Mike's ship, mostly going because Mike and Simon were going and twenty Roax soldiers. These men were mostly going to fulfil the need to find out what had happened to their relations on the missing fleet. Adrian amazingly was one of them. Simon intrigued had asked him why he was going, when he was so excited about seeing Salvation.

"It will still be there when we get back." He'd answered smiling, not wanting to abandon his new friends.

When the day arrived for the final sailing of the last sub back to Salvation, John who was the Captain of one of the ships, begged Simon and Mike to forget this expedition and return with him. Mike close to tears told him, no, saying how much he would miss them all on Salvation.

"Well good luck my friends, and remember we will send a sub through the portal in a year's time. It will stay here for twenty days starting on today's date. That's your last chance to return home. After that time, the portal will remain closed, and you will be trapped." John explained, hoping they understood.

"We'll be there John, don't worry," Mike assured him, as the sub made ready.

Watching the submarine sail out to sea, Simon and the rest of the crew stood silently all wondering if they'd done the right thing.

"Too late now isn't it!" Adrian shouted as the others laughed. Radon came forward and slapped Adrian on the back.

"Thank you all for doing this; I am honoured by your sacrifice," Radon exclaimed his voice for once clear and full of emotion. Many of them told him it was nothing that they were just along for the adventure. Simon and Kate saw the truth; Radon had become their friend, they wanted to get him home.

"Okay men let's go, there's no point standing around here!" Mike pointed out, as they all walked silently to the ship. Mike was just about to board when he looked up at the bow of the spacecraft seeing a name written there.

"I name her after Kate," Simon said, going slightly red as Kate beside him squeezed his hand.

"Good thinking Simon, it's about time we started naming ships again!" Mike grinned as they hurried aboard 'The Katherine'.

THE SURPRISE

"We're going to do what?" Radon's garbled voice asked shocked, as Simon told them of his plan to travel through a portal. Even though Radon knew Simon and Mike had been planning something, this was beyond his comprehension. He wasn't the only one. Crewmembers were looking at each other, trying to come to grips with Simon's plan.

"Is it possible to even do it?" a Roax crewmember asked, having spent some time working on the portal technology.

"I wouldn't try it if I didn't think we could make it. Also, it will cut our time away from our base here to weeks instead of months" Simon assured them, this time getting more positive looks.

"It's no good worrying about it, let's go." Mike smiled his confidence in Simon reassuring them all. Silently the crew made ready, Kate could see several still had doubts including herself.

"Simon, are you sure?" She whispered.

"Yes love it will be fine. I wouldn't risk anyone's life unless I were sure." He smiled reassuring her, moving to the portal controls.

Like their subs, the Roax spaceship could hover, which allowed it to escape the gravitational pull of a planet. Once the ship had safely reached several thousand feet, Simon engaged the portal, punching in the first planet's coordinates. The telltale whirlpool opened south of the Salvation portal alleviating one problem Simon had, which was could he open a portal in close proximity to another one. He remembered how the Roax entities on Earth had made them travel a good distance from the portal on Salvation, now he wondered why?

Moving on, he ordered everyone to strap in, as he positioned the ship above the portal and turned the shield on. Turning the ship vertical, Mike said a silent prayer, before dropping the ship into the swirling, tumultuous funnel. Once inside Simon ignited their engines slamming them forward through the turbulence.

"Well, that was easy!" Adrian shouted above the thundering noise, as the ship shuddering, accelerated forward at an ever-increasing rate. Some crewmembers laughed nervously, though most sat there quietly hoping they would survive. 14 hours of waiting and praying ended, as the ship burst from its confinement. Roaring into a dark night sky, the crew watched the sky illuminate, as they rose above the planet. Reaching a safe orbit, Simon cut the engines and closed the portal, as all on board breathed a sigh of relief.

Checking their instruments the whole crew went about the task of finding out if the planet was safe and if not if they were.

"Why'd you close the portal?" Radon asked Simon, as the others checked the planet and the surrounding solar system for life.

"For now, I'd like to keep the portal secret. In time others will learn of it, but for now, I like whoever we meet to think we travel here by the usual way."

"You are learning fast Simon." Radon smiled.

The initial scans found no intelligent life signs on the planet. Deep space radar also detected no ships in their system they had entered. Mike after getting an all clear, decided to take the ship in and land on the surface. Plotting a course to the surface, Kate spotted the ruins of a large city. Picking a flat area in the west of the city, Mike guided the ship down. Finding the air outside was breathable Simon opened a large side door in the ship. On guard ten crewmembers slowly checked the surrounding area before signalling the area was secure.

The city lay in ruins as Radon anxiously checked inside the buildings looking for any signs of life. After 5 hours of searching, Mike called the search off, returning the ship to orbit. Here the crew gathered what information they had gathered looking for clues to where the population had gone. The city hadn't been attacked, and it had belonged to Radon's people. Unfortunately, no evidence could be found as to why it had been abandoned.

"It is a mystery to me why they left this planet, as there is an abundance of food and material," Radon added sounding forlorn.

"They seemed to have left in quite a hurry as there seem to be a large number of personal belongings left behind." Kate pointed out.

"Maybe either the Roax or this unknown enemy turned up, that's why they left." Adrian put forward thinking that could explain it.

"Well let's try another planet tomorrow. Maybe we'll find them there?" Simon pointed out optimistically, gripping Radon's shoulder before everyone turned in for the night.

Sliding into bed next to Kate, Simon kissed her cheek lovingly, happy just to be with her. Her hand roaming over his body told him he could sleep later as he pulled her to him. They'd just gone to sleep when from seemingly a long way away, Simon heard the wail of a klaxon horn, as Kate shook him awake. Grabbing his pants, Simon swiftly dressed, as he and Kate scrambled to the bridge.

"What's up?" Simon asked, trying to read instruments over the crewmember's shoulders.

"Another ship coming in fast. I can't identify its design or propulsion." Mike replied, watching a monitor connected to the long-range detection system.

"Is it your people Radon?" Kate asked hopefully.

"I hope so Kate, but the design is unfamiliar to me, even though I've been gone a long time."

"They're in range to talk, why not hail them," Mike suggested, handing Radon his handset. After transmitting on multiple frequencies, no answer was received and a sense of foreboding settled on the crew.

"Bring us to battle stations," Mike ordered, looking at Radon. "They would have replied to your hailing if they understood your language or not my friend. Better to be prepared." Mike continued, his eyes glued to the screen. Radon acknowledged him with a nod.

The ship approaching was massive at least twenty times their size. As it bore in straight at them, the crew tried to gather as much information as possible about the ship. A close inspection of the hull showed it to be crystalline in appearance; it seemed to glow with power.

"They've just raised their shields, Sir." A crewmember informed Mike.

"Unidentified ship, come no closer, or we will open fire,"
Mike spoke clearly into his headset, hoping the ship would
stop.

"Couldn't we just open up a portal and leave?" Kate asked
sounding frightened.

"If they're the enemy the Roax encountered, they'd then
know we had a new form of space travel. It's better we stand
and fight, then give away our advantage." Simon answered,
secretly wanting to enter the portal rather than face this ship.
He knew that if this ship was part of an enemy fleet that
attacked the Roax, they'd know their ship was of Roax
manufacture.

"Sir, they're transmitting, but not to us!" One of their
crewmen yelled from the communications room.

"Calling for backup, or orders on what to do I'd bet," Mike
said out loud, getting a nod of agreement from Radon.

"They just got an answer, Sir, now they're hailing us," The
same crewmember informed them.

"Put it on speaker thank you," Mike replied, letting everyone
listen in on the conversation.

"Roax ship surrender and be boarded, or face your fleet's
fate." An arrogant voice commanded.

"Can I ask your name, Sir?" Mike asked politely, waiting.

"I am Commander Yoron of Flax's battle cruiser Blue
Crystal, now lower your shield!" Commander Yoron ordered.

"Never heard of you or your ship my friend? Now, this is
Captain Hayes of the Katherine, as I said before back off."
Mike replied smiling, as the enemy's ship fired its first volley.
The Blue Crystal's weapons fire was incredibly powerful, far
more powerful than the Roax's lasers. Most crewmembers
including Simon involuntarily flinched, when the first blast hit
their ship's shield. Despite some of their misgivings, the lasers
failed to penetrate Simon's shield.

"Now Commander it's your turn to surrender, or we will
destroy you," Mike ordered as the enemy ship fired again. "We
don't know what's going on here, so target his weapons
systems. Let's pull their teeth." Mike smiled, as their lasers
opened fire.

On board the Blue Star, Commander Yoron stared furiously at the Roax ship.

"Why are our weapons not penetrating their shields?"

"They're different from before Sir. Maybe we should move away?" the Weapons Officer answered.

"Nonsense fire again and keep on firing till they're destroyed!" Yoron ordered, as the first laser ordered fired by Mike, hit their ship. Unlike the Roax's lasers, Mike and Simon's improved weapons cut through the Flax's warships shield easily impacting. Panic broke out as laser fire racked the Flax's warship destroying their weapon systems. Sustaining major damage and unable to return fire, Yoron ordered his ship to turn away and take cover behind the planet. Once his ship's rear was revealed, Mike had the Flax ship's engines targeted, bringing the enemy ship to a halt.

"Are you still there Commander?" Mike asked merrily, as Yoron's men looked at their commander silently.

"You Roax bastards are confident, I'll say that for you," Yoron replied, failing to hold his anger in check at his defeat.

"Language Commander, and who said we were Roax?" Mike replied as a long silence followed.

"We know of your ship's design, it is of Roax manufacture," Yoron replied, his voice sounded confused.

"We hold the Roax planet, but we are a different race Commander. Remember that next time you attack one of our vessels." Mike answered.

"What do you make of that?" Yoron asked his second in command, not understanding why the enemy ship hadn't destroyed them.

"I'm not sure Sir. Their technology is now far superior to ours. If they come in force, I doubt we could stop them." He replied as Yoron stood weighing up the situation.

"No one is superior to our race Captain! This ship is some kind of one-off I'd say. Let's find out more about this ship the Katherine and her crew. We may find a weakness and at the same time, delay their departure, until our fleet arrives." Yoron smiled.

After smoothing over the whole confrontation, Commander Yoron asked politely if he could come aboard. This proved a huge problem, as Simon hadn't set the ship up for meetings in space. In the end, Simon and Mike decided to land on the surface again, while Commander Yoron brought a shuttlecraft down.

"Be careful Simon" Mike warned him as they walked towards Yoron's shuttle. "He's only meeting with us because we hammered them." Mike continued, as Radon and Kate came up behind them bearing laser rifles.

"They won't be necessary," Simon said softly, having no weapon himself.

"This time I side with Kate, you two worry too little," Radon growled sounding on edge, as Flax's shuttle opened up and twenty soldiers in formation, filed out.

Walking cautiously towards the four humans, Yoron came to a halt when he realised an Oregarthian, was part of the group.

"What is going on here? That creature is an enemy of our people and yours." Yoron bellowed, causing his men to spread out, covering the human group.

"He's our friend and companion and here under a truce commander,"Simon answered, as behind him Radon and Kate moved apart, so they could fire their weapons freely.

"Everyone keep calm," Mike ordered as Yoron ordered his men back. In the end, Yoron and one officer came forward alone, while Mike signalled Kate and Radon to stay put while he and Simon talked.

As they moved nearer to Commander Yoron, Simon realised that they were not quite human, even though they were similar. They were the same shape, but their skin was crystallized like their ship, giving them a glowing quality. Their facial structure was more pronounced, with larger noses and pointed eyebrows giving them a more aggressive look.

"So what are you doing here in a Roax ship?" Commander Yoron asked, looking over their ship, seeing no damage from his ship's weapons fire.

"Were explorers looking for our friend's people?" Mike replied neutrally.

"Well, you won't find them in this Galaxy. They moved on when the Roax and our own forces started hunting for them, many centuries ago." Yoron answered sarcastically.

"And why would you do that?" Simon asked bluntly, not liking Yoron's attitude.

"They attacked our home world aeons ago; we've been at war ever since," Yoron answered, sounding as if he was telling the truth.

"You seem to have a bad habit of starting wars commander, you were lucky this time." Mike pointed out, wondering why Radon's race would've attacked Yoron's planet in the first place.

"Yes, your shields are quite impressive as are your laser weapons. But you've only got one ship, and we have hundreds of these battlecruisers, which are heading here." Yoron replied confidently.

"So you were the race that destroyed the Roax fleet?" Simon asked studying Yoron's shuttle.

"Yes, though we lost many ships in the fight. We stopped them from reaching our main planet."

"The Roax were at war with Radon's people, why would've they attacked your world?" Simon asked sadly, having guessed the answer.

"They entered our Galaxy and refused to surrender as you did, we had no choice."

"And what would you have done in their situation commander?" Mike asked.

"We do not surrender to anyone!" Yoron replied, his sense of superiority evident.

"We don't mean you any harm commander, but sooner or later you're going to regret your attitude like the Roax did theirs," Simon answered turning away and walking back to

Kate and Radon. As Mike too turned back towards the others as well, Yoron confused wondered what they were doing.

"Don't you want to be our allies, or sign some sort of treaty?" Yoron exclaimed, not sure what was happening.

"Waste of time commander. Your race thinks yourself above other races, with that attitude you cannot be trusted to honour any agreement." Mike replied, before continuing back to the others.

"You'll regret that decision," Yoron shouted angrily, feeling slighted.

"I regret meeting you already." Mike laughed waving as he walked away. Yoron, his anger just kept in check, watched this new group of troublemakers walk away, not even bothering to look back.

"We should kill them all now, while we have the chance!" Yoron snarled, waiting for his second in command to back him.

"They have us under their guns, Sir. It would be suicide to attack now." The officer warned, watching their new enemy as they casually walked back to their ship.

"We'll see about that when the fleet arrives." Yoron spat out, not impressed with his fellow officer failing to support him.

Once Yoron and his shuttle had blasted off, Simon had Mike move the ship to the opposite side of the planet to the Flax ship. While the enemy warship was blind to what was going on, Simon opened another portal, which they swiftly entered. Yoron upon boarding his battle cruiser was shocked to find the alien ship gone.

"Where did they go?" He asked angrily, staring at the ship's sensors.

"We think they used the planet to mask their departure from this system." Yoron's navigator explained, seeing no other solution.

"Send a transmission to the fleet, this new enemy is looking for the remains of the Oregarthian's population. Order fleet ships to gather near known planets." Yoron ordered, before pushing the crew to get propulsion back online.

"Might be best to leave them alone sir. They do seem to be on a peaceful mission, and they could have destroyed us." Jeddah, Yoron's second in command suggested.

"They are our enemy Jeddah, there will be no rest for our forces, till they are forced to surrender, or destroyed. Have I made myself clear?"

"Yes Sir, as you order Sir," Jeddah replied, before leaving the bridge, to check on the repairs. Yoron glared at Jeddah, watching him leave. He knew there'd be an enquiry into this incident, once the fleet arrived. Yoron had no intention of being held responsible for his people's first defeat in over a hundred years. Looking around at the crew, busily bringing the ship back to life, a plan came to mind.

Carrying out a complete inspection of their laser installations, Jeddah realised how lucky they'd been. The damage was extensive with most of the weapons systems utterly destroyed. Walking back to his cabin, Jeddah speculated on what would have happened if the Katherine's captain had been as hungry for war as Yoron was. When he had met the representatives of this new race, he'd been impressed with how open they were. He knew it wasn't allowed, but he found himself actually wanting to know them better, especially the young male, somehow he seemed friendly.

'That isn't going to happen,' Jeddah smiled to himself, thinking of Yoron's embarrassment when the aliens had walked away ignoring him.

"Well, I'm not going to meet anyone unless I can get the ship moving," Jeddah told himself, resuming his work.

Once Mike had entered the portal and safety, a debate broke out on what action should be taken. The Roax members were all for going back and destroying the enemy, as they now held the upper hand.

"Look men that sounds good, but a large number of those ships firing at the same time might destroy us. Better we find

Radon's people and find out what's going on." Mike suggested, getting lukewarm agreement from everyone.

"They sounded close to human?" Radon said confused.

"Could be a distant ancestor, or an entirely different race, who knows my friend, better to move on back to our base and try again. Simon had remained quiet through the whole battle observing the enemies' weapon systems. Now the action was over, he asked for a private word with Mike. Once in Mike's cabin, Simon angrily asked his grandfather what was going on, much to Kate's and Radon's surprise who had tagged along.

"Those shields the enemy have are like the ones we had on Earth," Simon exclaimed seeing a connection. Mike at first seemed torn, wondering if he should answer.

"It's a long story, Simon. You better sit down." Mike suggested closing the door to the cabin. "Over a hundred years ago, your great-grandparents, my parents, came to Earth. That's right Simon; we weren't human, at least to begin with. Our family were part of the Flax confederate, which covers several Galaxies. Our grandfather was against the confederate expanding and attacking other Galaxies.

They had introduced Marshall Law to increase their fleets, making every planet under their control, contribute soldiers. My father refused to serve and was branded a traitor. With the help of some close friends, he repaired an old spaceship. Using advanced shields and weapons they had designed and built into the old ship, they'd fought their way free of the Confederation. Travelling outside the known universe, they entered their hibernation chambers sleeping for several centuries.

By luck more than anything, they awoke and found the Solar system containing Earth. Though primitive, they found the human population friendly, building their new lives here, keeping their past hidden.

"How did he change his appearance?" Simon asked.

"Several of his friends, who travelled here with him, were geneticists. Using advanced DNA mapping, they matched human DNA to their own life forms. It wasn't perfect, but it allowed them to move freely on Earth."

"Did grandmother know this?" Simon exploded.

"Of course she did. Your grandfather, although an alien, was an honest man; he told her everything before they married." Mike shot back.

"This explains much. I wondered why your weapons and shields were so advanced while your ships are primitive." Radon added still worried by his new friend's leaps forward in technology.

"Grandfather, when he reached Earth, kept his past hidden, including technology. When the war started on Earth, I was forced to reveal the shield technology to save the planet from complete destruction, pretending that I invented it." Mike admitted sheepishly.

"We're all glad you did Mike, or none of us would be here," Kate smiled.

"Yes, it was the right thing to do. Since then with your parent's help and you Simon, we've greatly improved on those technologies. Luckily the Flax's confederacy has not!" Mike pointed out.

"Is that why I'm so smart, because of two different races' DNA?" Simon asked wondering, as Radon looked on studying him.

"I'm not sure Simon. Your parents were both intelligent, your mother much more than your father. I think it may have something to do with it, but I wouldn't get too big a head over it."

"You are an enigma, Simon. Who else could take the Roax's most advanced travelling technology and make it work beyond what they thought possible." Radon put forward. Secretly he was worried for his friend, seeing the danger others would see in his inventiveness.

"Anyway, we're not getting anywhere talking about the past. Let's look at another planet." Simon suggested as they moved back to the bridge.

RADON'S PEOPLE

The Katherine visited four more planets finding no living sign of Radon's race. Twice they had to leave quickly as Flax warships closed on their positions. Hopes of finding the Oregarthian people were dwindling, when on the fifth planet they at last by chance, received their first break. Radon had deciphered a message left on a wall of a destroyed building. At first, no one had taken any notice of the message, till Adrian pointed out how amazing it was that the message had survived intact. Intrigued Radon found a secret code hidden in the message, indicating a planet, where the Radon's people may have retreated to.

The planet listed was not a known planet they had the coordinates for. One of the known Oregarthian planets was close, though it meant they'd have to travel across open space for several weeks to reach this new planet. Mike decided to put the plan to the crew to get their approval, as this mission would put them in far greater danger. Simon in the meantime worked on increasing their shield strength in case they voted to go.

When the time came to vote on travelling to Radon's people's location, he was surprised when the whole crew immediately backed the plan. It appeared Radon's situation had hit a note in the conscience of all on board. They all wanted him to find his people and were willing to risk open space. Still, Simon just in case, spent another week perfecting the quality of their defences and armaments.

As planned, they first travelled to the closest planet using the portal. Emerging from the portal to dry land this time, the ship settled into an orbit around the planet. Simon immediately scanned the surrounding galaxy looking for any sign of movement. Confident the area was safe, Simon signalled Mick to take the ship out into space. Before they left the planet, Kate had them look down into the portal that Simon hadn't closed yet. From space it looked like a giant circle of water spinning clockwise. Instruments showed it was energy, swirling around the entrance of the portal.

"That's amazing!" Mike grasped. "I didn't know it was possible to travel without water."

"I figured the Roax used water to mask their appearance on the planets they visited. I believe the portals will go to any place you have the position of, though you have to watch you didn't come out in a populated area." Simon pointed out.

"This could revolutionise space travel," Adrian exclaimed.

"Or enslave it." Radon put forward, seeing the danger.

The bridge was as quiet as a tomb, as Mike gave the order to head out into space. The only noise was the roar of Katherine's engines, as they accelerated faster than the speed of light, towards Radon's people's planet. After a week, Simon found space travel different to what he had pictured it. Instead of groundbreaking discoveries, he encountered the dark endlessness of travelling through the void between planets. Kate filled this time always with him as they spent time learning more about each other. Boredom became everyone's enemy, as days ground by and the feeling of confinement gripped the members of the crew.

To keep everyone alert, Mike organised activities and studies, as well as battle drills keeping the crew on their toes. Simon could see why hibernation had become such a huge part of space travel. They were only crossing a short distance in space, which would take just over three weeks and already the crew were bored silly. The Roax had spent over 500 hundred years just to reach Oregarth, only to find it empty. Simon knew that without Kate he would've opted to sleep.

Having crossed two-thirds of the distance to their destination, the first sign of life appeared, as an alert from the ship's sensors.

"What is it?" Mike asked the crewmember on duty on the long-range sensors, as the whole crew crowded into the bridge.

"Several ships have entered this Galaxy behind us near the planet we started from."

"Have they detected us?" Mike asked softly, as everyone in hearing distance stopped and listened.

"Hard to tell Sir. If their equipment is as advanced as the Roax's, I'd say they've got us."

"We can't let them follow us to Radon's people. Let's change course and see what happens, maybe we can use one of this Galaxy's suns to confuse them." Simon suggested as Mike ordered a course change, towards the nearest sun. For several earth days, they continued watching for pursuit, dodging around several suns, before continuing on. Boredom had been forgotten as the whole crew took turns, manning the ship's sensors, watching for pursuit.

While travelling on this new course, Mike noticed Radon kept checking the forward sensors, taking more and more readings in the direction they were heading. As time passed, he became agitated even nervous.

"Is there a problem Radon?" Mike sensed that something was wrong.

"We must turn soon, or we will enter the void."

"What's the Void?" Simon asked, he too had been studying Radon.

"It is an area of space where no one goes. To enter is certain death." Looking at the instruments, Simon saw nothing of any danger, just a small solar system of twenty planets orbiting a small sun. Looking at the Roax maps for this area, he was surprised when a warning came up indicating danger.

"I see no danger Radon, but the Roax maps indicate danger as well. Is it just your race that can't go there or the Flax as well?"

"For thousands of years, no one has entered that system, those who do never return."

"How long before we enter?" Mike asked.

"At our present speed, we have maybe two days. I am not joking Mike, we must turn soon." Radon sounded scared.

"Okay, I believe you. Will give it one more day then resume our course." Mike suggested as Simon continued to stare at the area called the Void. Going over the Roax records, Simon could find nothing to justify the no go ban. Records showed they had lost twenty ships in this area but not necessarily in the void. In bed with Kate that night he continued to think about the void wondering what was there that made it such a danger to every race.

Unable to sleep he walked to the bridge studying the space ahead, trying to pick up some hint to what was out there. Only a few crewmembers including Adrian were on duty, so Simon grabbed a headset, scanning frequencies. For over an hour he listened for anything out of the ordinary, while watching the long distance scanner array. Except for the twenty planets and the small sun, there was no sign of technology or life in the system. He found this strange, as the fourth planet from the sun had a similar orbit to Earth.

Yawning, tired of listening to background static, he was just about to turn off the communication system and return to bed, when a voice spoke through his headset.

"Come to us when all is lost Simon, we will help you!" Startled, Simon jumped to his feet, as the crew turn surprised by his sudden movement.

"Is everything okay Simon?" Adrian asked watching him.

"Must've fallen asleep, I thought I heard voices." Simon smiled, getting in return, chuckles from the crewmembers.

"We would have all heard it then. You've got the frequency open at the moment; we can all hear that static noise." Adrian smiled, as Simon turned off his headset.

Leaving the bridge, he returned to bed wondering about the voice, it had seemed so clear, and what did it mean, by 'when all is lost'. Mystified, wondering if it was just his imagination, he settled into an uneasy sleep.

After another day of travelling blindly away from their destination, and finding no sign of pursuit, Mike told them to resume course, much to Radon's relief.

"Well if nothing else, it will make the return journey a lot faster." Adrian put forward, the crew breaking into a rare session of laughter.

"I'm glad you came Adrian, you're a born clown," Mike replied smiling.

"Well thank you, Sir, I think," Adrian answered, not sure what a clown was.

After spending two weeks longer than anticipated, the Katherine arrived at the fifth planet. Kate in charge of the scanning equipment checked the planet, finding evidence of a large fleet of ships behind and on the surface.

"They're my people's ships alright. The problem for us is how do we tell them we've come in peace?" Radon put forward, knowing his people would already know of their approach.

"I suggest you hail them Radon. Let's face it you know them the best, it might help." Simon suggested, passing him the headset. Clearing his throat, which made an unholy guttural noise, Radon transmitted.

"This is Commander Radon Dargon of the Ninth, do you read me?" Simon for the first time became aware that Radon had been more than just a foot soldier in his race's army. Twice more Radon repeated his message before an answer came.

"Commander Dargon was presumed dead many centuries ago in a battle against the Roax. Who are you and why have you come to our planet?" A voice asked.

"The Roax are no more, only a small group remain. The people I travel with now control the Roax planet."

"Your ship though old is of Roax design, though your shields are different from theirs in many ways." The voice replied sounding intrigued.

"Who now rules?" Radon asked.

"Commander Caydon of the Fifth." The voice replied proudly.

"The Fifth! Last time I saw the Fifth, it was running towards the portal like Gerrom's, to escape a tidal wave!" Radon laughed, sounding like he was gargling. Silence followed Radon's statement as all on board wondered if Radon had insulted the Oregarthian leader's soldiers.

"What's a Gerrom?" Adrian asked Radon, as everyone waited.

"A brown crablike creature stands about 2mts tall with six legs. It can run like the wind and tastes like a chicken."

"What's chicken?" Adrian asked Radon's reply was cut short.

"Commander Dargon, how is it you survived?" Another voice asked

"I was trapped on the Roax planet near the portal's base. I rebuilt a hibernation chamber from one of our ships." Radon told them. Silence followed for several seconds.

"Follow the small ship approaching yours. It will guide you down to a landing field." The voice commanded, before continuing "Be warned my friend do not deviate from the flight path."

Landing safely, Radon suggested he go first. Outside, several hundred Oregarthians in armoured vehicles formed ranks outside their shield. Opening the hatch, Radon raised his hands showing they were empty, he then walked towards the welcoming committee. Mike not as optimistic as Radon had the crew train several heavy laser guns to target the small opening they had allowed in the shield. Simon excited to meet the Oregarthians followed Radon, angering Kate.

"Someday he'll regret jumping in without looking." She told Mike as they watched him catch up with Radon.

"Let me do the talking Simon," Radon whispered, seeing Simon come up beside him, as an Oregarthian came forward.

"Radon Dargon of the Ninth is it really you." A voice boomed out.

"You must be Caydon of the Fifth?" Radon replied, walking forward to stand in front of him.

"No, I am Kargol of the Sixth." He answered seeming embarrassed.

"Why isn't your leader here to greet me?" Radon snarled sounding offended.

"He thought it prudent not to expose himself in case this meeting was a trap," Kargol told him. To Simon, he appeared ashamed.

"Much has changed since the Tenth led." Radon pointed out, getting a nod from Kargol who turned and stared at

Simon. Seeing his focus moved to Simon, Radon knew it was time to introduce him.

"Kargol may I introduce Simon Hayes. He is the reason why I am here. I owe him my life." Radon confessed, shocking Kargol and the Oregarthian in hearing distance.

"No Oregarthian should make a deal with a Roax murderer." Kargol spat out.

"He is not a Roax, though his race now holds the Roax's homeworld." Radon replied just as angrily. Kargol confused studied, Simon. He noticed the boy, or he seemed to be a boy, wasn't afraid of him, or the large group of aliens facing him.

"Simon is it. Why have you come here with Radon?"

"In return for Radon's help with the Roax on our home planet, we agreed to return him to his people. When we arrived at Oregarth, we found it occupied by the remaining remnants of the Roax people. In return for letting them go home to our home planet which was once theirs, they allowed me to use one of their ships to bring Radon home to his people."

"Is he joking?" Kargol asked Radon. Finding it hard to believe an alien race would travel across the Galaxy to return one member of a different race.

"Simon's race is like none we've met before, honour is everything to them, as well as how do they say it, 'the common good," Radon said, smiling at Kargol's confusion.

"We have much to talk about, and time is short. Already our enemies gather. My people are worried by the arrival of the Roax ship Radon, so for now, only Simon can come with you to our base. Is that agreeable?" Kargol asked. Radon nodded his acceptance. While Radon went ahead with Kargol, Simon returned to the ship to brief the others.

"You can't go, Simon! Look at the way they're acting. I can't protect you there." Mike sounded worried.

"He's right Simon don't go. We did our job getting Radon here it's time to go home." Kate put in.

"Radon will be with me, and this race needs our help against the Flax's confederation. I'll be perfectly safe."

"You're a stubborn fool!" Kate replied turning and hurrying inside, leaving Simon with Mike.

"Simon you can't save every race. Out here in space its survival of the strongest. Since you're going to go no matter what I say, take my laser pistol, it's one of the old ones, it can't hurt to have a little protection." Mike told him, handing him the gun. Tucking the weapon into his pants, Simon hurried to catch up with Radon, as behind him, Mike yelled a warning. "Tell Radon if anything happens, I'll level this planet and destroy all their ships!"

"It will be okay," Simon yelled back, but Mike had moved back inside.

When Simon returned to the meeting place, he found Radon had gone ahead with Kargol with most of the troops. Twenty Oregarthian soldiers, in an armoured vehicle, had been left to escort him to the base. The troop carrier he was to travel in resembled early earth tracked vehicle. Of course, this one hovered just off the ground, using an advanced type of jet engine, like their hovercycles.

"Stand next to me and hang on." A soldier told Simon as he scrambled aboard. As they were talking, one of the soldiers at the front of the vehicle yelled something back to the soldier talking with Simon.

"What did he say?" Simon asked not hearing over the engine noise.

"He was wondering what you'd taste like." The same soldier grinned.

"I'm not sure, but there wouldn't be much of me to go around." Simon smiled, as the soldiers chuckled, as Simon's answer was passed forward.

"Are you from the fifth?" Simon asked.

"No, we are of the ninth. Only a few thousand of our army survived the invasion of Roax. We now serve Caydon of the Sixth."

"Then you are Radon's soldiers?" Simon pointed out, trying to make sense of the Oregarthian's customs.

"Radon, if he is Radon was once our commander. Now we are not sure." The soldier answered, as their vehicle entered a narrow canyon. Simon noticed the soldiers grow tense, many raising the weapons they carried.

"Is something wrong?"

"In this area lives a large beast, its body is armoured, making our weapons near useless. We only travel as we do, to stop our enemies picking up our spaceship's engines." The soldier replied, as he too watched the surrounding area.

Simon felt the soldier's unease scanned the surrounding area seeing nothing out of the ordinary. Smiling to himself, he realised that nothing was ordinary to him on an alien planet. He was just about to ask what the creature looked like, when the ground to the vehicle's right, suddenly fountained into the air. Rising from its lair a huge beast, rushed towards them, as screaming out its hatred, it moved to intercept them.

The scream sounded like steam escaping from a pipe. It filled everyone's mind with horror, as Simon crouched down away from the side of the vehicle. The creature at first appeared to be just a black lump, devoid of eyes or facial features. As it gained on their vehicle, Simon knew it must have some way of sensing their presence as it came in for the kill. Smashing into the side of the vehicle, Simon like everyone else fought to stay inside.

The armour panels at the front of the vehicle collapsed like paper. Four soldiers who had been standing near the front spilled out onto the ground. The driver seeing the soldiers fall, slammed the vehicle into reverse, as the creature's momentum carried it forward in the direction they'd come from. As the carrier came to a bone-jarring stop beside the four soldiers, the rest of the soldiers poured from the vehicle, forming a defensive position around their fallen comrades.

The creature surprised by the sudden stop, came to a halt, swinging around it rushed back towards them. Simon, who had remained on the vehicle, watched the creature charge in. At first, he'd thought it must have some type of natural propulsion like their hovercycles. Now seeing the creature clearly, he saw it was propelled by hundreds of tiny legs, hidden underneath its armoured body. Simon mesmerised, watched it charge towards him.

Below him the soldiers took aim, firing a long burst of their lasers rifles at the creature. Appearing unhurt by the beating they were inflicting on it, the creature roared its defiance. Pulling out Mike's pistol, Simon in desperation, took aim at the creature's legs. Firing a long burst, he saw several of the creature's limbs sever, as blood sprayed from its injured legs. As if the creature had hit a hidden tripwire it toppled forward, screaming in agony, before slumping onto the ground unmoving.

The soldiers looked from the creature to Simon; unable to believe Simon's small pistol had stopped the creature.

"That is impossible!" The soldier Simon had talked to earlier exclaimed, looking at Simon's little pistol. "Where did you come by such a weapon?"

"My grandfather and I made it. We were lucky this is an old version, not as powerful as our new ones." Simon pointed out, as the soldiers looked at each other, wondering what their other weapons were like.

The danger over, the four soldiers were quickly loaded back onto the vehicle, which continued on, the soldiers silent. Many cast brief looks at Simon as they whispered amongst themselves. Some had witnessed the human when he'd fired on the beast. They told how he had calmly drawn his weapon, lined up the creature and fired, showing no fear at all. It had impressed them.

After a brief examination of the four soldiers, it was found that none of them was severely hurt. Cleared by their medic, they approached Simon, thanking him. This he was to find out later was quite an honour, recognising his bravery. He was just about to answer, when the carrier came to an open valley, filled with spaceships. At least fifty huge ships lined the valley floor lined up in military precision, facing a vast cavern. This Simon concluded was the Orgarthian base.

"My God that's incredible!"

"Well, it's good to know we can at least impress you with something!" One of the soldiers exclaimed as the others laughed.

When they reached the base, the twenty soldiers spread the word about what Simon's old gun could do. The guards at the base, hearing the story, barred his way, until Radon appeared. After being told what happened, Radon burst into laughter, at his race's reaction to Simon's little gun. His laughter stopped when they still refused to let Simon in with it.

"They want you to leave it with them before you enter. If you do they'll copy it if they can. Better to return to the ship." Radon explained, upset by his race's welcome to his friend.

"No, they can have it, remember I came here to help. It's an old model anyway the new shields wouldn't be worried by it." Simon smiled, handing the gun to one of his escorts, before following Radon inside. Behind him, the Oregarthians gathered round to look at the weapon. It was then swiftly taken to a lab for examination. By the end of that day, the entire population knew of the new weapon and the new race that had come to help them.

THE OREGARTHIAN COUNCIL

By the time Simon and Radon's meeting with the council got underway, the whole council had been brought up to date with Simon's weapon. The fact he'd given it to them without a second thought impressed them. They told him of their history from the early times to the meeting with the Roax. Since their defeat on the Roax planet, they'd gone from one disaster to another.

First, there were reprisal attacks from the Roax fleet, then soon after by the Flax federation. In fleeing the Roax, they had entered the Flax federation home system. Like the Roax after them, their fleet had been annihilated, leaving the tattered remnants to scatter. Now, this small planet held what was left of a once powerful race. Simon could see defeat written on their faces, as an uneasy silence clouded the room.

"Look I can give you the means to defend yourself, but I don't want you going off to destroy them like they did you," Simon told them, seeing a continuing cycle of violence. The council looked towards Simon as if he was speaking a foreign language unable to grasp his idea.

"You expect us to do nothing to these killers when they come for us?" Caydon their leader answered.

"No, I expect you to defend yourself and your territory, not invade theirs."

"I see no difference," Caydon replied.

"I am suggesting you live in peace, not go looking for war," Simon said watching them.

"This concept is alien to us, we must think on it," Caydon confessed as he and the other council members left. Simon could see they didn't believe in his concept of peace. When Simon had first met their leader Caydon, he had felt uneasy as Caydon continually stared at him. It was as if he saw Simon as a threat to his rule. Now alone with Radon, Simon asked what problem did Caydon have with peace?

"The universe doesn't always do as you want Simon. My race has always conquered like the Flax federation does now. They want to be the victors, not the vanquished. As for

Caydon, he has led his people from one defeat to another. He needs a victory, or his reign will be over." Radon said smiling.

"I won't give them advanced weapons to conquer the Flax federation." Simon pointed out.

"Then just give them enough to survive, for my sake." Radon pleaded.

"Okay, but unless they change their ways, we can never be friends," Simon admitted, moving outside. Radon watched Simon walk outside, conversing with the soldiers from the troop carrier. They too saw Simon as a friend, willing to help them. Caydon didn't see Simon in that light. He saw him as a threat that one-day would have to be dealt with.

Arriving back at their ship, Radon and Simon told Mike of the meeting; Mike at first was reluctant to help.

"You're changing the balance of power Simon. Even giving them our old shields and weapons, puts them ahead of the Flax federation and the Roax. Only in numbers are they inferior" Mike pointed out.

"We can't allow them to be destroyed. They're the last of their race, it will give them a fighting chance to move elsewhere." Simon replied.

"Simon you can't save everyone. Someday trusting strangers will be your downfall." Kate said softly. She knew Simon for all his intelligence, had a weakness in never seeing the danger in knowledge.

"I am not a stranger Kate. I would never let any harm come to Simon." Radon assured them. Even with his shark-like teeth, everyone there knew he was telling the truth.

"We know you wouldn't Radon, and we'll help your people, but even you must have doubts." Mike challenged him.

"Yes you're right, my people don't trust you. On the other hand, they'll perish without your help." He replied honestly. In the end, Simon convinced them to help. Mike still wanted everyone to stay on board, while Simon upgraded the Oregarthian systems.

Spending the night with Kate, Simon found her unusually silent. Even when they'd made love, Kate although passionate seemed distant.

"It will be okay Kate. It'll only take me a day or two, to teach them the new programs and then we'll go home." Simon assured her.

"I'm scared, Simon. Each thing we do seems like a pile of blocks, one false move and they will fall." She shivered as Simon held her.

"Two night's time from now, we'll leave everything behind us and go home, don't worry," Simon promised, hugging her until they both fell asleep.

Early the next morning, Simon and Radon emerged from their ship to find the twenty Oregarthian's soldiers from the first day waiting for Simon in their vehicle.

"Seems you made some friends." Radon smiled, as they climbed on board. The soldiers excitedly showed Simon their new rifles, based on Simon's old pistol. He was impressed and at the same time made aware of how desperate the Oregarthians had become. To them, the new weapons gave their race a chance to survive before they faced extinction. Radon, like Simon, picked up the soldiers' excitement, singing along with them, as they crossed the mountains into the base.

Caydon and the other councillors were not there this time, having given the order to prepare to leave, once the new shields were uploaded. Ushered into a vast laboratory on board Caydon's flagship, Simon was introduced to their lead scientist named Jarob. Unlike Radon who was tall as the other soldiers, Jarob had a slight build like Simon. He found out from Radon that soldiers were trained from birth to be soldiers, while the intellectual members of the race, followed a different growth schedule. Radon of course as a commander followed a program made up of both systems. Simon found it strange, to say the least, that before birth your destiny for life, had already been laid out.

Jarob at first seemed uppity about Simon being in his lab especially after Simon had handed over the laser pistol that he'd found beyond his understanding. Once he'd broken it down and worked out how it functioned, he'd updated the program to their weapon factories on board their spaceships, where they altered their existing space weapons, plus reissuing personnel weapons for their troops.

Now he sat back in his own domain to be told about some new shield program by this young upstart. Wanting to prove that he knew something, Jarob showed Simon his latest version of a new type of computer he'd designed. The young man seemed fascinated by it, asking permission if he could use it. Jarob despite his misgiving, found the human to be an incredibly fast learner making the computer do things he hadn't thought of yet. He was also polite, not pushy, wanting for Jarob's input into the shield generation and implementation.

Lunchtime found Simon sitting with Jarob and the other Oregarthian scientist going over everything from power saving to growing and breeding livestock. Simon told them of his people and how they voted in a leader for a set term. It was well into the night before Simon and Jarob, and his team called it a day.

The shield units were already being deployed to the fleet. On the ships, engineers worked without stopping, until all their spaceships were protected and battle ready. Jarob, like the soldiers escorting Simon, felt a bond of friendship to this young man of a race they didn't even know. He'd expected to meet some superior member of an alien race instead he'd met an honest person just trying to help.

Jarob was smart enough to know his leaders wouldn't see it the way he and the soldiers saw Simon. They, he believed would only see an enemy to be eliminated at a time that suited them. It had never occurred to him that an Oregarthian could be whatever he liked, not what their race decided for them. Now after meeting Simon, he knew the truth.

The next morning, Caydon sat with his councillors watching a video of Simon's day at the base. He had asked all the commanders to attend this briefing, pulling them away from working on their fleets. The video started with their troops escorting Radon and Simon. Radon could be seen singing along with the soldiers while Simon looked on smiling. The councillors then viewed Simon conversing with the scientist lunching with Simon, Radon taking a back seat clearly lost in what they were talking about.

"This human seems to have a way of disarming anyone who talks with him." Caydon pointed out, watching the interplay between Simon and their leading researchers.

"They respect him for what he's done for Radon and our people Commander of the Fifth." Kargol Commander of the Sixth answered. At the moment Kargol held the second largest contingent of troops and spaceships, making him second in command. He'd been having breakfast with Radon when this meeting had been called. Suspicious he'd asked Radon to remain on his flagship while he attended.

"Simon and his race are a danger to us. I believe Radon is no longer to be trusted. He's become infected, with this human view on peace through mutual trust." Caydon spat out.

"He has given our people hope where there was none before. They are departing soon, as will we, so the chances are we will never meet again." Joal, Commander of the twelve replied, wanting no trouble.

"I asked for a vote to seize their ship!" Caydon roared daring anyone to oppose him. To his surprise out of the seven commanders including himself, only three backed him, making it four votes to three. In the history of the council, this was the first time the vote hadn't been unanimous. "We will attack when they come to say goodbye. Prepare your ships." Caydon ordered his surprise at the vote plain to see, as he stood and turned to leave.

"What if our new weapons fail to pierce their shield? Surely they didn't give us their most powerful weapons?" Joal added, uncomfortable with attacking the humans.

"Do as you are commanded!" Caydon shouted as a light above the entrance door started flashing. "What is it now?" He shouted as a soldier ran into the room.

"A large fleet has entered this solar system. They're heading straight for us." The soldier informed them. The room grew deadly silent as Caydon retook his seat.

"How many ships?" Caydon asked.

"At least three hundred, Sir."

"Tell the fleet to go to battle stations and launch all ships on the surface. The ships carrying women and children are to head away immediately. Use this planet to block the enemy's sensors." He ordered as the soldier rushed outside. "How many battleships are fitted with the new weapons and shields?" Caydon asked Kargol.

"Just over a hundred and fifty. The other thirty will take another day. I suggest they go with the women and children ships for some defence, in case we fail." Kargol suggested, getting acceptance from Caydon.

"What about the humans?" Joal asked

"I'll ask for their help." He replied.

"Weren't we just about to attack them?" Kargol reminded him.

"They can wait till after this business is dealt with," Caydon replied leaving his council members astonished. As the meeting broke up, Joal walked with Kargol to his shuttle.

"Kargol I have no faith in Caydon," Joal whispered. To the Oregarthians his statement amounted to treason, causing Kargol to freeze.

"It goes against our laws to denounce him," Kargol replied. In effect, he'd agreed with Joal by not reporting him for his statement.

"You have my support," Joal answered before moving on. Kargol watched him go; knowing Joal had just placed his life and his army in Kargol's hands.

Klaxon horns blaring woke Simon and Kate from much-needed sleep. Running to the control room, they joined the crew in taking up their battle stations.

"What's going on?" Simon asked Mike.

"Looks like we didn't lose those ships that were following us like we thought," Mike replied sounding anything but happy.

Their long-range sensors had picked up the incoming fleet at the same time the Oregarthians had.

"Where's Radon?" Simon asked.

"He went to stay the night with Kargol. I suppose he's trying to find a position for himself here." Mike answered. Simon for the first time realised that Radon wouldn't be leaving with them.

"Sir the Oregarthian fleet is breaking up. Two-thirds of the fleet is going to battle stations. The other ships are heading away from the incoming fleet." Adrian reported.

"Saving the women and children, I'd say," Mike suggested more to himself.

"Are we going to make a run for it?" Kate asked.

"No, we brought the enemy here we'll stand and fight with the Oregarthians!" Mike told them, getting a shout of support from the crew.

"Prepare the ship to launch into space," Mike ordered, as their radio came to life.

Caydon told them what was happening including sending their women and children away. Caydon wanted to lead the attack, but Mike convinced him to hold back behind the planet till they were engaged. Caydon agreed hoping these humans would be destroyed in the first volley.

Trying to encourage his troops, Caydon addressed the whole fleet. He told them they weren't alone, that the humans, who had given them advanced weapons, were launching to attack as well.

To his shock, the men shouted their support, banging their feet on the decks cheering Simon's name. On his flagship, Kargol heard the shout go up as well, and the realisation that his men knew of Simon's name hit him. Kargol realised he had a lot to think about.

On the Blue Crystal, Commander Yoron looked out through the bridge window at the massive fleet bearing down on the Oregarthians. 'This time we'll finish them' he smiled, plotting the course of the ships fleeing to destroy them later. In front of his ship was the Supreme Commander on the Jagged Crystal.

He'd come in person to witness the destruction of the enemy fleet. The Jagged Crystal dwarfed Yoron's ship. It was the most powerful ship ever built, four times the size of his cruiser. Yoron's smile faded as he recalled that it had been his ship to command until he'd had the run-in with the strange Roax ship.

He'd been passed over for promotion. Losing a battle, to an inferior enemy was unacceptable. No one believed the enemy ship was more advanced than theirs. It was put down to a malfunction on his ship, caused by the crew's neglect. Fuming at his mistreatment, Yoron had blamed Jeddah and the crew for everything. He'd had them all transferred, replacing them with another crew.

Jeddah once Yoron's second in command scanned the enemy fleet, looking for anything out of the ordinary. He'd been given temporary command of an old cruiser, called the Shining Crystal that was being decommissioned. On board was a high percentage of the Blue Crystal's crew having been demoted as well. Once the ship arrived back at the scrap yard they were all to be used as replacements, Jeddah to be court marshalled. They'd been given a reprieve when news of the enemy fleet had come in.

When the Roax ship had first been detected by a squad of 4 Flax ships, they'd been ordered to break off the chase and pretend they had lost them. Instead, they had followed the original course the Roax ship was on, spotting the Oregarthian fleet by its heat signatures. Holding back, they'd called up the rest of the Flax Southern fleet and waited. Now with overwhelming numbers, they hoped to finally finish the Oregarthians off once and for all.

Jeddah like many others conscripted to serve with the fleet was sick of the constant fighting. Most wanted to go home and leave the Oregarthians alone, maybe he hoped after this battle they would. So far the enemy hadn't reacted to their presence, except to send the ships he believed contained their women and children away from the pending battle. The only thing out of the ordinary was they hadn't deployed their shields.

"They could be low on power?" He mumbled to himself, as he continued to look for any sign of treachery.

A new power reading on the planet made him move his equipment to focus on the new contact. 'I've seen that signature before' he thought when like a blinding flash he remembered.

"Captain Yoron, can you hear me!" Jeddah shouted into his headset, calling Yoron his squadron commander.

"Of course I can hear you, so can the enemy if you yell any louder," Yoron replied seeing his new crew smile. Yoron had given them his side of what happened.

"The enemy Roax ship that we encountered before is on the planet preparing to launch. I suggest we retreat and reconsider our assault."

"That is not your decision to make Jeddah and are you sure it's the same ship?"

"Yes, I've compared its signature to the one recorded. The Supreme commander must be told." Jeddah warned. Not bothering to answer him, Yoron called the Jagged crystal.

"Supreme commander, Jeddah has asked me to inform you that the Roax ship we met before is on the planet. It appears to be getting ready to launch, and he thinks you should retreat."

"Commander Yoron, we are well aware of the small ship. It disgusts me that Jeddah still shows such cowardice in the face of the enemy. Order him to stay with the auxiliary fleet ships." The Supreme commander ordered, leaving Jeddah fuming having heard the conversation.

"Jeddah, you are instructed to reverse course, move away from the battle," Yoron ordered, a small smile appearing on his lips.

"Yes, Sir. I hope you and the Supreme Commander are victorious." Jeddah replied half-heartedly, ordering his ship to move away.

"Launch!" Mike commanded as the Katherine shot into space heading towards the enemy fleet. "Okay crew in ten minutes we'll be in range. We've got twenty lasers cannons, fire on as many different ships as you can. Though our shields are far superior, we can't afford to be hit by multiple weapons fire, it could overload them. So it's hit and run, we must at all times keep moving, does everyone understand." he asked. Getting a muted response as a little fear moved amongst the crew, he gave them a smile. "We'll get home yet my friends, so let's teach these bullies a lesson." Mike chuckled, as their lasers in range, stabbed out into the approaching fleet.

Onboard Caydon's flagship, he watched the small ship rocket into the enemy formation. 'They've got guts I'll say that' Caydon thought to himself, watching as twelve of the enemies' ships burst into flames.

"What just happened?" Caydon roared at his crew.

"The human ship just cut right through their fleet. I count twelve ships either damaged or fully destroyed." His second in command told him, the crew cheering wildly.

"Ordered the fleet forward while there's something left for us to shoot at," Caydon ordered, worried by what was happening.

On board the Jagged Crystal the Supreme commander looked at the battle taking place with horror. All that Jeddah had told them was true, as the small Roax ship, carved a path right through their fleet, escaping untouched. Then the outer units reported the Oregarthian fleet had raised their shields and were moving forward. To the Flax's astonishment, the shields were Roax. Although the shields weren't that much better than their own, the enemy's laser weapons seemed to have been improved, cutting into the Flax federation ships.

Three hours after the battle started the Flax confederation had lost over a hundred ships destroyed or out of the fight. The Oregarthians fleet was suffering too, having lost at least forty ships. While both sides suffered losses, the Roax ship kept attacking appearing undamaged. This caused confusion in the Flax formation, stopping them from organising a defence against the Oregarthians.

Seeing the Roax ship turning for another pass, the Supreme commander ordered the Jagged Crystal and Yoron's ship the Blue Crystal to intercept the Roax ship themselves.

On board the Katherine, Simon closely monitored the power to the shields. Several times he had been forced to cut the weapons power, to bolster the shields. Everything seemed to be working effectively, though the shields consumed massive amounts of power, when multiple weapons were firing at them. Simon tried to calculate how long their power reserves would last, at the moment they were holding.

"Sir the large cruiser I warned you about is coming towards us, with an escort," Adrian shouted, from the sensor array controls. Earlier Mike had discussed the huge ship, coming to the conclusion that it was the fleet flagship.

"Let's try and end this. All weapons concentrate on the two incoming ships and keep us away from the rest of the fleet if you can." He instructed the crew, as Simon watched the gauges dip, as the Flax's flagship fired everything she had at them. Something would have to give soon he realised, as the flagship's escort started hitting them as well.

When the battle had first started, Simon, like everyone else on board, wondered how a ship fought in space? Though all the ships present could reach the speed of light, high speed was impractical when closing in on an enemy ship. With all their advances in technology, space wars had become like early 16th-century sea battles, where ships broadsided each other, trying to score a fatal blow without being fatally hit themselves.

The Katherine was like a light cruiser fighting massive battleships. She only survived by manoeuvring around the larger ships striking quickly then retreating. The problem was sooner or later you were going to take a hit, slowing you down, which meant you'd be hit more often. Now with these two much bigger and more powerful ships closing in, Simon tried to think of a way to end the battle swiftly.

He'd come up with the idea that he thought would work, but did he dare use it? Going over the plan in his head he was convinced it would work, but thousands would be wiped out in seconds. Looking at Kate seeing the terror in her eyes, he knew he must act.

"Mike, turn our ship, so we're heading directly at the flagship!" Simon yelled as he pushed new commands into the ship's control system.

"Are you sure Simon? We can only fire our four front weapons."

"Trust me, do it now." Mike not knowing what Simon intended but trusting him, ordered the ship to turn towards the enemy.

On board the Jagged Crystal, the Supreme commander watched the small Roax ship head straight towards them.

"Does he intend to ram us?" He asked Yoron.

"He can only fire four of his weapons now, he must be damaged," Yoron replied happily thinking they'd beaten them.

"Continue to fire until this menace is completely destroyed." The Supreme commander roared, as a brilliant blue light, screamed towards them. "What is happening Yoron?"

Yoron too stared at the light, covering his eyes as a feeling of impending doom settled on him.

Simon watched the flagship loam up in front of them, as the whole crew stood silently, watching him. Mike to the side held his breath hoping whatever he was planning happened soon. Simon watching his instruments saw the required distance had been reached, so taking a deep breath; he turned on the portal switch. The blue light that Yoron had seen was a portal trying to open around him. Without a fixed address to open too, power built up swiftly imploding around the flagship, closing the portal.

In a blink of an eye, the flagship and Yoron's ships were gone. The Flax's fleet, seeing their commander and his escort ship vaporised, retreated. The Oregarthians too had been shocked by the ship's destruction. Unsure what had happened they stayed where they were, waiting for orders. Caydon, summoned his scientists, asking them how the humans had destroyed the flagship. Jarob, his senior scientist, who had been closely watching the battle and had seen the light, but like the others, had no idea what it was.

"Obviously it's a new weapon of some type. I don't quite understand why the humans didn't use it earlier."

"They could have battle damage and the weapons only used as a last resort," Caydon suggested.

"I'm not sure Sir, their shields are still up, and I see no battle damage." Jarob wondered where this was going.

"Gather the fleet. We will attack them while they're weak." Caydon ordered. Looking around he saw his men hesitate.

"But they've helped us, Sir," Jarob shouted.

"I gave you men an order!" Caydon screamed as he slapped Jarob, knocking him to the floor. The rest of the men looking downcast moved to their stations. "And take this man away he's under arrest for treason."Caydon continued, surprised by his men's hesitation.

Kargol receiving the signal from Caydon to attack the humans ordered his units forward, then contacted the other fleet commanders, before asking Radon to come to the bridge. He explained to Radon what was going on, asking his advice.

On the Katherine, the crew rested, thankful it was over. Simon had again become the centre of attention trying to explain what he'd done. Mike near the bridge was the first to notice the Oregarthian fleet closing on them. Simon and the rest of the crew's attention was drawn to Mike seeing him staring at the advancing fleet.

"People, they could be just coming to thank us, but stay at battle stations, just in case," Mike suggested, as the crew reluctantly resumed their positions.

"I wonder how Radon is," Kate asked, holding Simon's hand, as they all waited.

Caydon was just about to order his ships to open fire when he was informed the military council members had just docked with his ship. Angry at this break in protocol, he waited for their arrival. His anger turned to open fury when Radon entered with Kargol.

"How dare you bring that traitor onboard my ship!" Caydon bellowed, startling all present. Radon without hesitation drew his weapon and fired. Caydon taken by surprise failed to react.

Taking the full force of the blast, Caydon toppled backwards hitting the deck, his surprised crew drew their weapons shouting for Radon to drop his. Radon bent down placing his pistol on the deck, before raising his hands and turning to Kargol.

"Kargol, Commander of the Sixth, you are now the leader of our people. As Commander of the Ninth, I was well within my rights to challenge Caydon, after he called me a traitor, as all here witnessed." Several crewmembers nodded their support as Radon continued, "Caydon was about to attack the humans who gave us the shields and weapons to survive this battle. Does anyone here not think I speak the truth?" Radon asked.

"You speak the truth Radon. I for one came to stop Caydon from launching the attack. But you have spilt the blood of our leader, and you must be punished. I order you to leave our people, you are banished." Kargol declared. To the Oregarthians this was worse than death. Many turned away unable to look at Radon, some saluting Kargol acknowledging him as leader.

"You are now the leader Kargol, I will obey." Radon cried, his grief evident, as he turned and left. Kargol, his face blank, ordered two of his guards to escort him to his shuttle. In the meantime, Caydon's body was removed from the bridge, as Kargol took command. Ordering the fleet to stand down he explained to the fleet what had occurred, praising Caydon for his leadership. Once he knew there'd be no dissention, he hurried to the shuttle bay to meet Radon. Dismissing the guards the two commanders smiled.

"Is control now yours?" Radon whispered.

"Yes my friend, the other commanders have excepted me."

"Good, you will be a great leader Kargol, I wish you well." Radon smiled, gripping Kargol's hand as a fellow warrior.

"I'm sorry friend that you have to leave, but it was the only way to be rid of Caydon," Kargol confessed, having thought the plan up, to prevent a civil war.

"I will miss my people, but the Ninth is no longer a fighting force, my usefulness here is minimal. The humans though advanced, are a young race. With them, I find my guidance is appreciated" He smiled.

"Tell them as long as I rule, they are always welcome. And we will avoid the Flax federation as Simon advised." Kargol conceded as Radon boarded the shuttle. Familiarising himself with the shuttle controls, Radon was just about to launch, when Jarob and twenty soldiers appeared. Opening the door, the group boarded the shuttle sitting down and strapping in. Jarob coming forward sat down next to Radon.

"What's going on Jarob?" Radon asked.

"I was marked as a traitor by Caydon. The soldiers are the guards that were assigned to Simon as his escort, they were arrested as well. We all seek to follow you Radon; here we will not be accepted, even though Kargol will now rule." Jarob confessed.

"I am honoured. But you must know, we might never return."

"Somehow I know we will." Jarob smiled, as Radon chuckling, blasted off.

Transferring back to the Katherine was not easy. The ship was not designed to receive transfers in space; there was also the issue of dropping the shield while surrounded by questionable allies. Mike, in the end, took a chance dropping the shield, allowing the shuttle inside before deploying it around their ship and the shuttle. Squeezing together, Simon managed to open the large cargo door, allowing the shuttle to enter. Slamming the door shut air was pumped back into the cargo area. When Radon opened the door, he found Simon waiting.

"Somehow I knew you'd come back, Simon laughed, going quiet when he saw the soldiers and Jarob. "What's going on Radon?"

"We've all been exiled. Would it be okay, if they came too?" Radon asked.

"I suppose it's okay. We'll have to ask Mike, even though it's a bit late now." Simon pointed out.

"They'll do whatever you ask. They just want to be free."
Radon assured him.

Mike agreed that the Oregarthians could stay letting them
billet in an area not used by the existing crew. The crew at first
seemed on edge being outnumbered by the new arrivals.
Radon assuring them there'd be no trouble, won them over as
they prepared to leave.

Before they left, Kargol sent an official message of
friendship; giving them an address of a distant galaxy they
were heading for. The Oregarthian fleet then turned in the
same direction that they'd sent their women and children
earlier, accelerating away. Kargol assured them they'd be
always welcome.

"Well Radon, I suppose welcome back is the only thing we
can say." Mike chuckled, having just travelled across a galaxy
and fought a battle to take him home.

"It was necessary, unfortunately, but here I have a purpose,
there I'm no longer needed," Radon admitted.

"Well, I'm glad you're back," Simon added, Radon in return
gave a smile in his own way bearing his teeth.

"You're going to have to work on that." Adrian sniggered as
the long-range scanner sounded a warning.

Looking at the screen, Simon saw one Flax cruiser
approaching. What surprised him was its shields were down.
Radon told them how Kargol had once met with the Flax
federation vessel that dropped its shield as a sign they wanted
to talk. Mike, in the end, agreed to drop their shield opening a
frequency they'd used before and during the battle with the
Blue crystal commanded by Yoron.

"We come in peace. Is that Captain Mike?" A voice asked.

"Just Mike will do. Who am I speaking to?"

"It is Jeddah. I was once the second in command under
Yoron." Jeddah answered.

"How is Yoron?" Mike asked.

"Not well, he's dead. You killed both the Supreme
commander and Yoron when you destroyed those two cruisers
with the blue light."

"So, what do you want?" Mike asked.

"We would like your help in freeing our people from the crippled ships," Jeddah replied before explaining. "The military council which controls the Flax Confederation does not accept defeat. In any battle that the Confederation was involved in, the ships crippled were abandoned as a lesson to the other of the cost of defeat. To prove their point, no ship had life capsules fitted or shuttles for abandoning ship.

Of the ships engaged in battle, over a hundred were destroyed, with another hundred crippled. The surviving ships had followed orders and left, leaving the crews stranded on disabled ships to die."

Simon looked around at the crew gauging their reaction to a call for help, from a race that just tried to kill them. What he saw was concern for the trapped crewmen.

"Jeddah your ship isn't damaged why aren't you leaving?"

"I have had enough of killing; I will not leave these men to die."

"You're a good man Jeddah; I'll put it too my crew." Mike then asked them. "Well, what do you think men?"

"It is best to leave them. To their race, they're dead anyway." Radon told them.

"I think we should help them, if we don't, we're no better than they are," Adrian said getting support from the others.

"I agree with Adrian. We came here to help stop the war by helping the Oregarthians. They have decided to move away, rather than to continue fighting with the Flax Confederation. We have a chance here to make a difference, I think we must try." Simon explained as Kate held his hand supporting him.

"Okay then, how do we do it?" Mike asked. Simon sat down working on his computer while the crew stood there watching him. Ten minutes of crunching numbers and he had a solution. Mike went over his figures before giving him the nod. Calling Jeddah, he gave him the details of Simon's plan.

What Simon had worked out, was to get alongside a crippled ship and then encompass the ship inside in the ship shield. Because the Katherine was small compared to the Flax ships, he would have to do it from Jeddah's cruiser. Jeddah could then use his powerful engines to land the crippled ship on the planet the Oregarthians had just left.

To help where possible, Radon suggested using his shuttle as he could enter their ships as he had entered the Katherine. Some he pointed out were beyond trying to save, better to take off the crew.

"I thought you were for abandoning them." Mike pointed out.

"I was, as I consider it dangerous to interfere in another race's affairs. Since Simon doesn't seem to have that problem, its best to help and get it over with." He conceded.

"There is one problem Captain Mike. No one aboard my ship or the other ships knows how to expand the shields."

"That's okay. I'll get Radon to drop me off at your ship." Simon replied.

"Simon," Radon started to warn when he stopped him.

"I'm in no danger, let's get on with it," Simon told them all, as he walked towards the door. Behind him, Mike gave Kate and Radon a silent look, as Radon followed.

"Captain Simon, I know it means little, but you have my word no one will betray you," Jeddah told him as Simon boarded Jeddah's ship. Radon stood behind him giving Jeddah the once over.

"There is one condition with Simon staying on board. Four of my men will stay with him at all times." Radon told Jeddah watching him.

"While Simon is on my ship, none of my men will carry firearms, is that acceptable." Jeddah put forward.

"That is more than I expected Captain Jeddah. If you now tell me which of your ships are the most damaged, I'll start evacuating them." Radon answered.

"You an Oregarthian are going to help us?"

"Yes, Simon has a way of changing everything." Radon laughed reboarding his ship.

After Jeddah and his crew got over the fact that the Oregarthians were helping them, Simon was taken to engineering, the look at the shield projection computers.

Amazingly they too were of a binary system, similar to the Roax. Simon knew it was no coincidence. He found out from Jeddah later that the system was adopted from captured equipment. The shield program was an elaborate set up with power used to overlap one layer onto another. Simon was amazed how advanced the system was compared to how weak the shield produced.

Working on it for several minutes, he could see where they'd gone wrong, seeing the overlapping was causing interference within the shield. He knew he shouldn't change their shield's output, but he saw no other way to make the shield expand and keep its integrity. Finished, he had Jeddah manoeuvre his ship next to the first crippled cruiser. Deploying the shield, Simon studied his improvements seeing the shield maintain its strength. Signalling that he was ready; Jeddah ordered the ship to proceed to the planet's surface.

It took three days to rescue all the ships' crews. Not all the crews survived, some ships were just too badly damaged that even Radon couldn't get to them in time. In the end, the planet resembled a giant scrap yard where the Flax crews cannibalised some of their ships to make others fly. Helping as much as he could Simon, in the end, told Jeddah they must leave.

"We cannot thank you enough Simon. Most of the crews here owe you their lives" Jeddah told him.

"What do you intend to do now?" Simon asked.

"We are in disgrace Simon. We will try to fight our way to the central planet and overthrow the council. We will most probably fail, but we will die trying." Jeddah told him.

"Why don't you just go home?" Kate asked.

"By now we have been written off. Our families will have been told that we all died bravely. No, if we go home, we'll be branded cowards and imprisoned or worse, better to fight."

"How many ships does the council's Home fleet have?" Simon enquired.

"Four hundred cruisers, it will not be an easy battle." Jeddah smiled.

"Will the other fleets support you?"

"I am not sure. Wanting freedom when your family will suffer if you fail is a hard decision to make. I could approach several fleets before we make our move, but if it doesn't work, it will alert the council to our attack."

"Well, we wish you luck anyway Jeddah," Simon said before leaving.

As Simon knew the position of Oregarth instead of taking weeks, they used the portal and were back in days. Arriving at the Citadel, Mike landed the ship next to her sister ship, near the portal base. Making an entry point in the shield, the whole crew after checking their surroundings disembarked. Adrian walked down the deserted streets looking at the city that had once been the command centre of the Roax on Oregarth. To him, it seemed unnaturally quiet and devoid of life.

Actually, it teamed with animal life, as the planet's indigenous wildlife moved back into the area. This had been home to Adrian for all his life, only leaving this city for this adventure with Simon. Now he looked at it like it was a stepping-stone to his new life on his race's home planet. Hearing approaching footsteps, Adrian turned to see Jorab approaching.

"This must have been a fine place to live," Jorab suggested waiting for Adrian to answer.

"Yes it was, but I long to go home," Adrian replied. When the Oregarthians had first come aboard, Adrian, like the other crewmembers, had felt uneasy at having them inside their shield. Most had kept to themselves Jarob was different. He always asked questions, his thirst for answers was insatiable. He wanted to know anything and everything about their lives and their dreams. He broke down barriers, after that the crew accepted the new arrivals as allies.

Once landed, groups Roax, Oregarthians and humans had hurried off in different directions. Some went fishing, some hunting, while other groups just explored the new world.

"We have another six months Simon tells us, till the submersible from Salvation arrives, and we travel there," Jarob answered sounding excited.

"I didn't know you wanted to go with us, I thought you would start your new life here on your homeworld."

"We will in time, but first we must see Simon safely home." Jarob smiled. Adrian wasn't surprised that Jarob wanted to see Simon make it home. Ever since coming aboard, the Oregarthians treated Simon as if he was their leader, giving him the same respect as they would their Supreme commander. That was another thing they all had in common, Adrian too, thought of Simon as his commander. On this trip, many had come to realise how vital Simon was to their survival.

Kate and Simon wanting to spend some time alone together decided on taking a break. Borrowing the shuttle that Radon had arrived in, they flew to the far side of the planet. There located in a small inlet, sat a seaside resort, that the Roax had built for vacationing. Here in a deserted bungalow, they spent the next week on their own, enjoying the peace. Until now, all of their time together had been in the confined, shared space of submarines or spaceships. Being able to walk around and swim naked, was something new to them. Simon would always look back on this week, as the time he really got to know Kate.

Of course, it wasn't completely isolated with Mike calling every day, checking on their welfare. In the end, realising they missed the others, they returned. Taking a place near the waterfront where their sub had first docked, they went about their lives waiting for the sub to arrive. Simon had suggested instead of waiting, they should take the spaceship through a portal he could open, knowing Salvation's position. Mike decided against it for Simon couldn't predict where the portal would open.

They'd been back on Oregarth for three weeks when their peace was suddenly interrupted. The Katherine's long-range sensors triggered an alert. It had picked up two ships coming towards their planet. Jarob, on duty at the time, sent out warning messages, recalling everyone. Some were miles away taking all day to return, but by that night, all were assembled on board the Katherine. To Radon's surprise, the two large warships coming towards them were Oregarthian.

"Why do you think they've come here Radon?" Mike asked.

"I'm not sure, but there are only two ships, and they have their shields down, so it's unlikely to be trouble."

"I'm sure you're right my friend, but we should go to battle stations just in case," Simon suggested, Radon agreeing.

The room grew quiet as one of Radon's soldiers tried to raise the ships. After several attempts at different frequencies, contact was finally made. It appeared the two Oregarthian ships were the last remaining battleships of the Ninth. Radon's remaining soldiers and their families had opted to find their lost leader. Kargol had given them permission to try, allowing them to return if they failed. They'd spent the last two months crossing the galaxy, following Simon's ship's course. Their fleet Captain asked permission to land. All eyes turned to Mike.

"Hey it's Radon's planet, they're his people, it's his call." Mike pointed out.

"Thank you, Mike, we know it's our planet, but after what you and Simon have done for our people, they need your permission to land. It means a lot to them." Radon told him. Mike nodding his understanding picked up the handset.

"Of course you have our permission to land Captain. We look forward to meeting you all." Mike said feeling embarrassed. Radon then grabbed the radio telling the Captain to land on the other side of the planet where a village already stood. This was the place Simon and Kate had spent a week at.

"This will give them space to set up a settlement until you leave." Radon explained not wanting the humans overwhelmed. Giving them a week to settle in, Kate, Mike, Radon and the twenty Oregarthian soldiers, travelled with Simon by shuttle to meet the new arrivals. Landing between the settlement, Simon was surprised when the Oregarthian's children swamped the shuttle trying to see him. Word had spread to the women and children of the human who had saved them all from annihilation.

Radon too was greeted formally, as the two thousand remaining Oregarthian soldiers, lined up to be inspected by their commander. Humbled, Radon slowly walked down their ranks talking freely to the troops, happy to see them, as they were to see him. Wondering how they'd feed themselves, till they got settled, Simon found out that the vast warships, which usually carry ten thousand troops each, were filled with supplies.

"I'll say one thing for the Oregarthians, they can certainly organise." Mike smiled.

"Yes, being on the run for several centuries means you always carry plenty of supplies," Radon answered as the group moved back to their shuttle.

Getting ready to leave Kate noticed the twenty original Oregarthian soldiers pile on board. It was strange considering Radon was staying for a few days to organise his people.

"You soldiers can stay here if you like," Kate told them, getting confused looks in return.

"We are Simon's guards. We go where he goes." The soldier in command replied proudly. It was only then that Kate realised that except for their week away on their own, some of these soldiers had always been discretely around Simon.

"I think Radon told them to watch over Simon. I'd say they take it pretty seriously." Mike whispered to her.

"The way he's always charging off on adventures, without thinking first, it mightn't be a bad idea," Kate admitted as Simon unaware of what was going on flew them back to the Katherine.

Two months and the Oregarthians had firmly settled in, starting to build their villages. Having learnt their lesson the hard way, they knew that there'd be no consuming the entire planet resources and moving on. Adopting Simon's clean energy and farming the land, they intended to make this planet their home permanently. Even Simon and Kate considered keeping a place here to live, as with portal travel it was only a few days from Salvation.

On one of their many visits to the settlements, many of the children had asked to see the planet Salvation where Simon came from. Mike always happy to please the children on this visit had brought some movies from his early times on Salvation. The whole settlement had turned out to watch them, having no such device themselves.

"How do you record your history?" Simon asked Radon.

"We don't, we just passed down what has happened in the past from mother and father to sons and daughters," Radon answered not understanding. Getting on with it, Mike ran several discs of the transfer of the human race to Salvation from Earth, then onto the other worlds. The audience sat frozen as they saw the desperation and then the happiness as mankind endured the portal crossing. Mike then showed films of his family showing Simon as a baby with his parents than as a young boy watching his parents leave in their submarine called the explorer.

Simon remained quiet through the movies. Kate sat beside him, holding his hand, reassuring him. At the end of the movies the Oregarthians cheered, their joy at watching the movies plain to see.

When the young ones had turned in for the night, the Oregarthians put on a display of their dancing used during their mating season. It amazed Simon how similar the races he'd seen were, their customs although different were in some ways the same. Pointing this out to Radon, Simon asked had he met any race totally different in appearance.

"No most races are similar, but then they have to be to advance." Radon pointed out. Seeing Simon was having trouble with his explanation, he continued. "For a life form to advance, it must start from scratch, growing food and hunting. Then it clothes itself and makes weapons. As the numbers of its people grow, weapons become more important as well as education. Unless you have limbs to move and make tools, you wouldn't advance. Arm's legs and fingers will be found on all species as no matter how clever you are you have to be able to work. Then there are communications, you must be able to talk and have a language, and hear. That means you must have ears, a mouth and eyes. So any race you'll encounter will have all of these features to achieve space travel. They might vary but not to a great deal, as with our race and your race, even though yours is ugly." Radon laughed.

"Excuse me, Simon, may I talk to you," Jarob asked

"Of course you can what's up?" Simon answered.

"The submarine 'the explorer' from your movie, I have seen it," Jarob informed him. At first, Simon just stood there unable to respond. Kate beside him yelled to Mike telling him what Jarob had said.

"Where and when did you see it Jarob?" Radon asked softly.

"I know it holds great sadness for you Simon, but it was on a planet we stopped at over a year ago in your time."

"Were there any humans there?" Simon, recovering from the shock asked.

"No, the planet has a poisonous atmosphere, Simon, no one could survive. We only stopped there to hide from a group of Flax warship, before continuing."

"Do you have its coordinates?" Simon whispered.

"Yes, it's in the ship's database. I'll get it for you." Jarob informed him before moving off towards one of the Oregarthian ships.

"I've got to go Kate. I have to know what happened." Simon pleaded.

"I know Simon. Mike and I will come too." Kate replied hugging him.

"No it's too close to the portal opening; you and Mike must stay here. I'll take Radon and a few soldiers. That way if we're late, I can follow in the Katherine."

"I should go to Simon," Mike said grief making him look older.

"No, you've been through enough. This is a journey I must undertake alone." Simon answered as the group boarded the shuttle.

The planet was a long way out; Simon calculated looking over Jeddah's data. Since the night of the movie, Simon had worked to bring the portal system and the Katherine into readiness for this trip. Most of his friends wanted to go. Simon had politely told them no, wanting risk kept to a minimum. The rest would go home on the sub as he'd promised them. Adrian was torn between going with Simon and seeing Salvation.

Simon, in the end, convinced him to look after Mike and Kate till he returned. With only a few weeks till the portal opened, time was tight, so with a quick farewell to Kate, Simon boarded and prepared to launch. Once aboard Simon couldn't help noticing how many soldiers were aboard.

"I thought I said just ten soldiers?"

"I decided on a hundred, to give them a chance to crew the Katherine," Radon answered.

"It's okay this time, I haven't got time to argue so let's go," Simon ordered as another problem appeared. Where he had calculated to open the portal, waited one of the Oregarthian battleships.

"What now?" Simon asked angrily.

"I decided on an escort as well," Radon admitted sheepishly.

"What about protection here?"

"We still have one battleship and the backup Roax ship. They're more than a match for any enemy fleet, so I see no problems." Furious but out-manoeuvred, Simon reluctantly agreed, allowing them to come. Reaching orbit, Simon activated the portal, and the Katherine leapt forward into the vortex, followed by her escort.

Five days passed, before the Katherine emerged from the portal, streaking into the sky above the planet Jeddah had told them about. Moments later the escort ship emerged, taking up station above the Katherine.

"That was the most amazing thing I have ever seen!" One of the Oregarthian soldiers exclaimed.

"Get used to it, things like this happen all the time around Simon." Radon laughed, the others joined in. The laughter stopped, and the room became quiet, as they became aware that Simon had not heard them, as he stared out a window at the planet. 'Duelong' as it was called was a pink colour, caused by the toxic gas that circulated in its atmosphere. As Jeddah had said there was no life, though a shape of a

submarine could be seen, beached beside a large body of
water

To keep risk to a minimum, just Radon and Simon travelled
to the surface in the Oregarth shuttle. Radon had devised a
way to open the side of the spaceship where the shuttle was
stored. This made entering and exiting easier. Flying down to
the planet, escorted by a shuttle from the escort, Radon was
first to spot the sub.

It was his parent's ship all right Simon confirmed, as he
manoeuvred the shuttle landing right beside it, as their escort
shuttle hovered above. Donning their spacesuits, they left the
shuttle through an airlock walking to the sub. It was locked up
tight, and by its appearance, it had been there a long time.
Going to an escape hatch, Simon turned the outside door
handle opening the hatch.

Signalling Radon, they both got in, before he resealed the
door. Opening the inside hatch they cautiously entered. Power
was still on which surprised Simon as they carefully moved
towards the control room. Several bodies or what was left of
them littered the control room. Most appeared as if they'd just
lied down and died in their sleep.

"Affixation, they died of lack of oxygen I'd say." Radon
suggested breaking the silence. Walking on, Simon came to
the Captain's cabin, finding a woman and a man lying beside
each other on a bed. Looking closer, his eyes blurry from
tears, Simon saw the couple had their hands clutched
together.

"Is that your parents?" Radon asked softly.

"Yes my father was the Captain, it's their cabin." Simon
sobbed walking back to the control room. Moving to the
computer console, Simon removed the hard drive before
walking back to the escape hatch, glad to be leaving.

"What will you do with your parents and the crews' bodies?"
Radon enquired as they entered the shuttle, pressurising the
ship.

"My parents, Andy and Susan had their closest friends as
their crew. I'll leave them here together." Simon answered, a

part of his life finally closed, with the discovery of their resting place.

On board the Katherine, Simon uploaded the data from his parent's ship. He was drawn to the last entry his parents had left, a summation of events that led to their final journey to betrayal. It told how they discovered an energy anomaly on Salvation. Following it, they had found its source on the floor of the ocean, underneath a wrecked ship.

Extending their shield, they were able to get close to the base's shield but could find no way in. By accident more than anything, they opened a radio channel between themselves and the base computer allowing them to communicate. They found the base belonged to a race called the Roax. It told them it had been designed by a race to run the portal systems throughout the universe.

The whole crew was overjoyed by the discovery of the portal builders, as several of the crew had suggested it was not a natural occurrence. While Andy and the crew tried to find a way into the base, Susan being a keen historian, kept a dialogue going with the base computer, discovering they'd even been to Earth.

The computer seemed delighted by her interest. It told her of a race so advanced that they were worshipped like Gods, by many of the planets they visited, including Earth. It made it clear to Susan that the Roax expected all races they encountered to treat them as Gods. Susan intrigued by the Roax, told Andy of her conversations with the computer.

Instead of impressing him, it made him wary. He had a feeling that the computer they were talking to was more than just a machine. As a precaution Andy dropped the shield and moved away from the base, he was preparing to raise his shield again, when the base fired.

The base computer must have perceived the action as a potential threat. The base on the ocean floor immediately fired on our ship. It caused damage to their steering and power, but they were still intact. Raising the shield with all the power they had left, Andy warned the base that we would return fire unless it surrendered. The computer, sensing their weapons were offline, fired again, trying to finish them.

Fortunately, their shield held, as Andy and the crew continued to restore power to their weapons. They had almost completed the restoration of power, when a portal opened immediately in front of them, sucking them in. Andy sensing it was a trap, tried to turn the ship, but the pressure waves drew them further in, giving them no choice but to continue.

Clearing the portal five days later they found themselves stranded, as the portal closed behind them. After calling for help on every frequency they could and receiving no reply, they all knew their fate was sealed. Running low on air, the crew decided rather than suffocate they'd take sleeping pills. Their final message was for their son Simon, hoping he had a full, happy life.

At first, he broke down, sobbing at their loss, knowing that all hope of seeing his parents again had now been removed. Radon and the others remained silent, standing with him in support during this difficult time. Simon started to shake as rage surged through his body, knowing the Roax, in the Portal base, had sent his parents to certain death. The Roax realised they had underestimated this race when explaining their expectation to be recognised as Gods.

"The Roax have betrayed us!" Simon screamed. Rushing to the console, he immediately prepared to leave. He was just about to engage the portal drive when Radon shouted for him to stop.

"Look to the north of your parent's ship!"

Looking down Simon saw a portal opening about two kilometres from his parent's submarine.

"What do you think it means Radon?" Simon asked.

"I'm not sure, but it might be best if we wait."

"It could be open for days, and the portal back on Oregarth will open soon." Simon put forward.

"We know the Roax did this to your parents, why would they open the portal here again?"

"To trap someone else, something must be happening on Salvation. You're right, we're best to wait, or someone else will have the same fate as my parents." Simon murmured a feeling of doom settling on him.

Five long stress filled days passed, before the ship's sensors picked up a disturbance on the planet. Watching from orbit, the crew of the Katherine watched 8 submarines break the surface coming to a stop. Simon seeing the subs belonged to four different planets of the Gun barrel planets was just about to contact them when Radon stopped him.

"I'd suggest raising our shield first Simon. Remember we're in a Roax ship, they mightn't react well if they have been tricked."

"Good idea," Simon replied giving the order, as he started transmitting. "Can any of the submarines on the planet hear me?" Thinking they hadn't heard he was just about to try another frequency when all 8 subs opened fire. Fortunately, Simon's new shields were more than a match, as the subs seeing their lasers caused no damage stopped firing.

"Well, they must be able to talk to each other to all fire at the same time." Radon concluded.

"Yes, it seems you were right to raise the shield," Simon admitted, before starting over.

"I say again, can you hear me?"

"Yes we can, who are you?" came a blunt reply.

"I am Simon Hayes, son of Mike Hayes. If you look to your right, you'll see the wreck of my parents ship the Explorer. The Roax tricked them into travelling to this planet like I judged they did you." Simon informed them.

"Okay we're listening, how do we get out of here?" The same voice asked.

"I came here in my spaceship the Katherine. We had received a report that a submarine was stranded here. I left Mike and the other members of my crew on Oregarth waiting for the submarine to come and pick us up. The crew with me are all aliens, Radon the Oregarthian who was trapped on Salvation and his soldiers. I have a shuttle that we can come down and pick up two men from each ship to return here to discuss our next move. Do you agree?" Silence followed Simon's statement as the subs communicated with each other.

"Simon, why did you call your ship Katherine?" A voice asked.

"After Kate, a young woman from New America, who is travelling with me. As you most probably guessed we've become close." Simon answered. The silence continued as again the subs communicated.

"We're picking up another ship, are they with you?"

"Yes, that's my escort."

"Okay, Simon we believe you, mostly because no one down here believes you could make a story like that up. We'll be waiting for you." The voice assured him.

"Just make sure you wear protective suits, the atmosphere is poisonous," Simon warned them.

"Thanks for the warning, but we've worked that one out for ourselves."

Radon and his soldiers weren't too happy when Simon told them, that he was going down to the surface. He told them it was the only way, as they'd think something was wrong if Oregarthian's troops met them. Radon, in the end, gave in, letting him go, as long as the escort shuttle went as well. Arriving at the first submarine, Simon found the two men in sealed suits standing outside on the deck waiting with the shield down. Landing they picked these two up, before picking up the rest.

Arriving aboard the Katherine, the sixteen men were overwhelmed by the ship. Most of them then moved to the window, staring at the escort.

"My God it's a monster!" One of the sub-men said as they all looked out into space.

"It certainly is. Now gentlemen, if you could take a seat." Simon asked wanting to move on. As the group sat down, they took in the troops that operated the ship.

"Can they be trusted?" An officer from one of the subs asked.

"I trust them more than I do you!" Simon pointed out, silencing them. "So how did you all end up here?"

"We were told by the UN that someone had seized the portal base. Since these 8 ships were the only ones available that were armed, we travelled to the base. As we approached a portal opened up, and our ships were made to enter, transporting us here."

"What do you mean 'made'?" Radon asked, making all the officers look embarrassed.

"We'd all secretly formed alliances with Corban's breakaway group. He exchanged technology for equipment. We all received advance computer systems for our subs. In this upgrade was a virus and it took over our systems. Before we knew it, we were too far into the portal to turn round." Another officer admitted. Silence descended as everyone took in how stupid they'd all been.

"What about you Simon, you were thought lost, but here you are flying a Roax spaceship, with a crew of aliens."

"It's a long story, so I'll give you the short version." Simon briefly told them of what he'd been up to. After an hour, more than one face thought he was having them on.

"So not only did you fight a battle with another alien race, but you built your own portal system?" The Commander of the New America's two ships asked, his face clenched, trying not to laugh.

"Well I'd better have gentlemen, or your subs will never leave this planet," Simon informed them.

"I think you're full of shit?" The New Russia Commander shouted jumping to his feet, as Radon's soldiers drew their weapons.

"Sit down you fool!" Radon growled "I too found it hard to believe when Simon opened the first portal. Look where you are! You are sitting on a spaceship, in the middle of a distant galaxy, on a toxic planet and you want to know if the only way you can live is possible? Just do as you're told, or we will leave you here." After staring at them, daring them to say anything, Radon angrily walked away, as Simon signalled his guard to lower their weapons.

"You have a choice. You either follow us through the portal or stay here." Simon spat. "Now return to your ships and make ready." He ordered, as the sub commanders stood up and left without another word.

After two Oregarthian soldiers had returned the men to the submarines, Simon worked out the calculations to bring them out in the water on Oregarth. On the 8 submarines the crews watched spellbound as a portal opened, and two spaceships dived into it. Scared but having no other choice, the 8 subs dived after the Katherine following at their own speed.

Arriving at Oregarth, the Katherine roared into the night sky. Simon anxious to contact Mike tried the radio, getting no answer as the escort ship joined them in orbit. Radon was first to spot the rising cloud of smoke that lay over the citadel. The port city was on fire.

"Oh my God!" Simon moaned, looking down from orbit on the burning city. Radon came forward, holding Simon, escorting him to a chair, making him sit down. Signalling to the soldiers to watch him, Radon radioed his people. They were okay, having been warned by Mike, that something wasn't right. Landing near the warship left behind, Radon found their shields deployed.

After moving outside where they could see him, they lowered their shield running to him. Many of the women and children were hysterical at the loss of the humans and their kin.

"What happened?" Radon demanded as one of his Captains came forward.

"The Roax came through the portal in one of the human's submarines. They captured most of the people at the harbour. We couldn't fire for fear of hitting the hostages." He told him, upset because he'd done nothing. Ordering the women and children back aboard the battleship, Radon had the Captain gather his men. Marching them onto the other battleship, he then flew them to the Citadel. Landing near where the portal base had been, Radon took in the devastation as one of his Captains gave him a complete report on what had happened.

"The portal opened two days earlier than expected. Mike was surprised at first, putting it down to them wanting to know if we were all right. Four days after the opening, a huge sub surfaced, sailing towards the city. Everyone gathered his or her gear, rushing to the dock. Many Oregarthian women and children were there as well to welcome the submarine. We were just about to fly our battleship to the port city so everyone could watch when Mike called us warning us to get everyone aboard and raise our shields. He said that he'd spotted the Roax emblem on the sub. Screaming for everyone to run, Mike then raced to the reserve ship.

Whoever was on board the ship must've seen the people run, as they opened fire on the city immediately. Caught in the open most surrendered, others who reached the city went into hiding. Mike reached the ship and tried to power it up and return fire. Unfortunately, he couldn't get his shield up in time, and the ship was destroyed. It triggered a massive blast, which engulfed his ship and the portal. By the time we launched our ship and came here to help, it was all over. The sub had rounded up as many prisoners as it could, then set sail. With them aboard we couldn't fire on them. Since then we have remained at battle stations, awaiting your return." the Captain confessed.

"You did the right thing Captain. Now search the ruins, someone may have survived." Radon ordered, leading a search team out into the darkness himself. Simon left the ship as well, searching for Kate. Several guards went with him following in silence, unable to find words. She'd loved their house near the dock, but that was gone, so where was she? He'd been wandering aimlessly thinking when it came to him. He'd told Adrian to stay with her maybe he'd managed to move her to safety. Heading back toward the citadel he began checking some of the half standing buildings, screaming out her name. After four hours of searching, exhausted and running out of hope he found Jarob and his ten guards.

Before he'd left, Simon had secretly asked these men to watch over Kate till he returned. The fact they were here with Jarob meant Kate might be near. Telling the two soldiers to contact Radon, he checked the other soldiers. All were dead except Jarob. He was badly hurt, but alive giving the Simon some hope. Unable to speak, he pointed towards the Citadel, indicating Kate was that way. Radon soon arrived with his soldiers, who spread out, searching in the buildings. At one building they found stairs blocked with debris, leading down indicating a basement. Digging furiously, Radon suddenly shouted for everyone to be quiet. Standing still, everyone tried not to breathe, as a faint tapping came from underneath them.

"Dig!" Radon ordered as the soldiers dug with renewed energy. After an hour of digging and they broke through, allowing Simon to go down first. Radon silently came up behind him, passing him a bright light resembling a torch. There were several bodies at the bottom of the stairs, all crewmembers of the Katherine. Simon checking each one found that they were all dead. Moving on searching the ruins, Simon came upon the person tapping. It was Adrian.

"I'm so sorry Simon. They took her" He croaked out as Simon moved to him, checking his wounds. With him were twelve Oregarthian children and their mothers from the settlement. They'd excitedly come to the Citadel to see the submarine arrive. With Radon's help, Simon carried Adrian outside, the Oregarthians following. The soldiers waiting let out a cheer, at seeing Adrian and the children rescued. Moving swiftly they carried Adrian to a field hospital while the children and their mothers were taken back to the settlement.

Radon continued to search with Simon, knowing what Simon was going through. He had lost everything he'd loved on Salvation when his people tried to invade that planet. His wife and their two sons had travelled with him, only to be lost in that wall of water, which had drowned his army. For years the only thing that kept him going was the hate he had for the Roax. He believed the Roax pure evil until Simon had come along.

He'd showed him another way through trust and respect, that not all people or races were all evil. Looking at him staring at the ruins, Radon knew Simon's test was coming.

"Gather your soldier's Radon it's time we dealt with the Roax," Simon growled, walking towards the Katherine, leaving Radon staring after him.

"And so it begins," Radon said to himself, walking quietly behind him.

Adrian lay on his bunk on the Katherine, more upset with the betrayal than his wounds. Mike and Kate had been like family to him, he felt deep guilt over what had happened. He'd been hospitalised for over a week, today he felt strong enough to sit up. Sensing someone was watching him, Adrian looked up from his bunk. Simon was standing at the door, watching him.

"What happened Adrian?" Simon asked, sitting down next to him on his bed. Seeing Adrian trying to croak out an apology, Simon stopped him, passing him some water. Taking a mouthful, Adrian began. When he and the others heard the sub was coming, he'd grabbed all his gear racing to the dock. Katherine laughing at Adrian's excitement had gone with him telling him he had plenty of time. Arriving at the dock the group waited excitedly as the submarine came towards them. Mike between the reserve spaceship and the dock yelled a warning, pointing at the ship's insignia.

Adrian at first thought it was just a gesture from the Roax who had gone ahead. He was about to yell back telling him to relax, when looking closely at the ship he saw Corban on the bridge. Screaming for everyone to run, he grabbed Kate's hand pulling her towards some buildings, as the sub opened fire.

Adrian thought they'd die right there, as others on the dock raised their hands surrendering.

Slipping away running frantically towards the Citadel, he heard the shout to stop behind them. From nowhere, Jarob and ten soldiers appeared firing on their pursuers. Giving them time, they ran on only to see groups of women and children running opposite them. Grabbing Kate's hand, he sprinted to them while Jarob's soldier continued to fire. Gathering the children, they kept running towards the Citadel, when looking back, Adrian saw Jarob's soldiers were all hit. Yelling at the children to follow him, he led them into a building with a basement. Gathering them together he led them away from the stairs, telling them to hide.

Kate having been given a pistol formed a defensive line on the stairs, with several crewmembers. Adrian was just moving towards them to help, when an explosion rang out, collapsing the roof and blocking the stairs. Adrian hurt, crawled, back to the children. In the pitch dark unable to do anything they waited. They remained silent in the darkness for hours, fearing to make noise, until he'd heard the sound of people searching. In desperation, he tapped on the wall hoping whoever it was would save them. He had been shocked to learn that they'd been in there for nearly two days.

"I'm so sorry Simon I wish she was here instead of me!" He cried, as Simon patted his shoulder comforting him.

"You're one of our closest friends Adrian, you did nothing wrong," Simon assured him.

"Have you found her?" Adrian asked.

"No."

"Then they must have her Simon," Adrian said trying to get up.

"Stay in bed my friend you can do nothing until you're well. In the meantime rest, I'll need you when we go for her." He assured him.

Standing, Simon left him, his head thumping. He'd thought seriously of hurting Adrian when he'd first entered, for being of the Roax race. Now he felt nothing but anger at himself for being so stupid. The Roax crewmen of the Katherine had given their lives fighting their own race to protect Kate and the others. Sitting in the ship's command centre, Simon again cried, not just for Kate and Mike, but also for the others that had died for him. The day after Simon had seen Adrian, the 8 subs from Salvation surfaced. Following the smoke, they anchored in the port, as many of the crews standing on the decks, looked at the devastation.

"What happened?" the Commander of the New America subs asked as Simon met them at the docks.

"The Roax came to finish us off. I didn't get back in time."

"I'm sorry." Was all the commander could say.

"It's not your fault. Let's move on." Simon suggested distantly, leading the way towards the Katherine, in the distance an Oregarthian battleship came into view.

"Those things are monsters!" the Captain gasped truly impressed.

"She's an Oregarthian Battleship belonging to the Ninth army, Radon is their commander," Simon told the gathered humans, as they watched it land next to the Katherine. "Now Radon's here we'll have a meeting to discuss what to do about the Roax." He continued, wanting to get on with it, as he led them on board the Katherine for a war council. Behind him, several of the sub commanders looked at the warship with growing unease.

"The Roax can't be allowed to become a dominant race again. I will travel back to Salvation and free our people and annihilate them." Simon promised, his hate for them exposed for all to see. The gathered commanders looked at each other, sensing Simon was on edge.

"Simon we can't kill them all. First of all, it's hard to believe they're all involved. Like Adrian, most wanted peace." Radon pointed out, surprising the gathering.

"I'd thought you'd be happy to wipe them out." Simon snapped back.

"Once I would have killed them all. I was like you are now, full of hate. You showed me there was another way Simon."

Simon furious made ready to put Radon in his place for not backing him. As he was about to reply, he looked around the room and saw the way the gathered Captain's were looking at him. He realised his decisions were being driven by blind rage and a lust for revenge, the very things he'd fought against.

"You're right Radon, I'm unfit to command. Please relieve me and take command." Simon asked, moving towards the door.

"Is that wise to put an alien in charge of an assault on Salvation?" the Commander from New Russia asked, stopping him.

"I trust him more than any of you. Especially given that each of your planets sought an independent alliance with the Roax to gain an advantage. That act of self-interest and stupidity exposed all of our planets to domination by the Roax. He is in command while I'm recuperating. That's the end of the discussion." Simon told them.

"Who said you could decide who was in command?" The commander of New America shot back.

"You are alive because we saved you from certain death. Until Kate and other hostages are safe, I won't let your petty squabbles interfere with their safety. Once the Roax are dealt with, you can do what you like, until then you obey orders.' This silenced any further dissent, as he departed.

"Gentlemen, my race has moved out of this Galaxy, only what's left of my army will make this planet our home. We will help you now because of our respect for Simon and what he did for us. When this is all over we hope to be friends with the human race, but remember until Simon is well again, I am in command. Let's get to it and plan the rescue of our people." Radon stated watching them.

"We're with you Radon, anything's better than being on that planet the Roax sent us to." The Commander of New America replied as the others eyed each other quietly.

Simon walked along the foreshore trying to shake off the hate that filled his chest where his heart had once been. Kate and Mike had been everything to him, now he had emptiness. He had hoped to marry Kate when they returned to Salvation, now he just hoped she was alive.

Radon was right; until he got over his destructive burst of anger, he was a risk to himself and the millions trapped on the Gun Barrel planets. The future of many people, including his friends and loved ones would now be determined by his next actions. This would require him to walk the fine line between compassion and utter ruthlessness.

Turning back towards the Katherine he saw his personal guard disperse behind a group of burnt out buildings, trying to keep out of sight. Radon must have told them to keep their distance but remain close enough to protect him. Smiling for the first time in days, Simon remembered a saying Mike always quoted before chuckling insanely.

'Suck it up, and get on with it. No one gives a shit about your problems.' Feeling better Simon went back to the ship to work on rebuilding a portal base for the coming attack.

After spending a whole week working on a plan with the sub-commanders, Radon came to a conclusion, that none of them could be trusted. As much as he tried to work out a coordinated attack, petty squabbles broke out every time he allotted different targets to the four groups. Each seemed scared another group would end up with something strategic to hold over the others, once victory was achieved. Prudently he kept his observations to himself going along with the changes they wanted in the plan.

Finding out from the soldiers guarding Simon that he was back at work, he went to him sharing his conclusions. Simon immediately burst into laughter startling him. At first, Radon was worried, thinking Simon might be having a breakdown. It then occurred to him that Simon knew his people better than he did.

"You knew I'd have this problem, didn't you?"

"Yes, unfortunately, it's a curse of our race that we can't really get along at all," Simon answered.

"I don't understand how your race could achieve so much while being so divided?"

"We are very independent. We only join to together for the common good." Simon answered. Seeing he was losing Radon, he gave him an example.

"Look, if I told the planets our combined armies could rule the Universe, they would argue over who commanded and what each planet would get out of it. If on the other hand, I told them the Universe was under threat and only by combining our forces could we bring peace, they would without hesitation send every available man they had.

The human race had always come through when the future looked bleak. It's living in peace we have trouble with." Simon confessed, thinking about what he'd said.

"You are a strange race Simon," Radon answered as a soldier came running towards him shouting.

"What is wrong?" Radon asked seeing the confused look on the soldier's face, as he wondered who was in command. "It's okay soldier, Captain Simon Hayes is back in command."

"Sir, four ships have been picked up on our long-range sensors. They're Flax Federation cruisers, and they're coming in fast. Behind them are another ten cruisers, they seem to be firing at the first four."

"Go to battle stations. Get all the women and children undercover. Tell the two commanders of the battleships to launch." Simon ordered as they both ran back to the Katherine.

Arriving on the bridge, they found the commanders of the eight subs standing in the corner, as the Oregarthian crew briefed Adrian and four other members of the original crew about what was happening. At Radon and Simon's appearance, the sub-commanders, rushed towards him, wanting to know what was going on.

"We may be under attack, but we're not sure, so we are taking precautions. I haven't got time to drop you all off so talk to my communications officer; he'll put you in touch with your ships. Tell them to go to battle-stations and submerge. Once you've done that, move to the side and stay out of the way." Simon ordered, moving to the Captain's chair.

"This ship was originally under the command of Mike Hayes, who put you two in charge?" the Commander from New Asia asked.

"You're wrong, this ship was always mine. The Elders of the Roax people on this planet gave it to me." Simon shot back.

"I thought you were unfit to command?" Another asked as several of Simon's bodyguard moved between Simon and the sub commanders.

"Launch!" Simon commanded ignoring the comment, as the Katherine leapt into the sky.

Plotting a course towards the incoming ships, Simon watched the two battleships take station on either side of his ship. Reaching light speed, the ship trembled as they raced towards the incoming vessels. On the screen, Simon watched the tell-tale flash of weapons fire between the two incoming groups.

"Transmit to the incoming ships to stop firing immediately or be destroyed," Simon told the Communications officer. Seconds passed as all chatter on the bridge stopped, the only noise the muffled roar of their engines.

"Sir one of the first four ships is hailing us. He says his name is Jeddah, he is asking for sanctuary for himself and his followers, he's dropped his shields."

"Order him to move his ships behind ours. Tell the ships following to ceasefire, it's their last warning." Simon told the comm's officer. In answer, the ten ships continued firing on the four ships. With their shields down, they immediately took damage, one exploding.

"All weapons open fire!" Simon yelled as the Katherine, and the two battleships unleashed a massive barrage of lasers. The stabbing fingers of light travelled through the void between the incoming ships and themselves in seconds. To an observer it looked like a harmless light show, it couldn't have been further from the truth.

The ten enemy ships had obviously not been involved in the fleet battle with the Oregarthians, in which their Supreme commander was killed. If they had, they would've turned away and fled. Instead, they rushed in, firing on Simon's three ships. It was over quickly, with eight enemy ships destroyed, the other two disabled.

"Cease fire," Simon ordered as his crew sat at their post watching him.

"Any damage?" Simon asked.

"No damage to our ship Captain. The two battleships received minor damage to their outer hulls.

"Radon, when we get back, ensure that both ship's weapons and shields are updated to the ones used on the Katherine."

"Yes, Simon it seems we will need them." Radon smiled.

"Sir the two Flax ships damaged, do we ask them to surrender?" Adrian asked. Simon picked up a headset walked to the observation deck looking at the two ships.

"This is Captain Simon Hayes, why did you continue firing after I asked you to stop?" Simon asked putting it on speaker so all could hear.

"We take orders from the Flax military council, not you." A voice barked back defiantly.

"Which ship transmitted?" Simon asked the Comm's officer.

"The ship on the right, Sir."

"Destroy it."

"You can't do that they are no threat, you must ask for their surrender first." The commander from New Asia shouted, getting support from the other commanders.

"Fire!" Simon ordered as Katherine's laser lashed out blowing the crippled ship to pieces.

"Can the remaining ship hear me?"

"Yes, we can Captain Hayes." A voice answered politely.

"Will you surrender?"

"Yes, sir."

"Where do you stand in this trouble with Commander Jeddah and your Federation?"

"I am Captain Jardin of the Red Crystal, I am just following orders from our fleet commander. Our families are being held captive, so we follow orders."

"Then go in peace Captain. Do you need any assistance?" Simon asked.

"We've managed to repair one engine that will get us home. It is best we make it without your help if you get my meaning."

"Good luck Captain Jardin. I hope we don't meet again." Simon replied, watching as the remaining enemy ship slowly turned and limped away. Standing to the side, the eight sub commanders stood stone-faced, as Radon let out a battle cry. The whole crew celebrating the victory took it up. Standing down from battle stations, Simon turned to the sub-commanders and pointed to the briefing room. When they were all inside Simon closed the doors.

"You gentlemen are no longer on Salvation. Out here in space, there can be no bickering over a Captain's decision. I destroyed that ship to send a message, so next time the enemy will know what's going to happen to them if they fail to heed my warning. Don't ever interfere with my decisions in front of my crew again." He told them, before turning and leaving. Outside he found Radon standing near the door with his bodyguard.

"Watch them." Was all Simon said, getting a nod from his guards in return.

Once a thorough check of the ships was completed, Radon, Simon and his personal guard, travelled by shuttle to Jeddah's ship. Docking, they were greeted by a guard of honour as Jeddah stood waiting.

"I'm sorry you lost a ship Jeddah, but dropping your shields convinced me it was you," Simon admitted.

"Yes, I took a chance that the cruisers pursuing me would heed your warning to cease fire. Unfortunately, they didn't. The only good thing was the ship targeted had a small crew and was carrying mostly supplies, not families like the other ships."

"Why are you here anyway?" Radon asked.

"Going home didn't go as we had planned. After you left us, we managed to repair twenty cruisers and travel home. When news came that crews had survived and been left to die, riots broke out on several planets. It forced us to go home and rescue our families, instead of attacking the Home Fleet. When I tried to escape with my family, I was arrested and imprisoned for desertion. As news spread of my capture on my home planet, the population rallied for my release.

The Flax federation council angry at the unrest ordered the Home fleet to crush the rebellion. One of our ships intercepted a message indicating a squadron of sixty cruisers was travelling to my planet. Their mission was to pick me up and punish the population.

My second in command, Captain Morga, ambushed the squadron, as it entered the system. With your improved shields, they fought the Home fleet to a standstill; the Home fleet retreated after losing half its ships. Knowing they'd send the combined fleet, our remaining ships gathered their families and attacked the prison I was being held in. I travelled here hoping you still might be on Oregarth and able to help us.

Unfortunately, a squadron of cruisers detected us as we entered this Galaxy. All we want Captain Simon is a place for our families to live, while we continue to fight for our people's freedom." Jeddah explained.

"What happened to your other ships?"

"Ten ships, including the one commanded by Captain Morga, were destroyed in the battle with the Home Fleet. The ten left broke into two groups travelling here by different routes. We lost one when we first encountered the squadron, the other we lost when we dropped our shields. I still hope the others will make it."

"You know Oregarth is again under the control of the Oregarthians." Simon pointed out.

"Then I will ask their permission to leave our families here so we can return and battle the Flax military council. Our families will abide by Oregarthian laws." Jeddah promised.

"Sheltering you on Oregarth could cause the war between our races to resume." Radon pointed out, thinking before continuing. "That aside, your council didn't make the gesture of friendship as you did. That means you are our ally, not the Flax council so we will help you. One question though, how do you intend to fight back?"

"We have overwhelming support from the people. Some fleets would join us, but the military council controls the planets through oppression. I intend to attack the council in their stronghold on Craigure. It is a planet with no indigenous population, where our leaders and families live a life of opulence, protected by the Home Fleet.

Their fleet contains the most fanatical followers of the council. It is the best armed and is used to keep the entire confederation under control. If I can strike there, even if I'm not successful, it will show the other planets that they are not in complete control. Already word has spread of the Home fleet retreating from our ships. A more successful attack may bring the council down." Jeddah smiled.

"With three ships, it would be suicidal," Simon told him.

"By approaching distant squadrons on the way, I hope to garner more support. In the end, someone must try." Jeddah confessed.

"I will do my best to help you Jeddah, but at the moment, we have our own problems to resolve," Simon confessed as Jeddah nodding his acceptance, led them on a tour of his ship. News that the Oregarthians would allow them to stay spread through to the ship, causing celebrations. After spending several hours on board, Simon and Radon overwhelmed by their welcome, travelled back to the Katherine.

Jeddah who wished to see Simon's ship travelled with them. Radon, Simon noticed, seemed to hit it off with Jeddah. Once on board, Radon took him for a personal tour introducing him to the crew, while Simon checked on a problem with the shield.

As he was showing him around the bridge area, he noticed the sub captains watching them, so he introduced Jeddah to them. The Captains of the eight subs in return, gave only a lukewarm greeting, contributing very little to the conversation. Afterwards, when Radon and Jeddah were alone, Jeddah broached their strange behaviour, when meeting him.

"Yes I too sensed it Jeddah, they're not like Simon and the other humans I've met. In the future we will have to make sure Simon is protected, I fear that they see Simon and his friendship with other races as a threat to their petty rivalries."

"You have mine and my people's complete support Radon, while my people stay here, you are our commander," Jeddah assured him as they continued their discussions.

The eight sub Captains from Earth gazed silently out of the observation deck window. There, five huge alien ships appeared to drift along beside them, as they approached Oregarth. They'd all been shocked at how ruthlessly Simon had destroyed the enemy fleet. Now he had formed yet another alliance with a different race of aliens. They knew they needed his help against the Roax, the problem was, were they swapping one group of dictators for another. The Roax were at least human in appearance, these aliens were something else again.

"Gentlemen, for now, we need help to defeat the Roax. When that has been achieved, then we can deal with Simon and his allies. Remember, everything revolves around the portal system of Salvation, the Roax have shown us that." The Commander of the New America subs pointed out; as they watched the fleet come into land. Above them, a miniature camera saw and recorded everything.

Twenty days after the battle with the Flax squadron, three ships were picked up approaching Oregarth. Radon this time commandeered the Katherine while Simon continued working on the Portal base. As the long-range sensors indicated the vessels were Flax cruisers, Radon asked Jeddah to accompany him with two of his ships. Like before they met the incoming ships as far out as possible, warning them to stop. The three ships immediately dropped their shields, reversing their engines.

The three ships were part of the other five ships of Jeddah's original group. A patrolling squadron had attacked them, as they fled. Unable to lose their pursuers, two of their number had volunteered to stand and fight. Transferring family members, and excess crew, the two ships engaged the vessels following, allowing the other three to escape. Though Simon's shields had helped in the battle, superior numbers had overwhelmed the two vessels. They both had been destroyed.

Jeddah had been saddened by the news, his belief in freeing his people becoming clouded with doubt.

"It's not over yet my friend. Remember that you've already hurt their image of being all-powerful. Your people will ultimately be free." Radon assured him.

"Thank you for your support Radon." Was all Jeddah said, leaving the bridge? Radon watched his once deadly enemy depart. He had over the past weeks come to appreciate having

Jeddah's help in planning the attack on Salvation. He was smart and trustworthy, with a firm grasp of battle tactics. Both men enjoyed the opportunity as leaders of their people, to discuss and compare the difficulties arising from day to day management of their ships and settlements.

Returning to Oregarth, Jeddah escorted the new arrivals to the Flax settlement while Radon visited Simon. He was hard at work building the new base. Radon was impressed that Simon was avoiding using the Roax equipment. Instead, he was adapting Flax and Oregarthian unique combinations.

"How is your work progressing Simon?"

"Good, another month and we can test it. Then we can open a portal to Salvation. I hear more of Jeddah's people have arrived."

"Yes, they were lucky." Radon explained what had occurred.

"You like Jeddah don't you?" Simon smiled after Radon had finished.

"Yes, though it is strange for me to trust one who until recently, was the enemy."

"Would you trust him with your life?"

"Yes, I think I would." Radon replied, knowing some Oregarthians would think him naïve.

"Do you want to update his weapons and shields to the ones we're using? It would give him a huge advantage." Simon pointed out, watching his reaction.

Radon at first didn't answer. He stood deep in thought, mulling over what Simon had said. Sure it was a significant advantage and a morale boost for Jeddah and his men, but there was a downside. Jeddah's ship would be more than a match for any Oregarthian ship they met with the shields Simon had given them. He had now at his command six ships, while Radon had two and the Katherine, meaning he could destroy them easily if he betrayed them.

Doubt made him hesitate, as looking at Simon he saw a small smile creep onto the corner of his mouth.

"You're testing me? You knew I'd hesitate over giving another race your powerful shield and weapons." Radon smiled.

"Now that you've thought about it, what would you do?"

"Common sense tells me, no, but he needs them to have any chance at all. So the answer is yes, let him have the shields and weapons, sometimes you've got to have faith." Radon answered, sure he'd made the right decision.

After the meeting that night with the sub-commanders, Simon told Jeddah and his Captains to stay behind. Closing the doors, he told him of the upgrades Radon had proposed for his ships. Jeddah's Captains were overjoyed at getting the advanced weapons and shields all thanking an embarrassed Radon.

"I will never forget this act of trust from you two." Jeddah softly replied bowing to them, as his captains followed suit.

"But what about the Subs, do we strengthen theirs?" One of Jeddah's Captains asked.

"For now no, they have good shields already, more than enough against the Roax," Simon answered, his voice betraying his mistrust.

"We will help you free your people from the Roax, and then we will deal with the Flax military council." Jeddah proclaimed, as his men cheered.

CORBAN

When the Roax had first arrived on Salvation, Corban had been humiliated by their treatment. Unlike the elders, who accepted being treated as equals, Corban found this beneath him. Breaking away from the elders, he pleaded his case, demanding their own planet where they could continue as the Roax race. Nearly a half of the Roax population mostly military followed him, hoping to establish a world of their own.

While a planet suitable was being sorted out, Corban's group moved north of New Vancouver, in the opposite direction of the elders' group, which moved south to land near Mike's port. Corban in the meantime gathered as much intelligence as he could on humans. He found underlying mistrust between the planets and the UN, which governed them. Using this to his advantage he made contact with New Asia wanting to trade technology for equipment.

They were more than eager to form an alliance, wanting anything that would give them the edge over the other planets. Amazed at how effortlessly he'd achieved an alliance, he secretly contacted the other 3 disgruntled planets. Individually offering the same alliance, they all agreed, giving Corban an idea. He had observed that everything the humans had, revolved around Salvation. It was the hub that the other planets connected to.

Corban knew that to conquer all the planets, all he needed to do, was seize the portal cutting off or controlling access. The problem for him was gaining access to the portal base. To his great joy, he was contacted by the entities from the portal base that had retaken Roax form. Pretending to be aligned with the elders they visited Corban, on the pretext of convincing him to return to the Elders.

Instead, they sought his help, to enslave the humans. Corban told them of his plan and the groundwork he'd already begun, all they needed was the portal base. This they admitted would be easy as they revealed the base's weakness to him, which they had engineered.

A year after they had arrived on Salvation, Corban launched his attack. Having purchased four old submarines, secretly, from his alliance partners, the Roax set sail for the portal base. The subs though old had been updated with Roax advance technology. The weapons had been updated to their own designs, but the shields remained as they were. For some reason, which riled Corban, the human shields were far superior to their own.

No one had an explanation for this leap forward in shield generation. Like Corban, most Roax engineers put it down to a fluke, that Mike Hayes had been desperate during the war on Earth and had got lucky. It was one of Mike's shields that now protected the portal base. Since the base was essentially running itself, only a small crew of UN personnel and scientists were stationed there.

Arriving at the portal base, one of the Roax subs deployed its shield encompassing the base and its shield. Using a pre-set code, that Elena had told them off, the Roax cut the power to the base, dropping the defensive shield as well. With superior numbers it was over quickly, but not before the UN personnel sent an alert to the UN headquarters on Salvation. Since the UN lacked armed submarines, all the planets' representatives on Salvation were contacted.

As the perpetrators were unknown, at an emergency meeting, it was decided to send a fleet of ships to find out what was going on. Of the six planets linked to Salvation, Earth and Southern Ocean planets had no armed vessels. The other four had two warships each, which immediately set sail. All four of suspected the Roax, but no one wanted to admit they'd given the Roax a submarine in return for technology. Still, they were confident, as they believed the enemy had only one sub.

Approaching the base, all subs deployed their shields and weapons. The New Asia planet commander, being in charge of the fleet, ordered the people on the base to surrender, to spare any bloodshed. Corban answered, saying he was only taking back what belonged to the Roax. He guaranteed if the fleet surrendered no harm would come to them. The fleet commander unimpressed with his statement warned him he had one hour to lay down their arms or all eight ships would open fire.

Corban sounding agitated told them to give him one hour to talk to his men. The fleet commander thinking he was about to surrender ordered his subs to wait for his answer. The order had just been sent out when without warning, a portal opened right in front of the fleet. All 8 Captains immediately ordered their ships to reverse. Instead, they accelerated into the portal.

Their updated software so graciously supplied by the Roax, overrode their navigation system, preventing the shut down of their propulsion systems. The eight ships now committed continued through the portal arriving at Duelong four days later.

On Salvation, Corban couldn't believe how easy it had been. Turning off the main portal system, he closed the link to the other planets. Elena was the first to congratulate him. In one move, they had removed all armed opposition to their takeover. There were still UN soldiers with personal weapons, but Corban commanded the only remaining armed submarines.

"Now there's only one other threat to take care of!" Corban pointed out.

"Are you sure you want to travel to Oregarth again? Wouldn't it be better to just leave them stranded there?" Elena asked.

"I have unfinished business with Mike Hayes. When they're all taken care of, I'll settle with the Elders." Corban promised.

"Don't underestimate Mike Hayes or his nephew, Simon. We tried to manipulate them both but failed with Simon. There is something different about those two, they're unlike the other humans." Elena pointed out, remembering how Simon resisted their attempt to control him.

"Do not worry. I intend to destroy all present and their technology without leaving the ship. They will be expecting a UN sub to take them home so surprise will be on our side. I'll bring back some prisoners to put on display; it might help break the morale of the humans here." Corban smiled looking forward to the encounter.

"Okay, while you are taking care of them, we will move our three other ships to New Vancouver. I believe a decisive show of strength, should lead to a quick ending of hostilities. We will then take care of the Elders and Mike Hayes's friend south of New Vancouver."

"Yes the Elders must be dealt with, but be careful not to alienate our people. In the coming years, we will need their numbers, to police the six other planets." Corban suggested as the group broke up.

Arriving aboard his flagship, Corban asked for a portal to be open as the submarine prepared to dive. He had hoped to capture Mike Hayes and drag him back to Salvation to be publicly executed, along with anyone else with him. The entities had convinced him that it might just make him a martyr, so he decided on finishing him off on Oregarth. In front of his sub, the portal opened. Feeling great satisfaction that once more the portal system was in their hands, Corban ordered the sub forward. Travelling through the portal, Corban spent the next four days preparing his crew, making sure everyone was clear on their duties once they reached the Citadel.

Surfacing on Oregarth, Corban ordered the crew to ignore radio transmissions. Approaching the Citadel's harbour, he ordered the crew to man their weapons. Smiling he watched the remaining inhabitants of the near-deserted city, rush to the docks, waving wildly. They were just pulling into the dock when he saw the people start to flee.

"They've somehow detected us, open fire!" He yelled, not realising one of his crewmembers had proudly painted a Roax flag on the bow. Several of the people were cut down immediately as the crew fired, others returned fire with small arms. Their fire couldn't really harm the ship, but it kept his men's heads down until each shooter was eliminated. Docking, troops rushed ashore rounding up the people who had raised their hands to surrender. Corban looking for Mike

Hayes spotted him entering one of the Roax spaceships left behind.

"Target that ship!" Corban screamed realising he intended to use its weapons on his ship. The subs main armaments immediately opened fire hitting the spaceship through the entrance he'd made in the shield when they landed. Explosions rocked the spaceship, as flames quickly spread, until with a mighty roar the ship exploded flattening the buildings around it. Unknown to Corban, the blast also turned the portal base, into a mass of burning debris.

With casualties slowly mounting, Corban considering his mission accomplished ordered all patrols to return to the sub. He was in the process of going below, when the report of a giant spaceship flying towards them, came in. Seeing everyone was aboard he ordered the ship to dive running for the portal.

"Well, that's the end of that!" Corban triumphantly told his crew, as they travelled back to Salvation, the mysterious spaceship forgotten. Going to the rear cargo hull, Corban looked over the prisoners, seeing a large number of aliens amongst them.

"Well, well, well it looks like Mike Hayes was conspiring with the enemy, to invade Salvation."

"That's not true you traitor." One of the Roax crew of the Katherine shouted, as one of Corban's men knocked him to the deck. Walking forward, Corban drew his pistol pointing it at the unconscious man's head.

"What will your people think if you execute one of your own people without a trial?" A young woman shouted. Corban moved his aim from the man to the young woman.

"You aren't Roax, no one would miss you." He snarled, as several men and women rushed to stand in front of the young woman. A standoff developed as Corban faced a wall of stone-faced people united against him by the young girl. Backing down, Corban holstered his pistol, walking to the cargo hulls exit, his men locking the door behind him.

"Find out who that young woman is. I want to know why those people were willing to die for her." Corban ordered heading back to the bridge, his good mood gone.

In the hull, Kate stood shaking with fear now Corban had gone. Moving to the Roax crewman hit by the guard Kate knelt down checking his injuries.

"Thank you." He moaned giving her a smile.

"No thank you, you're a brave man," Kate told him as an Oregarthian woman approached.

"I'm a nurse, I'll look after him." She assured her, bending down and checking his head wound. Kate smiling sat down in the corner as several people approached her.

"Do you think Captain Simon will come to rescue us?" They asked sounding scared.

"Count on it." Kate smiled.

Elena and the other Roax's conspirators had in the meantime, moved on New Vancouver, only to find it abandoned. The UN, having been warned by the trapped fleet, had ordered everyone to move inland. When the Roax fleet surfaced, they found the population retreating towards Harmony.

"We could open fire and inflict casualties on the retreating population. It might make them cave in." One of the ship's Captains suggested. Elena not wanting a war hesitated, not sure. By the time she met with Rile and the other entities and decided to attack, the population was out of range. The humans they assumed would now make Harmony the capital into a defensive position, destroying rail and road connection to New Vancouver. This they admitted would take away the Roax's main advantage of their dominant submarine fleet.

Making another decision, Elena left one submarine at New Vancouver and sailed south to Mikes harbour to the south, hoping to capture the population there. It too had been abandoned with the fishing fleet gone. Infuriated by this tactic, Elena ordered the port destroyed, leaving only the fish-processing factory, as it was vital. The fishing fleet too was important for food production, so she decided to let it go its merry way at the moment. In time it could be tracked down and the crews punished.

The big question was had this group joined the others in Harmony or travelled inland to meet up with the breakaway Elders and the Roax sympathisers? Either way, Elena knew she couldn't split her forces, so angrily she set sail back to New Vancouver.

When Corban returned ten days later, he found Elena still sitting in New Vancouver trying to work out what to do. 'No wonder they lost the fight with the Oregarthians' he thought as he gathered the Entities and the four ships' Captains for a meeting. Here Elena explained the situation pointing out their troops were significantly outnumbered and would struggle in a drawn-out battle.

"You know, if you had hit them as they were retreating, you might have broken them." Corban pointed out.

"It might've hurt negotiations in the future." Rile suggested.

"Look, the fact that they are fortifying their inland city, means they're not planning to surrender. They're going to try and inflict casualties on us when we attack them. At the moment we've got the upper hand, but we lack numbers. Given time we can starve them out as we hold all the seaports. The question is, do you want to wait?" Corban explained trying to keep his anger under control,

"Our people want results now. I suggest we move what troops we have here inland." Rile put forward, Elena nodding her support.

"There might be another way. Does Harmony have a shield?" Corban asked.

"No, I doubt the humans thought they'd need one." Elena smiled.

"Good, we'll move the troops here to keep them pinned down. While that's happening, we'll prepare an aircraft to carry a laser weapon to wipe out their military, which of course they will deploy forward to meet our troops. That way we can dispose of their fighting forces and leave the civilian population at our mercy." Corban explained.

"How long will it take to build an aircraft?" Rile asked.

"The humans have some aircraft, but this one will have to be specially built to hold a powerful Laser and be shielded from their ground fire. I would say about two months if we have our engineers cannibalise the human planes to build it. That will give you time to either make them surrender or defeat them." Corban told them.

"Sounds like a good plan. Changing the subject, how did it go on Oregarth?" Rile asked. Corban gave them a complete rundown on the raid, impressing them with its detail.

"Can you add anything about the spaceship which followed you to the portal?" Elena asked wondering where it had come from.

"The information's sketchy, but it might have been an Oregarthian battleship."

"That would explain the Oregarthian prisoners." Rile put forward.

"And who was the girl they tried to protect?" Elena asked.

"It appears she is Simon Hayes' girlfriend or something. My guards told me they expect him to come after her." Corban laughed.

"Do you think he will?" Elena exclaimed thinking he was dead.

"Look we control the portal. Simon Hayes was off on some mission in the other Roax spaceship. He can't do anything but take centuries to reach us."

"I hope so. I have a nagging concern that there is far more to Simon Hayes than he allows us to see. For some reason, he scares me." Elena admitted. Rile, watching the concern on Elena's face, remained unconvinced that Simon was not a threat.

"Let's forget Simon Hayes for a moment and move on. He's just another human too focused on petty power struggles to see the big picture. Once we defeat the humans, we can either travel back to the planet and deal with him or prepare for his arrival in the far distant future. Either way, he's not a priority at the moment." Corban grumbled, happy to move on. Across from him Rile exchanged looks with Elena.

Two months of heavy fighting, saw both sides facing off two miles from Harmony. Corban's rebel soldiers had pushed the UN troops back into their final defensive positions. Up until now, the rebels had flanked the UN forces from their hastily constructed defensive positions. These were usually based on river crossings or other natural obstacles. Their defences this time had been purpose built over the past month using the civilian population. The Rebel force numbered over five thousand, while the UN could field six thousand.

The problem was the UN troops were mostly green troops, accustomed to checking people's visas not fighting a determined enemy. The Roax soldiers, on the other hand, had trained most of their lives, as a force to defend Oregarth from invasion. Elena thinking it had gone on long enough, asked for a ceasefire so they could talk. Walking across no man's land between the opposing forces, Rile, and Elena escorted by four soldiers, also hoped to observe the UN defences while they were there. Instead, just short of the UN line, the Roax elders greeted them.

"What are you doing here?" Elena spat out.

"As part of the Gun Barrel planets, we have joined the humans in opposing their enemies," Ileana announced as Goren and Borack came up to stand beside her.

"You are traitors to our race." Rile replied reaching for his laser pistol.

"I wouldn't do that if I was you. You are all covered by our men and are here under a flag of truce." Goren pointed out, as Rile reluctantly let go of his pistol. Both groups stood silently waiting for someone to say something, Elena started.

"I won't waste time bartering, we want your unconditional surrender immediately, or you will face the consequences."

"Maybe you can't count Elena, but we have committed an additional four thousand soldiers. Your forces are totally outmatched, plus we'll be fighting from prepared positions." Ileana informed them watching Rile closely.

"They will not protect you. We will give you the rest of the week to surrender, or you will all be annihilated." Elena told them, turning and walking away followed by Rile and their guards.

"What do you make of that?" Borack asked as they too walked back to their lines.

"Elena is too confident. Something bad is coming. Let's go warn the others." Ileana answered sounding worried.

At the UN council, Ileana told the gathered leaders of her talk with Elena. It was a sign of trust in the Elders that the UN had them meet with the rebel Roax leaders to find out what they intended. Ileana reported all that had been discussed. She observed that Elena, seemed confident, that even with the reinforcements of Elder's Roax soldiers, the UN would be destroyed.

"Do you think they have a more powerful weapon that they can deploy to the battlefield?" John, Mike's second in command and now UN military leader asked.

"Yes, though I'm not sure what it will be. Knowing Corban, it will most probably be able to fly and be heavily armed. Our defences are not built for heavy weapons I'm afraid." Ileana admitted.

"Well we knew this might occur, so what do we do?" Gordon, the head of the UN council, asked.

"I think it wise to abandon the city and disperse the population into the surrounding countryside. Though supplies will be minimal, we can have them travel at least another hundred kilometres inland where dense rainforest can protect the population from aerial attack. That way we can lower the chances of the Roax rebels being able to locate and capture them. Second, we should thin down the defensive line and where possible hide the men in prepared positions where they can thin out the attacking soldiers. I'd suggest withdrawing half the UN and half the Roax troops to form small units to ambush the Rebel forces if they break through." John put forward as the room lapsed into silence.

"Do you think it's time to consider surrendering, rather than have our soldiers and people killed?" Gordon suggested.

"Surrendering would mean many would die anyway and the rest will be slaves. Better to go down fighting." Ileana replied getting a grudging acknowledgement from them all.

"You know Ileana, you and the other Roax could join them." John pointed out, as everyone in the room froze.

"You took us in and made us welcome. You are our friends. Corban's group has betrayed the friendship you offered us all. They are now our enemies as well as yours. We will all live together as friends or die as allies against evil." Ileana answered leaving a silent room behind her.

At the portal base, a handful of Corban's rebel soldiers sat at their stations, fighting off boredom. With the portal closed, their only function was to guard the base and being at the bottom of the ocean gave them fair warning of any trouble approaching. Their only amusement was listening to the constant chatter from their troops at the front. With growing optimism, they kept track of the advance on Harmony. All that changed in an instant as the base warning system burst into life. It reported that a portal had opened south of their position.

"That's impossible!" One of the engineers screamed as secondary systems confirmed the opening.

"I thought we were the only ones with portal technology?" A soldier pointed out, as the engineer considered what to do. Making a decision, he sent a message to Corban passing on the sighting.

Corban at that moment was looking over his new air force. Instead of building one hover plane he decided to make three, in case there were any problems. The aircraft looked like flying tanks, but he was sure they'd carry out the plan they'd come up with, to humble the humans into surrendering.

"Okay, let's see how they fly." He ordered, as the three crews of five men hurried to their aircraft, to fly them for the first time. As the aircraft engines roared to life, Corban felt a ripple of anticipation. At long last, the Roax nation would again be superior to all other races. His thoughts were cut short when a soldier told him of an emergency at the portal base. Ordering the planes to stand down, he rushed to the situation room asking for a full report. What he heard left him speechless.

"What do you want us to do Sir?" One of his Captains asked worried by his silence.

"Send two of our planes when they are ready, to destroy the human capital Harmony. Leave the third here in reserve. With luck, that should make the enemy surrender! Instruct the portal base to watch for any submarines coming through the portal. I'll instruct Elena to send our submarines there immediately." Corban replied, a sense of foreboding settling over him.

When Elena was told, she too sensed trouble with the opening of the portal. Ordering three submarines south, she left only one at New Vancouver to back up the troops. Contacting Rile and Corban, she asked them to join her, going over what they knew of the humans who had been studying the portal system. In the end, they came to the only possible conclusion, Simon had taken a copy of the system.

"It's the only thing that makes sense. We know everyone else who studied the portal, worked at the base. Simon is the only one who carried out his work from his workstation on the sub." Rile concluded.

"Could he have built a base on Oregarth?" Elena asked.

"Maybe, there was enough of our technology lying about to copy our base here. Still, I find it hard to believe he could build one and a submarine to return here." Corban scoffed.

"We have always underestimated Mike Hayes and Simon. I feel there is a lot more to them than just being human." Elena put forward.

"You think they aren't from Earth?" Rile replied.

"I'm not sure, but it fits in with the shields they have. They're too advanced for the humans, either they're aliens or working with them. Either way, we should make ready in case they return." Elena suggested.

"Look even if what you say is true, I'm pretty sure Mike at least is dead as he was on the ship that blew up. This could be just an elaborate way of making us think they're coming, to make us react." Corban was convinced it was a bluff.

"We will know soon enough. In the meantime, Corban can continue his plans to attack the humans. We have four days to prepare, being the time it takes for a sub to travel through the portal from Oregarth to here." Rile pointed out, Corban agreed and left. Rile, and Elena watched him go, before continuing to discuss the situation.

"We should prepare for the worst. Corban can't see it because he sees us as superior to everyone." Elena pointed out.

"Yes if Simon comes he'll come for revenge. Best we have a backup plan in place just in case." Rile replied as they worked out a way to survive the coming encounter.

The three submarines sat on the bottom, watching the portal. They had just arrived and were preparing a plan for dealing with any threat that might eventuate. The portal had only been open for over ten hours, giving them plenty of time to set up. The base that was monitoring the portal suddenly came online, reporting seven objects moving at tremendous speed towards them.

"Could they be submarines?"

"No, they're much too fast, and six of the signals are at least four times as big as our largest sub." The base replied.

"Go to battle stations!" yelled Commander Johnston, the sub fleet commander. With a brilliant flash, the first of the ships roared past the surprised subs hurdling towards the surface. Seconds later a much larger ship roared past them followed by five more. They all joined the first hovering several hundred metres above the ocean's surface.

"Can you identify them?" Johnston shouted.

"Only three Sir. One is a Roax space cruiser. The other two next to the cruiser, are Oregarthian space battleships. The other four are unknown, probably newer designed Oregarthian ships" The crewmen replied, as the whole crew stood quietly looking at their commander.

"Fire on those ships immediately!" the Commander ordered, as the three submarines opened fire. After several minutes of firing, Johnston asked for a damage report.

"There appears to be no damage, Sir. Our weapons appear to have failed to penetrate their shields." The crewmen reported. Johnson stood gauging his crew's reaction, feeling an undercurrent of fear running through his men.

"Commander, we are receiving a transmission from the enemy ships." The radio operator informed him.

"What's it say?"

"Surface and surrender or be destroyed."

"Don't mince words do they? Tell them we are Roax and we don't surrender." the Commander smiled reassuring his crew.

"Shouldn't we inform Corban of this situation?" Johnston's second in command asked.

"Let's see how effective their weapons are against our shields before we panic," Johnson told him. Seconds later, his sub was ripped in half with the loss of all aboard.

The two other subs, witnessing their commander's ship being pulverised, promptly surrendered.

Simon sat in the Captain's chair on the Katherine, staring at the console, studying the boiling water where the Commander's submarine used to be. As he'd travelled through the portal, he'd wondered what he'd do once they reached Salvation. At first, he had planned to come through on his own in the Katherine, with a skeleton crew made up of the surviving ten Oregarthian soldiers of his security detail. Since Kate's kidnapping, the ten soldiers had elected to be his bodyguards, never leaving his side.

Radon had bluntly refused to let him go with so few soldiers to protect him. Simon had explained that the eight subs were going too, giving him a significant fighting force. Radon, however, had spotted the lie. The subs couldn't travel even one-tenth of Katherine's speed, meaning Simon would be alone for at least three days. Radon, in the end, had won the argument bringing the Oregarthian warships and four of Jeddah's ships as a backup. Jeddah knowing he needed time to prepare before his attack on the Flax council had joined Radon in support.

Leaving the Oregarthian and Flax women and children inside the new portal bases shield for protection, Radon had brought what was left of the ninth along with him. In a way, it was closure for them that the Roax, who had destroyed their army, would now be brought to justice by its remnants. Simon had left Adrian in charge, to watch over the planet until they returned. He had been none too happy about staying behind until Simon had pointed out that he didn't want him firing on his own people.

When they had first encountered the Roax submarines, Simon had wanted to wipe them all out. Radon had suggested giving them the option to surrender first. It had proved the right move, with the loss of only one sub. Leaving a detachment of Oregarthians and Flax troops on each Roax submarine, the Katherine and the Oregarthian ships flew north towards New Vancouver. The four Flax ships in the meantime were to head to the portal base and secure it.

Arriving at the base first, Jeddah had given them the same demand that Simon gave the subs. This time the base immediately surrendered already aware of Commander Johnston's submarine's fate. As before a handful of troops were transferred to the base, as Jeddah headed for New Vancouver to join Simon.

Corban failing to hear from his submarines sent the third aircraft to check on the portal base. As the aircraft travelled south to intercept the enemy ships, it tried to contact the portal base for an update. To their surprise no reply came as the aircraft came face to face with the three ships, cruising towards New Vancouver. The crew knowing they had no chance, changed direction, fleeing back to their base, warning Corban.

Meanwhile, while the third plane flew south, the other two commenced their attack, targeting Harmony. After an hour of firing their lasers, the city was consumed by fire. John with his UN and Roax soldiers, looked down from the surrounding hills in horror, having only evacuated the population two days earlier.

"You were right to evacuate John," Ileana whispered, standing close to John, as he turned to his radioman.

"Instruct our troops to withdraw!" John told him knowing holding the line was now impossible.

The two aircraft finished with the city moved towards the frontline. Targeting the human defensives, they supported the Rebel soldiers as they moved forward. Unable to hold, the UN soldiers and their Roax allies retreated in disarray.

So absorbed were the planes attacking the troops that they didn't see the three spaceships until they opened fire. Running ahead of the enemy troops trying to organise a defence, John hearing an explosion, looked up. He saw the two aircraft burst into flames. Turning, looking back towards the Enemy troops, he saw laser blast rip into their ranks, as three huge flying ships came to a stop over them. Over some type of broadcast system, the vessel told the Roax to lower their weapons.

For several minutes some Roax troops fired back at the ships. Laser blast hitting the ground around the Rebel troops brought a swift end to the resistance.

"What do you make of that Ileana?" John asked, wiping sweat from his brow.

"I've never seen ships before like the big ones. The smaller one though is the cruiser Simon was repairing on Oregarth." She smiled.

"Well let's help them round up the Rebels. Whoever they are, I bet they'll head for New Vancouver." John smiled, yelling at his men to change direction.

"Ileana!" Barack screamed, running towards them. Short of breath, he ground to a halt next to them.

"What's wrong?" John asked.

"Those two giant ships are Oregarthian." He stammered out, shaken.

When Corban received a transmission from the plane telling of the spaceships coming towards him, he couldn't believe it. Next came a field report telling him the army was in full retreat, his two planes destroyed. Trying to raise Elena and Rile proved fruitless as their sub had set sail, leaving New Vancouver. Giving orders to his men to fight to the last, Corban ran to the plane, past surprised ground crews. Once aboard he ordered the crew to fly immediately to the portal base.

Casualties on both sides were heavy, as John, with three hundred troops, stormed into New Vancouver. The two spaceships continued to provide cover fire, neutralising any threats that materialised from the Roax. It had taken five days, but at last the Roax troops were surrendering, and the war appeared over. Word also reached them that the 8 missing subs had returned and were steaming towards New Vancouver.

After the last resistant had been crushed, Ileana stood with John, as the three spaceships came into land beside the waterfront. Many Roax and humans gathered around as the enormous ships opened their doors and Oregarthian troops poured out. Both humans and Roax soldiers reacted differently. The humans, stood surprised by the alien. The Roax recognising the Oregarthians fearfully raised their weapons.

"Lower your weapons!" A voice exploded from the Roax cruiser. "These are your allies who have come to help you." Simon's voice roared over the crowd. A hush fell over them all, as Simon appeared with Radon. Spotting John in the gathered crowd, Simon walked over to him.

"What's going on Simon, where's Mike?" John asked as Ileana tried to mask her fear of the Oregarthian troops.

"He's dead. Corban came to Oregarth and attacked us. Many prisoners were brought back to Salvation, including Kate and some Oregarthian women and children." Simon told him.

By now most soldiers had lowered their weapons, though an unease hung over the crowd at the alien troops' presence. Radon beside Simon felt the disquiet too, as speaking into his headset, he ordered the majority of his forces back onto the ships. As the alien troop numbers lowered John and Ileana asked Simon why the alien forces were here.

"They're my friends. They came to help me, and they'll leave once we have secured the release of our friends and family." Simon answered, unimpressed by the thanks they'd received.

"You could have warned us," John replied.

"To what end? Simon asked, before continuing. "Anyway I have to leave, Kate and the others are still being held, prisoner. There's one sub still missing, the prisoners must be on board." Simon pointed out, hurrying back aboard his ship.

"Can we come too?" John asked.

"Of course," Simon replied as John and a reluctant Ileana boarded the ship.

"The base is the only logical place they'd head for, it's their last refuge," Simon concluded once the ship had lifted off. Ileana and John stared out from the viewing deck marvelling at the ship as the Oregarthian crew brought them refreshments.

"Thank you," Ileana said her eyes watching the Oregarthians.

"You are perfectly safe Ileana. I vouch for all my soldiers." Radon assured her, seeing she was still uncertain.

"It's just such a shock, to meet a race that has been an enemy for over a thousand years" Ileana admitted.

"Yes, it required some time for me to be comfortable with the concept of trust and friendship between enemies," Radon confessed.

"And who are the other race?" John asked, having heard the Flax ships were at the base.

"They are a group of galaxies known as the Flax Confederation. Jeddah, their leader, is at the moment involved in trying to free his people from a corrupt military council that rules them." Simon informed them.

"What happened to Mike?" John asked.

"Corban came through the portal pretending to be there to pick us up. Instead, he opened fire on the people gathered at the dock. Mike was killed when he tried to return fire from the sister ship of this one. Kate and at least a hundred

Oregarthians and friends were captured. I came here to take care of the Roax traitors." Simon spat out.

"They are not all evil Simon," John replied, sensing Simon was no longer the carefree young man he remembered.

"I know that John." Simon snapped back. He was about to continue when a crew member raised the shields and triggered an alarm.

"Sir, the eight subs from Oregarth are coming upon us, their shields are up, and they are charging their weapons. All eyes turned to Simon, including John and Ileana's.

"Contact them, tell them we are going to the portal base. Ask them to stay in New Vancouver and help the people there. Keep the shields up." Simon ordered. No answer came as Simon's ships flew south while the submarines passed underneath them, sailing towards New Vancouver. Silence settled over the bridge, John and Ileana saw the crew's stone-faced reaction to the subs ignoring Simon.

"They mustn't have heard you," John suggested as Radon beside him looked at him scoffing.

"Your petty squabbling will be the end of you all," Radon said softly, walking away.

They were close to the base when Jeddah contacted them. He told them a submarine had approached the portal base, it said it had all the hostages on board.

"Pull your troops back from the portal. We will be there shortly." Simon replied turning to his crew. "Go to battle stations and increase speed," Simon ordered as the ship surged forward.

Arriving at the base, Simon saw the sub had projected its shield over the portal base. Through their outside cameras, they watched the Roax lead the prisoners into the base. As they watched, they observed a plane approach from the north, it was communicating with the base. Moments later they received a message.

"Simon Hayes, we order you to let the plane reach this base, or hostages will be killed." A female voice announced.

"If one hostage dies Elena, I will liquidate the entire rebel Roax population on this planet. Then I'll track you down and cut you to pieces." Simon promised. Silence followed as the plane docked with the sub, continuing on as if Simon had capitulated.

"Simon." Ileana was about to suggest a course of action.

"Be silent! Simon warned, "Who is on board that plane, I need to know?" Simon shouted at the crew.

"From voice analysis, we believe it is Corban." A Roax crewmember informed him smiling.

"Are the prisoners inside the base?"

"Yes, Sir."

"Target the sub. Burn it." Simon shouted.

"Simon that crew should be offered a chance to surrender." John pointed out.

"Like they gave my parents or Mike a chance? Fire" Simon ordered, as the Katherine weapons came to life.

On board, the submarine Corban had just left the sub after they'd docked the plane. It had been tricky flying the plane underwater to the sub, as it had not really been intended to submerge. The design, however, was made for space travel, meaning it was completely sealed. Corban knew it was risky, but they'd pulled it off right under the nose of their enemies. Giving the crew a well done, Corban started to walk to the base.

"Once I'm in the base, I'll convince Elena to use the hostages as a shield against these humans and their allies." Corban smiled as a roar started behind them. Not even looking back, Corban screamed in terror, knowing what was happening. Elena and Rile, saw the sub hit, fear making them freeze, as one of their engineers, seeing the danger, raised the base's shield.

Corban had nearly made it to the entry door when he impacted with the shield. Knocked to the ground; he looked back towards the sub, which superheated, erupted like a volcano. Lava-like flames flooded towards him across the once wet seabed at an incredible rate, as a scream formed in his mind. He never got a chance to yell his terror, as he was burnt to death.

"Sub destroyed Sir."

"Take us down to the base. And deploy our shield around it." Simon ordered.

"Simon we are vulnerable with the base inside our shield," Radon told him, as Simon nodded his understanding. Picking up his headset he signalled to the Comm's officer to open communications.

"Elena once the shield is in place, I will meet you outside the entry door. If you try anything, the ships above us will target your power supply then launch an attack." Not waiting for a reply, Simon walked towards the outer door, followed by Radon and his bodyguard.

Rile, and Elena had watched Corban's last moments, knowing their fate if they didn't meet with Simon.

"Any suggestions?" Rile asked her.

"I wouldn't hand over the hostages, it's the only reason we're not dead." She pointed out.

"I suggest we meet him with his woman, he'll be more reasonable if we threaten her." Rile smiled, Elena, agreeing.

On board the Katherine, Simon quickly conversed with Radon and his men before opening the outside door. He was just moving away from the sub when John and Ileana joined him.

"We are coming too. It will help you to have us there to negotiate an acceptable solution." John said backed up by Ileana. Simon just stared at them, as if seeing them for the first time.

"Yes, it might help to have you there." He replied as the group moved towards the portal base.

Kate sat with the other hostages praying for a miracle. Their treatment had been merciless Oregarthian's and crewmembers alike had been tortured and worse as the war dragged on. Several had wounds, and many were malnourished, fed only on scraps. Kate, herself, had suffered. She had been beaten and stripped naked before the entities, as they sort to humiliate her.

When they'd been moved from the sub to the base, many sensed their usefulness was at an end. They'd been led down into the bottom tunnels of the base, left in total darkness, told not to talk or they'd be all killed. After being there for just two hours, a massive explosion had made the whole structure shake. Moments later a squad of soldiers had appeared. Seizing her, they dragged her away, as the others screamed in fear for her. Several laser blasts fired above their heads quietened them, as Kate was handcuffed and taken to the entrance.

Moving outside, her eyes tried to focus after being in the dark for so long. As they cleared, she saw Simon and his guard with John and Ileana standing in a semi-circle twenty paces from her. Excited at seeing Simon, Kate went to move forward, only to be knocked off her feet by one of her guards.

"Touch her again soldier, and I'll burn your entire family at the Roax settlement," Simon shouted, as the thirty soldiers with Elena and Rile, all took in his words.

"You haven't got the guts." Rile laughed, calling his bluff. Simon spoke into his headset, as above them just visible through the water, they watched the Oregarthian battleship turned away, moving north.

"Radon is taking his men to your settlement as we speak gentlemen. I can assure you the Oregarthians look forward to arriving there." Simon replied.

"Simon we came here to negotiate." John cut in.

"Okay Elena, what do you want in return for the prisoners' release?"

"We want you to surrender your ship with the portal device. Or you'll never see Kate alive again." Elena promised.

"It will never happen. What do you soldiers want?" Simon asked addressing Elena's men.

"They want what we want!" Rile growled watching them.

"Yet, Rile and Elena have no family at the settlement, and they intend to take my ship and flee. Where does that leave your families?" Simon asked.

"I see no reason why they can't have your ship, Simon. We still have the portal base, and you can build another ship." Ileana pointed out trying to salvage some type of truce.

"I tell you what, if you promise to hand over the prisoners right now, I will recall the Oregarthian ship and give amnesty to every Roax soldier," Simon announced. As Rile pointed his weapon at Kate.

"One more word and I'll shoot her right now." Rile smiled, forcing Kate to her knees.

"Look we came here to stop any further bloodshed. Let's all take a step back and rethink." Ileana suggested as a Roax soldier behind Rile knocked his weapon from his hand. Moving forward the soldiers secured a shocked Elena and Rile.

"I am Captain Bores; do I have your word that our families will be safe?"

"You do Captain, I will also move you and your people to a different world if you wish," Simon promised.

"Then we accept your terms, though most of us would like to stay here on Salvation." The Captain answered as his men dropped their weapons, freeing Kate. Simon rushed to Kate's side picking her up, cradling her in his arms.

"Are you okay my love?"

"Yes Simon, I knew you'd come." She said smiling, as one of Simon's bodyguards rushed up taking her from him.

"Where are the others?" Simon asked Bores, as Kate was carried to the ship.

"They're in the lower levels. They haven't been well treated." The Captain admitted embarrassed.

"I know you were following orders Captain. Can you have some men go and release the prisoners for me, thank you." Simon asked. Using his radio Bores relayed a message to his men inside, asking them to bring them out and updating them on what had happened. Twenty minutes passed before a group of ecstatic freed prisoners burst from the base entrance running to Simon. Crying for joy, Simon's bodyguard and additional soldiers from the ship, escorted them aboard.

"Are you going to recall the battleship?" John asked unimpressed with Simon's devious plan in ending the siege.

"It was never sent. It just travelled north enough to convince them I meant it" Simon told him, as Bores, beside him, burst into laughter.

"Then you were bluffing?" Ileana barked knowing he had used them, never intending to negotiate.

"It was necessary. These men have families they love, Elena and Rile, have forgotten what that is."

"What do you intend to do with them?" John asked.

"I intend to gather up their followers and banish them to another planet," Simon answered as Elena for the first time since being secured looked at him her eyes showing surprise.

The UN having regained control, sent a team of technicians to restart the Portal system. The Roax under Captain Bores, who wished to stay, was given one of their submarines to travel home, while forces loyal to the Elena and Rile, were escorted aboard the other sub. Many including Radon thought Simon was making a mistake in letting them go unpunished. Simon assured them that they were travelling to another galaxy where they could do no harm to Salvation. Elena and Rile once aboard smiled at each other.

"Simon Hayes has made a grave mistake in underestimating us. Once we reach our new home; we build another portal and seek our revenge." Rile told their supporters, as Simon on board the Katherine, opened a portal. Once they entered it, Elena knowing they couldn't touch them, sent a message warning Simon they'd be back.

"Simon you did the right thing. Letting them go was the only fair thing to do." Ileana assured him, as she left with John on a UN sub for New Vancouver. Radon and Kate watched them all depart before turning to Simon.

"Where'd you send them?" Radon and Kate asked at the same time.

"Duelong"

Four days passed before the Roax submarine exited the portal, the whole crew shouting for joy, prepared to start their new lives. Heading for the surface, their sensors picked up another submarine to the east. Rile cautiously decided to take a look through the periscope. It was an abandoned sub he told the others, reassuring them that it was no threat. He then saw its name. White-faced he turned to the gathered crowd of high-spirited people, unable to speak.

Returning to New Vancouver, Simon was greeted by Gordon the UN President. Coming forward he embraced both Radon and Jeddah thanking them on behalf of the people of the Gun Barrel planets. Unlike before the people warmly welcomed the Orgarthian and Flax soldiers, they were grateful the ordeal was over. Simon received a hero's welcome; he was also given the keys to the city for saving them from slavery. Thanking them, Simon assured them they could always count on their allies for assistance, praising interplanetary friendship for defeating the rebels.

Gordon had arranged for several days of celebrations in honour of Radon, Jeddah and Simon. Unfortunately, Simon declined, as Kate's condition had deteriorated and he had to get her back to Salvation. As the ships launched, Radon and Jeddah on the Katherine with Simon, looked down on the waving people. Many on the ships waved back their earlier misgivings with the human soldiers forgotten.

"You know that's the first time I've received a welcome like that," Radon admitted, smiling happily.

"Yes, it was certainly different from my welcome home." Jeddah chuckled, as the ship travelled to the portal base. Arriving, Simon punched in the Oregarth planet co-ordinates opening the portal. Without a second thought, the vessel accelerated forward.

With a flash of light, Simon's small fleet erupted into the sky above Oregarth. Flying to the Oregarth village first, Simon saw both Oregarthain and Flax women and children rush from their homes to meet the ships. Like on Salvation, the crowd cheered as the ships landed. The sight of the rescued woman and children sent the crowd wild with joy at their safe return. Since the Oregarth village had the best medical staff and facilities, Kate remained there under their care, until she recovered.

Simon stayed as well until Kate was strong enough to return to the Citadel. Leaving the shuttle for Simon's use, Jeddah in command, flew Katherine's crew home. While Simon was settling Kate in, Adrian arrived from the Citadel. Briefing Simon on what had happened in his absence, Simon suggested to Adrian that he might want to travel to Salvation, now things had settled down. To Simon's surprise, he'd answered that he now had a home here with his crewmates on the Katherine, Salvation could wait.

"Salvation will always be there waiting for me when we're finished here." He told him, wanting to stay with his friends.

A month of watching over Kate found her little changed, after suffering from pneumonia. True her colour looked good, but she was still extremely weak, unable to walk. Jeddah in the meantime was preparing his ships to travel back to the Federation. The new shields and weapons had been installed and tested. Morale amongst Jeddah's men was excellent. Simon when taking a break from watching Kate helped them prepare.

He like Radon had spent many hours with Jeddah enjoying the reluctant leader's honesty and friendship. Simon secretly wished he was also going with them. Close to the day when Jeddah's fleet would leave, Simon found Radon was preparing to go with him as well.

"You're going too?" Simon asked wondering why Radon would put his men's lives in danger for Jeddah's people.

"He wants to bring freedom to his people. That, in turn, will help my people to stay at peace with the Flax confederation. He is also my friend."

"I would like to go too, but only after Kate is well again."

"We understand my friend. We will keep you informed of our progress, you can join us later."

"She needs rest when she is strong, I will come," Simon promised, watching his friend make ready.

"Simon, you have helped enough, stop thinking you have to do everything. Remember we're big aliens we can look after ourselves." Radon chuckled, moving towards his ship.

Jeddah was more than impressed with his weapons and shields. His fleet had also climbed from six to eight ships and Radon, who was coming, was a gifted tactician. He knew Simon too would come when he could, that was his greatest weapon. Simon's name had become widespread throughout the confederation for not only saving the Oregarthians from defeat but helping save the crippled fleets' crews.

Jeddah knew he was a good Captain and well liked by his people, but he was no military genius. Now he had Radon backing him, he felt more confident. He now thought he had a chance to free his people and bring peace. When the fleet was assembled, Simon brought the Katherine up into orbit, opening a portal for them. Bidding him farewell, one ship after another accelerated into the portal. In the end, only the Katherine remained.

"Wish we could go with them," Adrian said out loud, the rest of the crew agreeing.

"Give them time to recruit others. We'll join them soon enough." Simon assured them as they returned to Oregarth.

Since returning, Kate spent most of her time in bed, her body slowly recovering. Simon was always there, looking after her. Several of the Oregarthian women she'd grown close to during her imprisonment visited often. Before her ordeal, she opposed Simon's meddling in the affairs of other races. Now after hearing of their suffering during the endless wars their races had been involved with, she saw Simon's efforts in a new light.

When Simon had come to her wanting her support in helping Jeddah, she had to his surprise, urged him to go. She realised her lover had a gift for openness, which disarmed the races he met. They trusted him, something her own race seemed to have trouble with. She could see he wanted to go, but wouldn't until she was better. As Kate lay there she thought of her time with Simon and what they had achieved, her only doubts were about Salvation.

John, Mike's closest friend, had trouble with Simon's relationship with other races. Kate after her rescue had seen John's wariness around Simon. Ileana too had difficulty hiding her misgivings regarding the presence of Oregarthian soldiers on Salvation. How could the human race hope to survive, if it based trust on your appearance, rather than your motives? Being abused and mistreated had a way of changing your opinion. Kate's eyes had been opened to the narrow-mindedness of her people.

As the fleet prepared to leave, Kate with Simon's help, watched with all the other women and children, waving as the ships lifted off. As a precaution, Simon had enlarged the shield around the new portal base, allowing the Oregarthians and the Flax people plenty of space in an emergency to find protection. He had also set up an array of sensors to detect anyone approaching from space or through a portal. This allowed everyone to go about their daily chores without being confined.

It was the first time Kate and Simon had watched friends depart for what could be a full-scale war. She felt the fear from the women around her as they held their children who like all children everywhere, wanted to play with their father, not stay with their mothers.

"They will be okay Kate, don't worry," Simon assured her, seeing the look on her face.

"Yes Jeddah said it changes everything having Radon with them, and soon Simon will join them too." Jeddah's wife told her smiling, holding her hand. As Kate stood there, a tear ran down her face, which she quickly wiped away. It had never occurred to her, how vital Simon was to these people, she felt guilty that he had remained with her.

While Radon and Jeddah's fleet raced through the portal, on Earth, the UN had convened a special meeting. Many of the planets after what had happened wanted Salvation fortified, and the portal technology shared. All the seven planets had their representatives attend, plus Ileana, Goren and Borack. They had no vote and were only there to supply information. John was also present along with the commanders of the eight submarines, who had travelled to Oregarth. The planet's leaders, led by New America wanted the ability to open their own portals thus reducing the possible threat to Salvation if it was again invaded.

They presented good arguments; pointing out how isolated each planet had been when the rebel forces seized Salvation. Gordon, the head of the UN, listened to the arguments with growing unease. They were right of course they were vulnerable if Salvation was attacked. The likelihood of an attack being successful was now low, given the level of preparation recently completed. He saw it differently; the planets wanted the portals to expand their influence. If a vote was called, Gordon knew it was down to him to decide. As head of the UN, he had his own vote.

When the UN was first formed it was decided to give the UN a deciding vote to equal up the three neutral planets, being Salvation, Earth and Southern Ocean Planet and the armed planets New America, New Europe, New Asia and New Russia. Knowing it would be a tie; Gordon asked Ileana if she had an opinion. Standing she addressed the council.

"I can see why you all would like to have this technology, but I for one would not want the system duplicated. This portal system could be used to invade planets and cause war. No matter how strong a planet is, it would be vulnerable to this form of attack. Portals can be opened anywhere, all an enemy has to do is open it in a main city or military area to inflict massive casualties. At the moment this technology is secure, once you start handing it out to all the planets, it will only be a short time before someone outside the government can copy it.

Our race was hundreds of years ahead of yours, yet an enemy that came through the portal destroyed us. I would think carefully about what you really want it for?" Ileana informed them, sitting back down. When the vote was carried out, many were surprised to find the vote was five votes to three against copying the portal. Gordon was relieved, as his vote hadn't been the decider.

Moving on, New Asia asked what the UN intended to do about Simon Hayes' portal and his alien allies.

"Why do we need to do anything?" Gordon replied.

"He controls unspeakable power in his advanced weapons and shields. He also has alien allies who we know nothing about, and he has his own portal device. What's to stop him from bringing them back here and making Salvation his colony." The representative of New America exploded.

"Didn't he just free us from the Roax?" Gordon pointed out, remaining in control.

"He only came to save his woman. I doubt he'd have lifted a finger otherwise." New Asia representative put in.

"Gentlemen you would have a hard time convincing the people that the man who rescued them from slavery, is planning to enslave us himself." Gordon smiled.

"If it pleases this council, I would like to call the sub-commanders who were on Oregarth, to tell what they saw." The New Asia representative asked. Seeing no reason why they shouldn't, Gordon granted them time to tell their story.

All eight captains told how Simon had taken command, making clear they had to follow orders. They told how Simon had wanted to wipe the Roax out completely, only stopped by Radon. He had then handed over command to Radon being unfit to lead. When another alien race had entered his Galaxy, he had immediately taken back command, wiping them out and killing the survivors who had surrendered.

Before the raid on Salvation, Simon had given Radon his latest shields and weapons making their ships superior to the Gun Barrel planets' defences. After he'd finished others were called backing up the first Captain's statement. Gordon didn't have to look at the gathered officials to know how they'd vote.

Trying to salvage some middle ground, Gordon asked John for his opinion. John hesitantly got up.

"Simon Hayes I'll admit has changed. The death of his grandfather Mike, and the kidnapping of his girlfriend, Kate, hit him hard. He's grown into a man who is now accustomed to command. When I was on his ship, I observed the crew follow him with absolute loyalty. No matter if they're alien, Roax or human they respect him for what he's done. He can be brutal and is inflexible once he's made a decision, but a danger to Salvation I'd find hard to believe." John told them.

"You may be right John, but you have to admit he's become extremely powerful, and he has no right to make treaties without the UN's consent." New Europe's representative replied. John unsure didn't answer, as everyone sat waiting.

"Gentlemen I think John like everyone else isn't sure and even if New Europe's representative is right how do we stop him? His forces are unassailable, and even if we seize his portal base, he can build another." Gordon pointed out.

"Not if he's dead." The Commander of the New Russia sub suggested, bringing a murmur of anger from the people assembled.

"There is no call for that type of solution, I'll hear no more of it." Gordon angrily replied, silencing the room. "He's a hero to the people remember that." He added ending the meeting. John looked at the people gathered, knowing most had taken an interest in the sub commander's solution, as Ileana approached him.

"I too am scared of Simon's relationship with the Oregarthians, but to suggest killing him is a solution Corban would've utilised," Ileana confessed.

"Yes, I might have my doubts about Simon, but to talk in this assembly about breaking our laws so openly worries me. Maybe Radon was right when he warned us of our squabbling.

"Can you warn Simon?" Ileana whispered.

"I'll do my best." He replied squeezing her hand before kissing her lightly on the cheek.

"See we're proof that different races can love each other." She smiled.

THE FLAX COUNCIL

"What do you think Jeddah will do?" the Council President asked their military adviser.

"With only a small number of ships, he is isolated. Even if he tried to rally support the Home fleet would crush them." Grom, his advisor, smiled.

"What of his ship's new weapons and shields. Do we know how he came by them? They severely hurt our Home fleet's reputation as being invincible."

"We're not sure Sir. Each ship fought to the end leaving nothing to examine. Their new weapons are only a hindrance nothing more."

"Well are the people under control at least?" the President barked thinking the advisor too cocky.

"Yes, Mr President. Your order to quell all dissent was carried out without mercy. None of the planets will again dare protest Jeddah's arrest." He replied politely sensing the President's anger with him.

"Has Jeddah been located yet?"

"No Sir. Since the loss of one of the outer squadrons, nothing has been heard. He may have perished in the battle, or teamed up with that renegade Captain Simon?" Grom put forward.

"Yes, the loss of those ships and the earlier loss of the Supreme commander's fleet has allowed this human named Captain Simon to escape punishment. Once we're at full strength again, I want him hunted down and his supporters enslaved." The President ordered, moving on to the next matter.

Radon's two battleships floated motionlessly behind a moon on the planet of Oberon. Jeddah's six ships were out in the open, as a squadron of ten ships approached. Jeddah had asked that only Flax ships be visible when he met with his fleet's ships.

"I am Jeddah and am seeking allies to stand against the council." He began watching the ships closely as they moved into an attack formation.

"You have been named a coward, we ask you to allow us to board." A voice demanded.

"I don't want to fight you, but I ask you to join me in opposing the military council." Jeddah watched them raise their shields, as silence followed his offer. "I ask again will you join me in freeing our people." As the ten ships moved into range, Jeddah ordered his fleet's shields raised.

"This is your last warning Jeddah, surrender!" The same voice demanded, as six of the incoming ships turned away. The four, which continued opened fire, lashing Jeddah's ships with lasers. Many of the crew winced expecting the worst, only to see the beams hitting their shields repulsed.

"Fire our main weapons," Jeddah commanded, unable to watch as the four ships disintegrated, under the concentrated fire of Simon's new lasers.

"All ships destroyed Sir. We're being hailed." A crewmember reported.

"Captain Jeddah here, who wishes to speak to me?"

"I am Captain Doran of the Crystal Deep. My ship and the other five wish to join you."

"Why did the others attack?" Jeddah asked.

"They were just following orders. Fear of rebelling against the council forces us to obey. We believe you can free us, though we are few."

"We are not alone Captain," Jeddah replied, as signalling Radon for the two ships to join them.

"They are Oregarthian ships Sir," Doran replied, his voice sounding unsure.

"They have decided to help us along with the human race that will join us soon. Once our Federation is free, they will then leave." Jeddah assured him. Captain Doran had heard of this new race called the humans, but like many, he considered it just a story.

Arriving by shuttle at Jeddah's ship, Doran and the other five Captains were met by Radon and Jeddah. After being introduced, Doran noticed the crew was made up of Oregarthians and Flax. Jeddah explained his plan to build their numbers, as they'd travelled through the Galaxy. Once a large enough force was gathered, they would jump to Craigure, through a new way of travelling. Doran like the other captains was sceptical. Radon, the Oregarthian leader, explained they needed more support before jumping to Craigure.

Doran told them of the position of the northern fleet. It was made up of about 200 cruisers, and Doran believed that the Commander was a good man. After asking if anyone had anything to add, Jeddah wished them all good luck before they returned to their ships. On the ride back the six new rebel Captains discussed their alliance partners. None were happy about the Oregarthians being here, but the human if the human Simon appeared, that was something else.

"This human could be a myth to gather support." One Captain suggested.

"Maybe, but where'd Jeddah's shields and lasers come from? They're beyond anything the Oregarthians have, so someone must have made them. I for one believe the human Captain Simon does exist." Another Captain added. "What do you think Captain Doran?"

"I think our people deserve to be free. If we have to turn to a former enemy and an unknown race to achieve it, well so be it." Doran answered, the others nodding their support. Back on board Doran and the other Captains briefed their men. Many were sceptical. The vision of the four ships being destroyed without effort left them unsure of the future of their race.

For another two months, Jeddah's small fleet continued on gathering ships to his cause and fighting others. The ships that joined them though loyal remained wary of their new allies and the non-appearance of the human race. Their fleet now numbered fifty ships though they'd lost ten in battles. Even with superior weapons and shields, there was a limit to how many ships you could fight at once. On Jeddah's ship, Radon met to discuss their next move.

"It's no longer working to approach small groups of ships. They panic at our approach, as now our numbers impose a threat.' Radon pointed out.

"We have to approach a main fleet. It will be risky, but we have no choice.' Jeddah replied becoming depressed with battling his own race. He was just about to continue when Captain Doran radioed a warning. He'd been patrolling to the east when a large circle of water suddenly appeared in the distance. He wanted to know what it meant.

"Captain Simon Hayes has opened a portal. Soon he will be here" Jeddah informed him, as he signalled for the fleet to head towards Captain Doran's position.

Like Doran the whole fleet stared at the revolving circle of water, waiting. They'd been waiting for two days watching the mirage wondering if it was real when their instruments picked up something travelling at high speed inside the mirage. Moving clear of the front, several ships raised their shields as the Katherine roared past them before turning and coming back.

"That is truly amazing!" Doran said into his radio, his whole crew staring at the ship unable to comprehend what had happened.

"That's nothing Captain. Wait till you enter it!" Jeddah replied laughing.

Radon and Jeddah couldn't help feeling elated by Simon's appearance. Studying the Katherine, Jeddah found it strange that the shields were down. Contacting the Katherine, Radon cautioned them against being too casual. Adrian who was in command at the time reported Simon's new shield was up and working perfectly.

"Are you sure, we detect nothing," Jeddah told him.

"Fire at us Jeddah. I'd like to see how effective this new shield is" Simon's voice ordered."

"Are you sure Simon, we have your new weapons." Jeddah reminded him.

"Give it all you've got," Simon replied.

"Fire on the Katherine with all weapons," Jeddah commanded as a nervous Radon beside him watched the result. Jeddah's ship shuddered as all weapons fired, while the rest of the fleet looked on in horror, wondering what was going on. Radon wasn't the only one shocked when the laser beams seemed to disappear as if the shield was absorbing them.

"My God that shield is sucking our power reserves dry," Jeddah informed Radon, as he ordered his weapons to ceasefire.

"He never fails to impress does he!" Radon laughed as Jeddah's crew joined in.

Captain Doran had to admit he was a little in awe of this new race and the demonstration he had just witnessed. Like most Captains aboard the Katherine to meet this human, he had expected the Katherine to be destroyed when Jeddah had fired unexpectedly on the Katherine. He like most had watched astounded at how easily the Katherine had withstood the beating.

Their first impression that this Simon was just a myth had been definitely proved wrong. He was young to command Doran considered, although Radon and Jeddah both seemed to hold him above themselves as they all were introduced. Doran when introduced, found Simon easy to talk to, explaining how everything worked, from the shields to the portal.

He told him how his soon to be wife had been captured and badly treated. He'd stayed with her when Jeddah and Radon had left, making sure she was okay before he travelled to meet them here. He also asked many questions about the military council wanting to know what they were like and what they would do once they were free of them.

Like Radon he did not intend to stay here once Jeddah had freed his people, admitting he was getting tired of travelling, wanting to stay with Kate at home. Doran realised he was in the company of an exceptional being, open and genuine, simply there to help a friend in need.

Once the introductions were complete, Radon went over their plan to contact a fleet, preferably the Northern fleet. It was commanded by Commander Hague, a well-liked and respected leader, someone who the people could support.

Jeddah had already indicated his reluctance to have anything to do with leading his people, so Commander Hague was the obvious choice.

"What if he says no?" One captain put forward.

"Then we'll find another. We have to start somewhere." Jeddah told them getting approval.

"Prepare your ships men, we leave in the morning," Simon told them as the meeting broke up.

"Before we go, Simon, can I ask a question?" Captain Doran asked. Seeing Simon nod, he continued.

"When you explained the portal, you said the portal device was on Oregarth. How is it you can open portals now from here to the North fleet and not to Oregarth first?" This question surprised Jeddah and Radon as well, as both hadn't thought about it.

"Because this ship has the portal device built in and does not rely on the portal base at Oregarth." Simon smiled explaining. After the attack on Oregarth by the Roax, Simon had thought long and hard about defending the portal base. When he started rebuilding the portal, the idea came to him to make two, one mobile allowing its use from different locations. The Katherine though not as large as Flax and Oregarthian ships had adequate space, so he'd built it onboard. The base on Oregarth was a backup and mainly used now for the protection of their people, while they were away.

"New shields and now a portable portal, how do you come up with all this?" Radon chuckled.

"Let's just say I hear voices." Simon smiled, as the group broke into laughter.

As planned, the Katherine moved out in front, opening a portal. The Flax ships' crews were taken aback when the huge rotating blue hole appeared right in front of Simon's ship.

Accelerating forward the Katherine dived into the projection followed by Jeddah's ships and the Oregarthians.

"Follow the other ships!" Doran ordered, as his ship and the gathered Flax ships warily followed Captain Simon into the unknown.

THE NORTHERN FLEET

The Northern fleet was patrolling along the border of the Flax confederation's most distant settlement when a scout ship reported a colossal circle had formed, near a distant unpopulated planet. Sending a report of the strange occurrence to the council, Commander Hague then ordered his two hundred cruiser fleet forward. Arriving at the anomaly, Hague stopped the fleet at a safe distance, while his engineers examined it. No one could tell him anything about the circle except the water like surface was just a projection, the tunnel behind it was pure energy.

"Is it a natural occurrence?" He asked.

"No, I believe the artificial water like surface, has been engineered to cover what is behind it." The chief engineer answered.

"Sir, Sensors report objects moving inside the anomaly. They should be visible shortly." a Crewmember shouted.

"Go to battle stations!" He roared, as over fifty ships appeared out of the watery surface, coming to a stop.

"Sir the ships are asking to talk to Commander Hague."

"They know my name? Can you identify the ships?"

"Sir, over fifty are Flax Federation cruisers, two are Oregarthian battleships, and the last is a Roax cruiser. It is the same ship involved in the destruction of the Supreme Commander's fleet."

"Well, this is a strange group of ships. Have the fleet stay at battle stations, while I talk to them." Hague ordered picking up his headset.

"This is Commander Hague, who am I talking to?"

"It is Captain Jeddah, I mean you no harm. I seek aid in overthrowing the military council."

"You have been branded a traitor Jeddah, and you are here with enemy ships. Can you explain their presence?"

"They are my friends and allies. They have come to help only."

"How did you arrive here?"

"The human allies, who command the Roax ship, have a new way of travelling, called a portal. It can transport ships across a Galaxy in days instead of months."

The Commander was about to reply when four of his ships broke ranks moving forward opening fire. Their target was the Roax ship, Hague instruments told him that the Roax ship hadn't raised its shield. After several seconds of sustained fire, on the Roax ship, Hague noticed no damage was being inflicted. He was just about to order his ships to fire on the four renegade's ships when with Roax cruiser fired on all four ships at once destroying them instantly.

"All ships hold your fire," Hague yelled into his comms gear, knowing why the four cruisers had opened fire. The Captains were related to members of the council. The council since the trouble with Jeddah's arrest had sent ships to every fleet to keep watch for any signs of mutiny. They had now paid the price for disobeying his orders he smiled. "Has the Roax ship been damaged?"

"No sir, Even though I can't detect their shields, the attack failed to penetrate them at all."

"Can you identify the type?"

"No Sir. The shields they are deploying are totally different to every race's shields we have encountered." Changing frequency, Hague again talked to Jeddah.

"Sorry about the attack Jeddah. Those ships were loyal to the council."

"Not anymore Commander. Do I have your answer?"

"I want the Confederation free like everyone else. Let's see your plan first, and then we'll see. I'll bring my shuttle to the Roax ship, you can meet me there." Hague suggested.

"As you wish," Jeddah replied, wondering why he'd picked the Roax ship.

Commander Hague docked with the Katherine to be greeted by a guard of honour, made up of two men from each ship's crews. The only one not in uniform was this Captain Hayes. Hague was impressed, to say the least, as Simon gave him a rundown on his ship, pointing out changes he had carried out to make the ship stronger. Jeddah walked beside

Hague engaging him in small talk, but Jeddah could see the Commander was fascinated with Simon.

Hague had met many different races over his lifetime, for some reason this human intrigued him. It was the way he showed him weapons and shields as if they were just for defence as if he never considered the concept of conquering. The Roax had been similar in appearance, though Simon had none of their arrogant traits. He was if anything too open, too willing to help as if he saw everyone as needing his assistance.

When they arrived back at the bridge, Simon talked to his crew as if they were family. Hague could see deep respect in his crew, a willingness to do anything to please him. Moving to a small control panel, Captain Simon outlined how the portal worked. Hague looked at the panel with wonder, seeing the military application to this new form of travel. At the meeting Jeddah laid out his idea for attacking Craigure, hoping to destroy the council in one mighty blow. This he hoped would stop the populations suffering reprisals. Radon then laid out the plan to attack the Home fleet in coordinated waves.

Using the portals, they would confuse the enemy by appearing in different areas around them. It was a good plan. The only thing, was why did they need him? Their ships were more than a match for the fleet why build up numbers, in the end, he asked?

"Your people need a strong leader to free them. How would it look if a fleet made up of aliens attacked the Home planet?" Radon pointed out.

"I see. You want me to form a new government once this is over. Why not you Jeddah?" Hague asked.

"I'm a good Captain, but that's all. The people will need a strong leader; I think you will do the job well." Jeddah told him.

"How do you know I won't become a tyrant like the council?"

"We don't, but then we can always come back," Simon assured him, smiling.

CRAIGSURE

"Any word from the Northern fleet, or the ships we sent to keep watch?" The Council President asked.

"No Sir. Not since they reported the anomaly." Grom answered.

"Do you think we should alert the fleet?"

"Why Sir? Its two months travel for our ships at their fastest speed to the fleet's position, I see no urgency."

"Something feels wrong. We've had high losses in our smaller units, and now a whole fleet isn't answering. Alert the fleet!"

"As you command Sir," Grom replied, with a tone that indicated he thought it was a waste of time.

To gain the element of surprise, Simon's first portal took them just out of reach of Craigure, where Jeddah assured them they wouldn't be detected. The next portal would take them right to the edge of the Home planet allowing them to exit just after they'd opened it. Here Simon calculated the exit points for three separate portals.

Because the jumps were so close he only had to open the portals for several minutes each to allow the groups of ships to move through. By having three exit points, he hoped to completely confuse the enemy fleet that was orbiting the planet or nearby.

On board the Northern fleet flagship, Commander Hague looked out over the ships gathered. Travelling here had been quite an experience he smiled, remembering the look of horror on his crew as they entered the portal. He too had been apprehensive. He trusted Jeddah and hoped that this plan would free their people. In the back of his mind, he was worried about the alien presence, wondering if he was being set up. Now as he looked out on the gathered ships, he saw a real chance of success.

"Bring the ships to battle station, deploy shields and prepare weapons! With luck men, our people will soon be free"

He broadcast to the surrounding ships. 'God I hope this works,' he thought as in front of him the first portal appeared.

Grom had just arrived aboard the Home fleet's flagship when the ship klaxon's horn screamed out a warning. Running to the bridge, he found Commander Tarwin trying to verify what had occurred.

"What is it, Commander?" Grom asked his stomach in knots.

"A large circle has just appeared near one of our outer squadrons. We asked them to verify the sighting when they reported they were under attack by Flax cruisers. Since then we've heard nothing." The Commander told him.

"The Northern fleet reported a circle of water before communication ceased," Grom exclaimed, as a feeling of impending doom settled on him.

"I've called in all the surrounding squadrons, we'll concentrate here." The Commander informed him when without warning a circle appeared to their right. Like the rest of the crew, Grom's eyes were drawn to the circle of what appeared to be water. Beside him, Commander Tarwin too stared at the image. He was wondering what it could be, when suddenly a Roax cruiser and two Oregarthian battleships burst from it, opening fire. Close on their heels six Flax cruisers appeared, all firing at a frozen enemy.

"Engage the enemy!" Tarwin screamed into his headset. Getting over their shock the fleet reacted. The Home fleet though scattered throughout this star system still had over three hundred ships within range of the intruders. The concentrated fire made many cover their eyes as their sensor's screens overloaded and blanked outgoing white.

"What's happening?" Tarwin shouted trying to see if the ships had been destroyed, as crewmembers tried to reset their monitors.

"They are still firing Sir." A crew member yelled, as one of the Home fleet ships to his right exploded showering his shield with debris, making his ship rock violently.

"Get a damage report from the fleet," Tarwin ordered calming himself, trying to work out a course of action.

"Time seemed to slow, minutes felt like hours, as reports flooded into the flagship.

"Sir twenty ships are severely damaged, another thirty have failed to answer. There is also the squadron that saw the first circle. I believe those ships have been totally destroyed.

"What?" Tarwin stuttered stopping himself, feeling panic starting to grip him. The battle had only been going for an hour since the first circle opened, and already he'd lost over twenty percent of his fleet.

"Sir the Northern fleet is approaching from another one of those circles to our rear, they are calling on us to surrender." A crewmember shouted as the room grew quiet.

"Tell all ships to cease fire," Tarwin commanded as the order was passed on to his fleet. Amazingly as soon as his ships ceased fire, so did the enemy ships. Grom who up until this point had remained quiet broke the silence.

"Commander, what are you doing?"

"Gaining time you fool! Now shut up."Tarwin growled studying the enemy fleets. "How many ships has the enemy lost?" Tarwin asked Captain Bevain his Intelligence Officer.

"The squadron that was first engaged reported damaging several ships before being completely destroyed. Their shields were the same as ours. The Flax ships in this battle formation in front of us, have the same shields as the Oregarthian's, they have some damage though nothing major. The Roax ship doesn't even register having a shield, and even though they've been hit by a massive amount of firepower, there is no damage whatsoever."

"So what are you saying, spell it out," Tarwin ordered.

"We might be able to inflict fatal blows against the Northern fleet and the cruisers from the first attack. The ships to our front may be overwhelmed in time, but the Roax ship in time will destroy us all."

"How can it possibly keep firing like it has and defends itself, Bevain?"

"From what my people are telling me, and it's only speculation, they believe the Roax ship is somehow absorbing our laser fire and using the energy to fire back at us."

"That's impossible."

"My men agree, but they're doing it just the same."

Tarwin stood in a sea of anxious faces as Grom beside him considered his options. Grom knew he was finished if Tarwin surrendered. He'd been personally involved in too many reprisal raids on planets, which had rebelled. Next to Tarwin, he was the most senior officer here; all he had to do was remove him. Moving to the Communications station, Grom asked for a line to be open to the council. Once he told the council what was occurring, they'd have Tarwin removed giving him command.

Bevain watched Grom move to the Communications area. He could almost see his mind working, knowing what he was up to. Bevain had been an Officer in the Home fleet for most of his adult life. Like many others he had supported the hardline of the council, knowing it was the only thing that kept the hundreds of planets in line. Over the past few years, punishment handed out to the planets, had become excessive.

Any type of complaint would cause a murderous response. Even the most zealous of the Home fleet knew something was wrong, that there had to be some sort of compromise.

Catching Tarwin's eyes, Bevain looked towards Grom, as Tarwin nodded his understanding. Commander Tarwin wasn't a man to give up easily, neither was he a fool to get his men killed for no reason. Looking around the bridge, he gauged his men's reactions to what was going on. Signalling to two of his most trusted guards, he motioned for them to come closer.

"Arrest Grom, do it quietly, but do it now," Tarwin ordered, as the two soldiers swiftly covered the distance to where Grom was just about to be connected with the council. A laser pistol pushed hard into his back made Grom freeze.

"Move towards the door." One of the men whispered into his ear. "If you try to yell I'll pull the trigger." The guard continued, as Grom silently let himself be led outside. Nodding his thanks to Bevain, Tarwin picked up his headset signalling for his Comm's Officer to give him a frequency to contact the enemy ship.

"This is Commander Tarwin. Who am I talking to?"

"Commander Hague, here of the Northern fleet. As you can see we have you at a great disadvantage. Though we are prepared to fight if necessary to free our people, we would rather have you surrender."

"Why are the Oregarthian and Roax ships here?" Tarwin demanded.

"Captain Jeddah has formed an alliance with them. They have assured me that they will leave as soon as the conflict has ended."

"Jeddah is a traitor, how can you trust him?"

"Jeddah's crime was saving members of the Southern fleet from certain death. In a fair court, I think you would have trouble convicting him. The Roax ship you see out there is under the control of Captain Simon Hayes, a human. He helped Jeddah save those men after our fleet had attacked him and the Oregarthians. As you can see, he gave his advanced shields and weapons to Jeddah's ships. Jeddah now has an equal footing with the Oregarthians in a fight, that doesn't sound like a thing an enemy would do if he intended treachery." Hague pointed out.

"If I surrender the fleet I want assurances that no action will be taken against the men who were just following orders."

"That is acceptable, though the ones who ordered the atrocities against civilians, must face trial."

"Give me 6 hours to put it to my men," Tarwin replied.

"You have it Commander," Hague replied switching frequency. "Jeddah did you hear all that?"

"Yes Commander, do you think he will surrender?"

"We'll know soon enough. It might be best to pull your ships back, give them room to think." Hague suggested not wanting a hothead on either side pulling a trigger. Simon also listening gave the order to move back.

When Radon had first proposed the plan, Simon had secretly had his doubts. He worried that the number of weapons firing on their shields might overload them. Talking to Radon and Jeddah, Simon had suggested only firing when they exited the portal and after the enemy took a break from trying to fry them. It had worked although some of Jeddah's ship had received severe damage, along with both the Oregarthian ships. Simon's shields hadn't even been ruffled by the intense concentration of weaponry, but then they were totally different.

While waiting for Kate to recover, he'd had time to look at the shield program from Jeddah's ship. He'd thought about combining the two different types of shields. In theory, they should have been twice as strong as Simon's, the problem was no matter how hard he tried, he couldn't get a result.

Abandoning the project Simon went to sleep that night thinking about what to do. Somewhere between sleep and wakefulness, he'd heard the voice again from the Void, warning him that his time was coming to travel to the void. Simon having nothing to lose aired his problems with his shield. Similar to when he was overpowered by the Roax base computer, a series of programs flowed into his mind, overwhelming him.

Waking in the morning with a splitting headache, Simon at first thought he'd dreamed the whole event. Going to his computer, he quickly recorded what he remembered about the voices' solution. At first, it made no sense, so advanced was the concept. Even Simon didn't recognise the program's functional ability until he put it to the test. It was the perfect protection. Nothing could penetrate the shield while allowing the shield to absorb the incoming enemy's weapon fire.

Once it had processed the energy, it funnelled it back into its own weapons system. In other words, it used the enemies own weapons fire to fight back. Deploying the shield, he found it remained undetectable to his ship's sensors. The only thing that worried him now, was the voice he heard was real and not imagined, and that scared him.

When his ship had exited the portal near Craigure, Simon had targeted most of the ships and destroyed them, while taking the brunt of the return fire.

"What if they don't surrender?" Radon asked Simon. He had arrived for a conference with Simon and Jeddah.

"We target the ship talking to Hague. It has to be their Commander's ship; its loss would cut off the enemies' head."

"You have become hard Simon. The Simon I first met would have had second thoughts."

"You once told me that the Universe doesn't always do as I want it to. I have learnt the hard way that some diseases can't be cured, best to cut them out." Radon was about to answer when Jeddah arrived.

"How are your crewmembers and ships?" Simon asked.

"Good thanks to you. We received damage to the hull, but few casualties. Your plan of concentrating on maintaining the shield worked."

"How is it that while we were holding the shields intact, your ship managed to fire continually, while appearing invisible?" Radon whispered clearly wanting the information kept between just Jeddah, Simon and himself.

"I had help from that voice from the Void," Simon replied softly, as both Jeddah and Radon laughed thinking he was joking.

"Radon bet me you'd turn up with something new then make out you didn't do anything special," Jeddah told him. It was clear both thought he was joking. Jeddah didn't seem too worried at losing the bet.

Commander Tarwin arranged a conferences link to his fleet Captains explaining the situation. The great majority agreed, though a small percentage refused to listen. Understanding their position Tarwin gave them till the time limit expired to leave. Jeddah was the first to notice thirty ships of the Home fleet breakaway, heading to the planet. There they stopped briefly, before accelerating away leaving the Galaxy. Simon watched them leaving, he asked Commander Hague what he intended.

"I sent two of Jeddah's ships with the improved shields, to shadow them. I judge the council has fled with what is left of their loyal Home fleet ships. Once hostilities have ceased, we'll track them down; they really have nowhere to go."

Commander Tarwin at the appointed time surrendered his fleet. To his surprise, Hague left him as its Commander while the transition to an elected body to govern the planets was set up. Hague was convinced that despite the hostility between planets in the Confederation, most would vote to stay inside the system. The wars with the Oregarthians and the Roax had shown there were other races out there that in the future might re-emerge as a threat. There was also trade, many planets made their living by the exchange of goods between planets let alone the planets that constructed transport ships and military vessels.

Landing on Craigsure, Jeddah found most of the infrastructure was intact. The only thing that seemed to have been destroyed was the archive where all incriminating evidence against the council would've been located. Also as they suspected, the treasury had been looted. Sending out a message to all fleets and military units, Hague informed them of the rebellion, ordering all units to arrest the council members and the thirty ships under their control.

He then contacted the planets, having the news broadcast to the inhabitants. Hague knew there would be a lot of supporters of the council still out there, but without military support, he saw no insurmountable problems with them. During this time Simon and Radon had kept in the background letting Hague become the leader of Flax Confederation's interim government.

Four days after the end of hostilities, Jeddah and Commander Tarwin arrived aboard the Katherine for a meeting. Jeddah's two ships that were tailing the Council reported that they had met up with several ships allied to the council. They number now around fifty ships; Jeddah and Hague both considered this growing fleet a threat. Hague had suggested Tarwin as a sign of trust bring the council members back to stand trial.

Tarwin knowing how the portal worked from experience asked if he could travel aboard the Katherine with Simon, using it as his fleet flagship. Jeddah and Radon's ships plus fifty Home fleet ships would accompany them. Tarwin knew Jeddah's ships and Simon's would do the most damage, so he decided to use them as a vanguard, the rest following.

Simon agreed though he was anxious to return home. He told Tarwin this was his last mission, after this action they would leave.

Early the next morning, Hague turned up to wish them luck handing both Radon and Simon peace treaties. It was symbolic only, as the Confederation still didn't have an elected government, though both Simon and Radon were pleased.

Tarwin stood on the bridge next to Simon as he opened the portal. It was exhilarating to watch the portal take shape as Simon ordered his ship forward into the watery circle. Hague had told Tarwin that Captain Hayes was an enigma. Standing next to him on the bridge Tarwin saw what he meant, as his crew eagerly carried out his commands. Tarwin, unlike Hague, had been on a Roax cruiser before.

During the battle with the Roax fleet, Tarwin had been a junior officer on an old ship, the Deep Crystal. One of the vessels had been captured intact after the enemy had left it dead in the water, its engines damaged beyond repair. It had been a foolish move, as the ship the crew transferred to, had been hit and destroyed while picking them up. They were beautiful ships, elegantly designed and far more advanced than the Confederation's mass-produced ships.

Looking around the Katherine, Tarwin now thought the Roax ship he'd seen was an antique compared to this one. When Simon had told him he'd updated all the systems during a refit, he wasn't kidding. Though the systems consoles were similar, each one outperformed the old systems, processing data at an unbelievable speed, giving the ship a faster reaction time, in defence or offence.

He had to admit he was a little scared of this unassuming human. In such a short span of time, he has changed two totally different races, from aggressive nations at war to peaceful coexisting civilisations. Talking to Jeddah, he'd found Simon was not popular with his own race, even after saving them from the Roax. Yet through all this, he hadn't asked for anything. Tarwin told himself; that once this trouble was over, he would travel to Oregarth to learn more about this Captain Hayes.

Two days travelling in the portal brought them out on the western boundary of the Confederation. Jeddah's two ships were waiting to bring them up to date. The council's fleet was in orbit around a planet called Ardore. It was a planet where space cruisers were assembled. The council had come here to seize what armament they could, increasing their numbers. The workers and families were being held on the planet as hostages.

Deploying the Northern fleet's cruisers to intercept any breakaway units; Tarwin took the Katherine in, accompanied by Jeddah's ships and Radon's two battleships. The council ships seeing them approach formed a barrier between themselves and the planet. Tarwin wanting to avoid bloodshed opened a line.

"This is Commander Tarwin. You are asked by the Flax Federation to surrender."

"I'm amazed they didn't shoot you Tarwin. How dare you come here to detain us! Move any closer, and we kill all the workers down here on the planet." The ex-President of the military council snarled. While Tarwin had been talking, Simon had the transmission from the ex-President traced.

"He's transmitting from the main building in the shipyard," Simon told Tarwin.

"It's too easy. I know the President, he would've had his transmission bounced off another position." Tarwin answered thinking. "Can you pick up high concentrations of Dolum?" Dolum was the Federation's equivalent of gold.

"Yes, there are four ships with large amounts in their hulls," Simon replied.

"Which one is the closest to the planet?"

"Three are in formation in front. The fourth is in orbit around the planet."

"Target that one." Tarwin ordered as Simon told his crew to fire."

It was one of those defining moments that tipped the scales in the Flax Confederation's history from war to peace. As the laser beam shot out from the Katherine, it was as if time slowed, as both warring sides watched the speeding beam of pure energy striking through the sky towards the heavy cruiser with the Flax's most advanced shields. Seconds later the ship exploded the beam passing through the shield as if it was made of paper.

The enemy fleet for several seconds sat in space staring at what was left of their untouchable leader's ship. Any thought of unity fled at that moment, as the majority of ships lowered their shields, surrendering, while others tried to flee. Not one escaped as the cordon of cruisers surrounding them, opened fire on the fleeing ships. Tarwin was more than happy with two-thirds of the ships captured without casualties. The other enemy ships, in their attempt to run, were wiped out. This eliminated any further attempts to stage another coup.

Thanking Simon for his help, Tarwin transferred to one of his cruisers, wishing him well. Back in command, Simon opened a portal for Tarwin and his fleet to travel back to Craigure. Once the fleet had departed Simon again opened a portal, this time back to Oregarth.

It was a quiet return with Radon and his men returning to their village while Jeddah and his men returned to pick up their families. As the Katherine landed near the portal base, a crewmember reported a submarine in the harbour.

"Keep the shield in place," Simon ordered, studying the sub. It was small compared to most subs he thought when in a flash of recognition, he saw the name on its bow.

"It's Mike's old sub the Penelope," Simon said out loud. Seeing the sub's shields were down, Simon lowered theirs letting the crew disembark. Calling over his personal guard, he told five to stay on the bridge and keep a discreet watch on the sub. The other five he told to stay near Kate once they left the ship.

When the large cargo bay door in the side of the Katherine slid sideways, it revealed a happy group of friends and family waiting. Kate was one of the first to move forward, her relief in seeing Simon back safely, clear to everyone. Simon after kissing and hugging her to him, glanced past the joyous crowd, to the submarine. It sat at the dock, under the watchful eye of a full detachment of Oregarthian troops. Kate feeling his attention elsewhere brought him up to speed.

"Your early warning system went off four days ago. It had located a portal opening. As a precaution, we moved everyone inside the portal base's shields. The sub contacted us once they exited. It's John and Ileana, they want to talk to you urgently."

"Let's go see what they have to say." Simon smiled, as his five shadows moved with them.

John looked at the devastation around the dock area caused by the Roax attack. He'd remembered the first time he'd come here to help resettle the Roax population back to Salvation. The place had been beautiful with well-designed houses lining the shoreline. Now there was just burnt out ruins, although some had been cleared to allow rebuilding. Using his binoculars, he looked over the remains of a Roax spaceship similar to Simon's. 'This must have been the one that Mike tried to fight back from,' John surmised, as in the distance Simon's cruiser touched down. He'd been on some type of mission Kate had told them, giving little away.

'She doesn't trust us' he thought to himself. In the distance, next to the Katherine a crowd had formed. John saw the waves and hugs as crewmembers met their loved ones, everyone seemed happy to be home. About twenty minutes later, John saw a group moving towards them.

When they'd first arrived on Oregarth, they'd been told to proceed to the dock area and await Simon's return. They were also told under no circumstance were they to leave the sub. John smiled at the order. It had come from Kate herself, and

John wondered what had happened to that carefree girl he'd first met.

"How do we greet Simon when he arrives?" Ileana asked as she watched the crowd approaching.

"As you would a friend."

"He is the leader here John. He might not know it, but these people would die for him."

"Yet he's still Mike's grandson and despite the change in him, I regard him still as a friend."

"I hope you're right my love. A lot depends on how he reacts." Ileana pointed out, as Simon and Kate came aboard.

Kate too, had stressed to Simon, to act friendly, wanting no trouble with John, Mike's closest friend. Simon already suspected what the problem was, as a subdued John welcomed him.

"Hello Simon, I hear you've been off again, changing the Universe."

"No, not this time, I just went along with Radon to make sure Jeddah's people gained their freedom."

"Was Jeddah successful?"

"Yes, I have a treaty of friendship and mutual support from the interim government to our government."

"That is good news Simon, it's also one of the reasons I'm here. Quite a few of the planets are worried by your representing them without their say so."

"Yeah, I thought they seemed a bit unimpressed with my methods. Maybe they could send a representative here, and with the use of the portal system to send them to meet the different races and forge new agreements."

"I'd think they'd like that Simon. The other problem they have is your advanced shields and weaponry. The fact you've given it to your allies and not your race worries them." John told him waiting.

"The shields the Oregarthians and Flax's ship have been given to them, as a show of trust. It also helped them succeed in bringing peace to this Galaxy. In time the Gun Barrel Planets will be given this technology, as well as the ability to construct cruisers when they learn to live in peace."

"They want you to return to Salvation to answer questions about your activities and methods." Something in the way John told Simon of this demand made Kate react.

"Is there something you're not telling us, John?"

"There could be danger in returning, some fear you, Simon. Threats were made at the UN that your demise was an option." John confessed as Kate beside Simon reached across to him, taking his hand.

"It could be just talk Simon. You know how the planets like to push their points of view." Ileana added, trying to water down the threats.

"I have done nothing but try and bring peace to the different races I've met, yet my own people are threatened by me," Simon concluded sadly, thinking of Mike and the others who had paid for his meddling.

"Maybe if you invited the UN council here to see what you've achieved, that could help?" Kate put forward.

"No, I should travel back to Salvation and straighten this all out. It's what Mike would have done. There's also our wedding Kate, we both wanted to be married in New Vancouver." He added squeezing her hand.

"It's too dangerous. I'd rather be married here." Kate confessed.

"I think Simon is right Kate. Facing the council would stop the backstabbers from plotting in his absence. Most of the people believe Simon, a hero for stopping Corban. Showing them your side of the argument might stop their nonsense." Ileana suggested.

"We'll think about it," Simon said, ending the discussion. After talking for another twenty minutes about home, Simon and Kate wanting to catch up after his time away left.

"That went better than I expected," John added watching Simon and Kate leave.

"Yes he seems to genuinely care about what his people think, I just hope they listen to him," Ileana answered holding John.

"They'd better. Did you see his personal guard watching us? I think if we'd tried to touch him, they'd have killed us."

"You're right, I've never seen such loyalty, they really love him," Ileana added both amazed and worried.

"You are not going, it's too dangerous!" Radon exploded when Simon told him of his meeting with John.

"I have to clear my name my friends, they're my people."

"We know how you feel Simon, Both Radon and I have been in the same situation. But on Salvation, you will be vulnerable." Jeddah pointed out.

"While I'm there I am going to marry Kate. I thought you two plus a few of our friends here could accompany us." Simon suggested.

"That sounds better. We'll bring our ships." Radon replied.

"No, only the Katherine's going. So keep the numbers to a minimum." Simon ordered knowing what Radon was up to.

"You're right we'll bring just what we think is necessary," Jeddah answered nodding to Radon.

Giving John ten days to travel back and arrange a meeting with the UN, Simon busied himself preparing his arguments. Kate helped him, by arguing the case against him from statements made by the sub commanders. Several times he lost it, as Kate baited him with the way he commanded his ship. Sometimes he realised, that his decision had been made on his intuition rather than facts.

His targeting of the disabled ship seemed ruthless, but it was calculated, to prove to the enemy that if he didn't surrender immediately, he would be destroyed. That's why he'd let the other ship leave untouched, knowing his brutality would be passed on by the survivors. Next time he knew the enemy would surrender knowing their fate, saving lives. Like many decisions made by commanders, you had to be in their shoes to understand why they acted as they had.

Sitting with Kate with two days to go, Simon received two special visitors. Jarob recovered, arrived with Adrian who'd been looking after him on and off since the Roax attack. Both had been invited to Simon's and Kate's wedding. Jarob though excited about travelling to Salvation, voiced his concerns about security. Simon played down their worries telling them how Radon and Jeddah were looking into it. Jarob unconvinced, looked around the room secretively before pulling out a small electronic device from his pocket.

"What is it?" Simon asked as Jarob passed it to him.

"It's a personal shield. It's only good for a short time, maybe ten of your minutes, but it will stop any laser blast or projectile weapon." Jarob assured him.

"This is ingenious. How did you come up with it?" Simon asked.

"While I've been convalescing, I've been studying the portable shield you used on Salvation. It occurred to me that individual shields may have a purpose when meeting untrustworthy enemies."

"How many have you made, and what's the range?" Simon enquired.

"This one is a prototype, it's the only one. It will easily enclose one person. Two people would have to stand right next to each other." Jarob explained.

"We thought during the wedding ceremony, and at the council meeting, you could stay close to Kate. That way in an emergency you could both be protected." Adrian suggested.

"Good, take it to Kate, make sure she knows how to use it and let's keep this between us for now." Simon smiled, as his friend departed. Outside Jarob was unhappy.

"I really wanted Simon to carry it. He's the one at risk."

"Kate's clever, she'll put it to good use," Adrian assured him.

"I hope you're right; I've got a bad feeling about this trip."

"Like you did when the Roax sub arrived?" Adrian smiled.

"Hey, that took us all by surprise, smartarse." Jarob chuckled, as the two friends went to locate Kate.

THE RETURN TO SALVATION

Unlike the last time the Katherine had arrived, this time no one was waiting in ambush. Cruising leisurely towards New Vancouver, the Katherine was soon surrounded by a flotilla of small aircraft, excitedly waving as they flew past.

"Well, that's a good start?" Simon smiled, as Radon beside him remained quiet.

"Sir we're receiving a message." A crewman shouted. It was Gordon head of the UN. He personally welcomed Simon and Kate home, before cordially inviting them and their friends to an impromptu lunch at the UN capital of Harmony. This surprised Simon, having seen the destruction of the City following the attack by the Roax planes. Accepting the invitation, Simon changed course, deciding to stop at Mike's home before arriving at Harmony. Like many of the homes here, Mike's had been levelled by the Roax when they attacked.

Landing near the burnt out remains, Simon surveyed the damage. Nothing remained of the home that he'd grown up in. The only visible reminder was the charred front gate and the rough line of the concrete walls. Walking through the ruins, Simon looked for any memento that might have survived the fire. Unfortunately, nothing remained, leaving him empty.

"Let's go, Simon. It's no good thinking about what's passed." Kate told him, reboarding, he signalled to the helmsman to proceed to Harmony.

Coming in over the city, Simon saw a huge amount of rebuilding had taken place. Landing in a prearranged area, Simon surrounded by his bodyguard went down the boarding ramp, to be met by President Gordon.

"Thank you for coming Simon, I can assure you you've done the right thing in returning," Gordon told him.

"It's good to be back." Simon smiled, as Ileana and John came forward.

"Good to see you again Simon. I've arranged for Kate's parents to travel here from New America, with some of their friends and family. They were surprised to hear Kate was getting married as they haven't heard from her for some time." John pointed out.

"My God, with all that's happened, I haven't called them," Kate admitted crestfallen.

"I'll take you to them, while the men talk and eat." Ileana smiled as they left together.

"Bloody hell. I haven't been to see her father either,' Simon said out loud, making some of the crew chuckles, as they made ready to travel to the function.

Of course, not all the crew left the ship. Radon and Jeddah had brought as many extra soldiers as the ship would hold including several armoured vehicles like the type Simon had travelled with when he first met the Oregarthians.

"Where'd they come from?" Simon asked.

"We will need transport. These vehicles carry a great many people." Radon replied defensively.

"Okay, you win this time. It might also be best to maintain a force around the ship as well, just in case." Simon suggested Radon nodded his agreement smiling.

"I will stay here. You don't need me to help you eat." Jeddah pointed out, having already arranged it with Radon.

"Okay, you're in command Jeddah, let's get going," Simon told them climbing into the first vehicle.

Radon stayed next to Simon as they drove towards the reception. Simon he noticed, seemed surprised by the crowds that lined the road, waving to them as they passed. The Oregarthian and Flax soldiers seemed at first uncomfortable with people waving and cheering, having never experienced it before. In the end, they waved back, enjoying the welcome.

In the centre of the city outside the UN council building that was being rebuilt, stood a large marquee. It had been erected in a large plaza surrounded by new gardens. Simon remembered this area as once being filled with stores. Obviously they'd been destroyed during the attack.

Dismounting, Simon followed by Adrian and Jarob moved towards the huge marquee. Here he was introduced to members of the council and the ambassadors from the different planets that made up the Gun barrel planets. Like most politicians, it was hard to judge what they were thinking. Most seemed friendly, though some seemed put out to be here. Turning, Simon noticed Radon hadn't entered.

"Where is Radon?"

"He's decided to stay with his men. He said the crowd made him feel claustrophobic." Jarob answered. Simon knew the real reason was that Radon didn't trust the people here, but let it go, he just nodded to Jarob instead. The night became a blur of faces. The New America ambassador was unusually chatty talking about the coming wedding of one of their citizens to Simon. He asked if shortly Simon would be visiting New America. Simon candidly told him he was yet to talk to Kate's father, something always done in the old days. The ambassador assured him he could arrange a visit to their embassy in New Vancouver where they could meet. Simon thought him a little too eager.

Answering that he'd think on it, Simon broke away from the ambassador seeking out Gordon. Asking Gordon's advice on the matter, he was surprised when Gordon told him bluntly to keep away from all the embassies.

"Once you enter their compound you are on their soil. They could arrest or imprison you, and there was nothing the other planets or the UN could do." Gordon pointed out.

"What do you suggest?"

"Get them to meet you here, its neutral ground, and I'd be happy to arrange it." Gordon volunteered.

"Thank you but wouldn't that affect the council's outcome?"

"They've already made up their minds on that," Gordon whispered moving away. Simon watched him go, wondering if the head of the UN had just warned him his trial was fixed.

Kate nervously waited for her parents in the lobby of a hotel in the New America compound. Unlike Simon, she could enter without risk of arrest though she still had to watch herself. Ileana, sat next to her smiling at the passing people, her thoughts masked.

"I hope this goes okay?" Kate confided in Ileana as they sat waiting.

"Don't worry. I think they'll be impressed with your choice." Ileana smiled.

"Yes, he's certainly been busy."

"Is Simon okay?" Ileana said softly watching Kate.

"I know you have your doubts Ileana, but I can assure you Simon's heart is in the right place."

"Yes, it's just that it scares me how much he's achieved in such a short time," Ileana confessed her mask removed.

"It frightens me to death too Ileana. Though he's managed to change the Galaxy, we're in from two warring nations to two races at peace. But there's something else," Kate whispered looking around. "A race called 'The First' talk to him when he's asleep. At first, I thought he imagined it, but they also give him information. It scares me." She confided.

Ileana's eyes grew wide at Kate's confession. In her race's early history she remembered talk of 'The First'. They were supposedly, an advanced race, which settled the known universe. She like many thought it was just folklore, now she wondered if she had proof the ancient race may still exist. She was just about to ask Kate if she knew anything more when a middle-aged couple appeared at the door. Kate spotting them, jumped to her feet, running to them.

"It's been a long time daughter." Kate's father Bill told her, hugging his girl. Her mother Linda then took his place.

"Well you're the talk of our planet Kate where's this madman or hero who wants to marry you?" Bill smiled.

"He's meeting with the UN president at the moment, trying to work out what all the fuss is about." She answered trying to make light of the situation.

"He seems to do whatever he likes Kate, does he treat you okay?" Linda asked.

"He was prepared to fight a war to free me, mum, I'd say that answers that question."

"Yes, the Roax seizing this planet was a bad thing. We didn't know till we arrived here that you'd been taken, prisoner.

On our planet news seems a little vague about what exactly happened here." Bill whispered, looking around.

"Funny you whispering dad. Simon always saw a problem with each planet trying to dominate the others. I was once like you, scared to see another view of the situation. Why should we be frightened to speak out?"

"Because we have laws to enforce our way of life, that's why." A voice boomed out behind her. Turning around, Kate found two plainclothes men staring at her.

"We still have freedom of speech in New America don't we?" Kate spat out, angry at their intrusion.

"You are on New American soil while you're in our embassy, you'd better remember that." One of the men snarled moving in close. Bill swiftly moved between his daughter and the two men as Ileana raised her hand for them to stop

"Are you prepared for war, my friends? If one hair is touched on her head, her future husband would level New America to a barren wasteland in seconds." Ileana warned the two men stopped as if hitting a wall. "Now leave us!" Unsure both men stood staring defiantly, before retreating, throwing a parting comment.

"We'll see how tough your future husband is soon enough." One of the men shouted, the other chuckling.

"Thank you, Ileana, for a moment there I thought they were going to arrest me," Kate admitted.

"I was bluffing Kate. I suggest we take your parents for a walk outside of this compound." Ileana suggested with a tremor in her voice, wondering what the man had meant by his comment.

Once outside Kate asked her parents were they really happy on New America. Both seemed reluctant to answer, in the end, Bill confessed they'd come under a lot of pressure since Simon put down the Roax uprising. Linda told them how government men had visited them several times, to make sure they insisted Simon visited their home on New America.

It appeared the government-backed papers had run a scare campaign, aligning Simon Hayes' relationship with alien races as a direct threat to their sovereignty. Many articles had been printed giving the sub commander's impressions of Simon's huge fleet and the danger he represented.

New America like the other planets had introduced conscription doubling their armed forces. Bill believed that each planet had secretly sent large armadas through the portal; they now waited on Salvation, to see what happened at the trial. Bill pointed to a bag he carried given to him by the ambassador. They'd told him to give it to Simon telling him it was an official letter from their President, warning Simon to surrender his ship to the UN authorities.

Both Ileana and Kate showed dismay at the growing fear that misinformation was causing. Ileana suggested Kate warn Simon.

"No he can't see the danger, but I know who will." She smiled picking up her communicator. "Radon, it's Kate."

Radon at the time of Kate's call was sitting with Simon's bodyguard near their armoured vehicles. He knew he should've been inside, but he couldn't handle the fake smiles of the people who greeted him. He was also worried about the security here. Instead, he'd left the close screening of Simon to Adrian and Jarob, who didn't seem to mind the politics of the humans. When his comm gear buzzed, and Radon saw it was Kate, he raised his hand bringing immediate silence to his men.

His facial expression said it all, as, with a simple hand gesture, Simon's bodyguard swiftly moved into the marquee locating Simon. While this was occurring, Radon spoke one word out loud, a code word to get Kate. Jeddah on the Katherine received the code from one of Radon's men. Hitting the battle station button the crewmembers outside raced to the ship, as weapons swung back and forth searching for danger. The crowd of people gathered for a glimpse of Simon scattered, all sensing something was wrong.

As soon as everyone was aboard, the Katherine rocketed into the sky, flying towards New Vancouver. Ileana and Kate had taken an hour to travel by hover car to New Vancouver from Harmony; the Katherine arrived in five minutes. Locating Kate by a beacon Radon had placed in her purse, Jeddah had the ship hover over her while a shuttle was sent to pick her up. Bill and Linda at first were taken aback, as Oregarthian and Flax troops poured from the shuttle, surrounding them.

Kate was just calming them down, when a laser beam shot out from one of the surrounding buildings, knocking her from her feet. Shocked, the soldiers ran to her fearing the worst, only to find they couldn't touch her, as she was encased in a shield. Telling them, she was okay she got to her feet, as Katherine's laser cannons fired, pulverising the building where the shot had come from. Ushered inside, Kate, her parents and Ileana sat down while the shuttle rapidly climbed to the Katherine,

"That was close." Kate smiled dropping the shield.

"I can't believe you're still alive," Bill said wiping tears from his eyes, hugging her.

"Yes, I was lucky. One of Simon's friends invented this personal shield for our wedding. I turned it on when I had trouble with those two men."

"Lucky you did Kate. Whoever fired that shot, meant to kill you." Ileana shivered a premonition of doom settling over her.

"My God, he named his ship after you!" Bill exclaimed looking past her at the window, as they flew past the bow of the Katherine.

Once inside, the ship's cargo bay was pressurised allowing them to enter the ship. Bill and Linda silently moved along behind Ileana and Kate as they conversed with the crew. It was clear to them that Kate was held in high regard by these soldiers, as they were led into the command centre. There, Jeddah introduced himself and key members of the crew to them, welcoming them aboard. He had heard about the attempt on her and was far from happy.

"We should destroy their entire compound." He suggested, waiting for her okay.

"No, we can't be sure it was sanctioned by the New America's Government. It could've been anyone." Kate warned him, her parents silently fearing their people were responsible.

"Anyway this is no welcome for your parents, let me show them around," Jeddah said moving on, having already contacted Radon about the incident.

Bill who was a programmer, was overwhelmed by the advanced equipment running every facet of the ship. He'd seen diagrams of the Roax ship, but seeing it up close was entirely different.

"She's a beautiful ship Jeddah," Bill said as Jeddah showed him around the bridge.

"Yes our ships although advanced, seem roughly made next to the Roax designed ships.

"I've seen Roax equipment from the settlers who came to Salvation, but yours seem to have been improved. Did you do this?" Bill asked.

"No, all improvements to this ship and ours, came from Simon. Both Kate and Simon are special to both my race and the Oregarthian's." Jeddah said softly, Bill taking his meaning.

"On my planet, they painted him as a madman, a danger to our race."

"Do you think my people and the Oregarthians, who were sworn enemies, would both trust him if what you say was true?"

"No you're right, but do you think my daughter is safe with him?"

"That is a hard question to answer. He risked everything to save her, yet Kate was kidnapped because Simon is feared and she was viewed as his Achilles heel. On Oregarth she is in no danger. Here on Salvation or on your planet, it's another matter entirely." Jeddah told him moving away. Bill watched him go, liking the alien who had been painted as an enemy of the human race. Looking across at his daughter as she talked to her mother and Ileana, Bill realised the decision wasn't his to make.

Simon had just finished talking to the ambassador from New America, when his personal guard rushed in, surrounding him.

"What is going on?" He asked as Adrian and Jarob joined him.

"Kate contacted Radon there is danger here, we must leave now." One of his guards warned him, as the group moved towards the entry. They were halfway to the door when Gordon rushed to his side asking what was happening. Simon's answer was cut short as an explosion erupted at the back of the Marquee, where Simon had been standing earlier.

Confusion filled the marquee, as screams of the hurt and dying filled the air. The gathered dignitaries in a state of panic, rushed for the exits, trying to get away from the danger. Several of Simon's bodyguards hit by shrapnel were knocked to the ground, as well as Gordon.

"Grab them, leave no one behind!" Simon ordered to his men, as in the entrance UN soldiers flooded in, racing to Gordon. Taking Gordon from Simon's soldiers, they carried him outside, while others attended the other guests injured by the bomb.

"We've got to get away Simon," Jarob yelled supporting Adrian who'd been hit as well. Nodding his understanding, Simon ordered his bodyguard to carry their wounded outside. When the blast occurred, Radon formed his men into a circle. He was just about to take a squad inside to find Simon when Simon's group emerged from the marquee.

Waving to Simon to hurry, his eyes were drawn to a line of about forty UN soldiers approaching from the hill above the marquee. Two UN officers, who had been talking to Radon earlier, also saw their approach. Not recognising them, one officer called for them to identify themselves only to be shot down. Simon's entire bodyguard dived for cover, pulling Simon and the others down, as a vicious firefight erupted. Radon's soldiers immediately opened fire, as the surviving UN officer ordered his confused men to fire on the imposters.

Whoever had planned the attack had good Intel on the location. Holding the high ground, they fired on the mass of people near the entrance. Their problem was no one had known Radon's armoured vehicles would be present. From behind the thick skins of their vehicles, Radon's soldiers poured heavy weapons fire into the imposters. Staggered by the avalanche of return fire, what was left of the group retreated, leaving their dead and wounded behind.

An eerie silence fell over the area. This was punctuated by the moans of the injured and dying. Simon lying next to Adrian and Jarob breathed a sigh of relief, glad it was over. Standing with the others, he made to move to the vehicle when he felt something hit him in the side spinning him back onto the ground. Touching his side feeling something wet, Simon stared at the red liquid that covered his hand before blacking out.

"Simon's hit!" Jarob screamed as everyone looked towards him.

"Get him aboard!" Radon shouted as Simon's bodyguard came to life carrying him to the vehicle.

Racing towards the descending Katherine, Radon looked down at his friend as his medic swiftly applied a field dressing.

"How is he?" Radon whispered

"I'm not sure Sir. It's not good." He whispered back, as Radon filled with anger and frustration, cursed himself for letting Simon come here. As the cargo doors on the ship opened, Radon told his drivers, to drive straight in, telling the ship to lift off immediately, As the doors started to close, several laser blasts hit the Katherine, making her stagger and veer of course. Her shield now deployed, she stabilised herself, as her weapons batteries, fired on positions of her attackers, flattening the area.

Adrian, his hand bandaged, found himself on the deck of the Katherine looking up at Simon's bodyguard. Like many others, he'd been knocked over by the laser blasts. One of them seeing him on the floor pulled him up. All the guards looked towards Simon, as he was loaded onto a stretcher. Adrian saw failure written on their faces.

"Simon!" Kate screamed, running through the crowd arriving at Simon's side. Sobs made her body convulse, as Jeddah and Ileana appeared holding her, as Simon was led away.

Radon gave Jeddah a complete rundown on what had occurred, guilt written on his face as well.

"All of you have nothing to be ashamed of. No one saw this coming. Simon decided to come back here, so stop blaming yourself, move on." Jeddah told Radon and the others, as the silent guards followed Simon inside. They hadn't even cleared the cargo bay, when another explosion shook the ship, throwing everyone to the deck. Jeddah getting to his feet grabbed Radon pulling him towards the door, as they both rushed to the bridge.

"What has happened?" Jeddah shouted, as the bridge crew seeing Jeddah, all tried to answer at once. Radon raising his hand to silence them pointed to the senior officer.

"There's been an explosion in the accommodation section of the ship. The hulls been breached allowing the outside air to fuel a large fire." The senior officer reported.

"Seal the area. Take the ship out to sea." Jeddah commanded as the ship leapt forward.

"What are you going to do?" Radon asked.

"We can't fight a fire in that area, there is too much combustible material. We'll take her down into the ocean, lower the shield and flood the area." Jeddah suggested. Laser fire from submarines at sea started to strafe the ship. The shield stopped any damage, but the weapons system had been damaged, stopping return fire.

"Get away from these enemy ships first Jeddah. Otherwise, we can't drop the shield." Radon pointed out as they continued on for another tense ten minutes. As the ship lost height, turbulence increased, as the ship, in the end, hit the ocean. Sinking to the bottom Jeddah swiftly scanned for enemy subs, before dropping the shield. It became deadly quiet as the crew thought about the people still trapped in the area, which was rapidly filling with water.

"Were many crewmen in that area Jeddah?" Radon asked softly.

"No, most were at their post. Unfortunately, Kate's parents were there, settling in. Someone will have to tell her." Jeddah whispered Radon speechless failed to answer.

For twenty minutes no one said anything until the fire alarm indicator suddenly stopped flashing.

"Deploy the shield, get us to the surface," Jeddah commanded his anger just held in check. "Are there any subs in the vicinity?"

"We have ten closing in on us from the direction we came from," Adrian informed him having resumed his station.

"When they're in range, give them one warning to stop. If they don't stop or respond, destroy them. Adrian, you're in charge." Jeddah growled as both he and Radon left the bridge.

When the explosion rocked the Katherine, and the hull was breached, a massive cloud of smoke burst from the ship. The smoke continued to bellow out, as the Katherine losing height, travelled out to sea. The people who'd planned the attack thought the ship was crippled.

"Have our ships chase her down and finish her." The officer in charge of the joint operation commanded.

The submarines off the coast, opened fire on the Katherine as she passed overhead. When the Katherine hit the water to the south of their position, the group of subs gave chase at full speed. When they arrived, they found the Katherine floating on the surface, still trailing smoke.

Unfortunately for them, Simon's new shield couldn't be detected, so they presumed it was damaged. When Adrian ordered them to stop, or they'd be fired on, they took it as a bluff rushing in, opening fire. Ten minutes after the attack started the ten subs or what was left of them sank to the ocean floor.

"Okay men, now that's over, let's get this ship repaired," Adrian ordered as the crew started to work out what needed to be repaired first.

Kate lay in the bed next to Simon heavily sedated. Both her parents were dead, killed in the explosion. A search of the damaged area showed the blast had occurred in her parent's cabin. After putting together what had happened, Jeddah and

Radon both came to the same conclusion, that the so-called document from the New America president was, in fact, a bomb. Kate had moaned in pain at the news, fainting, before being sedated.

"I should never have asked John to go see Simon. This would not have happened if we hadn't told Simon to come back to Salvation and plead his case." Ileana sobbed.

"Sooner or later Simon would've returned. At least you warned him there could be trouble." Radon pointed out.

"What do we do now?" Jeddah asked.

"Take them home to Oregarth, they're not safe here,"Radon answered.

"That is not possible. The ship needs major repairs."Jeddah pointed out.

"How about using the shipyards near Mike's home to the south where the fishing fleet was built? I'm sure John wouldn't mind, and you'd be safe there." Ileana suggested.

"It would do I suppose, though this ship is more complicated than a fishing trawler," Jeddah added.

"Okay, we'll head there. Ileana, you contact John and tell him what's happened, I'll take the shuttle and visit the UN. I want an explanation for what has happened." Radon barked.

All the planets in the Gun Barrel system voiced their shock and anger at the attack on the UN and Simon. Gordon recovered from his injuries, called an emergency meeting of the council condemning the attack. Who was responsible for the attack remained unknown, as the identity of the attackers couldn't be confirmed. Gordon suspected all four armed planets were involved by the size of the attack. In an unprecedented decision, Gordon demanded that all the planets withdraw military units from Salvation, instructing the UN ships to be fitted with shields and weapons immediately. It came down to his vote in the end, but it was passed, whether it happened was another matter.

Radon's arrival brought a hush to the gathered representatives. He told them that the attack was an act of war against the Oregarthians and the Flax confederation. He threatened to bring their fleets through the portal, wiping out the planets responsible. Gordon felt the fear as the gathered planets weighed up Radon's statement. He also noticed that no one got up to argue. Asking to speak alone to Radon to defuse the situation, Gordon dismissed the council.

"How is Simon?" Gordon asked.

"He's alive at the moment. If he pulls through is another matter."

"Is everyone else okay?"

"We lost thirty crewmembers and soldiers at the marquee and during the explosion on the ship. Kate's parents were also killed, by a bomb they unknowingly brought aboard."

"Poor Kate, today's events will be a heavy burden to bear."

"How are you going to deal with these rogue planets?" Radon asked.

"You heard me tell them I'm arming the UN?" Radon nodded he had. "Unfortunately it was just a bluff, as we have no way of knowing what military capacity is already here."

"We can supply you with our shield and weapons technology. That will make your ships far superior to theirs. We will also enclose the portal base with Simon's new shield. It will make it impregnable, against any future attempts at controlling it."

"Thank you, Radon. I know it doesn't mean much, but I will personally see that all allegations against Simon are dropped, and the people responsible for this attack are brought to justice."

"You're a good man Gordon. I hope everything goes well for you." Radon replied, shaking Gordon's hand and starting for the door.

"You weren't really going to wipe out their planets were you?" Gordon enquired, a little afraid of Radon's threat.

"No, I was bluffing. The people on their planets have nothing to do with their leader's complicity in this madness. But they don't know that do they." Radon smiled leaving.

Boarding his shuttle Radon waved goodbye to Gordon, as he departed. Airborne, he looked at his men seeing the suppressed anger they held following the attack on Simon. He had lied to Gordon back there about only bluffing to wipe out their planets. Given a chance he knew he would make the guilty pay for what they'd done to his friend.

John stood at the shipyard, watching the Katherine slowly drop from the sky landing in a disused dock. Like many others after the attack by the Roax, Mike had set up a makeshift home till his house was rebuilt. The Roax rebels had really done a job on Mike's harbour, levelling every home that bordered it. The only structure they had spared was the fish cannery and with it the shipyards.

When the attack on Simon had occurred in Harmony, John had been luckily outside arranging a place for him and Ileana to stay for the night. Unarmed, he'd hit the ground, keeping down till the shooting had stopped. By the time a resemblance of order had been restored Simon, and his group had left. He spent several frantic hours trying to find Ileana, eventually returning to his home and waiting anxiously. It wasn't until the next morning when Ileana had called him that he knew she had survived.

Bringing him up to date on what had happened, Ileana asked if Radon could use the docks. Telling her it would be okay, John rang as many people that he knew who would be needed to help repair the ship. He also called the local hospital secretly having a medical team brought to the cannery on the presumption that someone working there was hurt and trapped.

As the ship landed, John watched the side doors slide open. Soldiers and armoured vehicles streamed out, taking up positions around the dock area. One vehicle came straight towards John, pulling up next to him. Ileana, jumping from its side ran to him. Holding him tightly, she began to cry telling him about Kate and Simon.

"It will be okay love, don't worry." He assured her. Radon was also on the vehicle. Hopping down he looked at the people gathered, before walking to John.

"Do you trust them?"

"They're all friends of Mike and Simon. Of course, I trust them." John shot back.

"Thank you for your help John, it's just hard to trust any of your people, after what has occurred."

"I understand Radon. How's Simon?"

"Not good. The sooner we leave for home the better." Radon replied.

"Well let's get to it then," John answered signalling for his people to start.

Replacing the metal was their first problem. The ships alloy was not known to the engineers, meaning they'd have to make do with what they had. Patching the hole with a lightweight aluminium alloy seemed the best idea. Radon explained that when they got back, they could use plate from the ship destroyed by the Roax. Although it had nearly blown in half, large pieces of the outer skin of the ship had survived.

With a bit of thought and a little guesswork, the welders had managed to weld the patches to the outer hull. It wasn't pretty, but it did allow the crew to pressurise the ship. The inside was another matter. It would take some time to repair the living quarters. Radon settled for just making the ship liveable enough to travel home.

While preparations were made to leave, the surgical unit arrived from their local hospital. John explained what was going on as the surgeon nodding his understanding, went aboard to examine him. Simon's remaining bodyguards, kept a close eye on the unknown surgeon and his team, while their own doctor observed. Jeddah who had remained on the bridge kept Radon, who patrolled outside continuously, up to date on repairs, while monitoring the early warning sensors.

John and Ileana sat quietly outside the ship. They could taste the tension in the air, as the Katherine sat defencelessly. They both felt somehow responsible for the whole mess. Radon, seeing them sitting there, walked over.

"It was destiny, my friends. There was nothing you could've done to change what occurred."

"I thought it was just talk, I didn't think we'd sunk so low," John confessed.

"I at first thought the same of your people John. Yesterday when we arrived, and the crowds cheered us, I realised the problem is the ones who covert power not the everyday people. Maybe now the UN is taking a more hands-on approach, something good will come out of this misery." Radon suggested, as his headset crackled. "The surgery is finished we can see Simon."

Jeddah was waiting there when the three of them arrived. His face told it all, saving them asking.

"How bad?" Radon finally asked.

"He is paralysed, unable to move. The doctor gives him six months." Jeddah stammered out his emotions bare. No one said anything for some time, as they each came to grips with the pain they felt.

"Who's going to tell Kate?" Jeddah asked apparently not wanting the job.

"Let's give her some time to recover, she's been through enough."Ileana pointed out. As they continued to sit in silence, Simon's doctor approached Radon.

"He's asking for you, Sir. Please be quick." The doctor suggested moving away. Looking at the others unable to say anything, Radon got up walking slowly into the operating theatre.

Simon lay upon the table, looking as if a statue had been laid down. There was no sign of movement; even his eyes wide open, didn't blink. Moving up to the table, Radon saw a tube entering his side pumping air into his lungs that barely moved.

"Is that you Radon?" Simon gasped, his voice tied to the rhythm of the oxygen pump.

"Yes, my friend I'm here," Radon whispered.

"Take me in the Katherine to the void." He croaked out choking. Radon held him as his body convulsed. He continued to hold him, for several minutes until the shudders stopped.

"I don't understand Simon why would you want to go there?"

"The voice told me to."

Coming out of Simon's room, Radon still wondered what Simon had meant. He was swamped by questions from the others. Telling them what Simon had said, left them all speechless.

"What do we do then?" Radon asked breaking the silence.

"What he told you to do!' Exploded a voice from the door, as Kate still in a hospital gown stumbled into the room. Jeddah being the closest ran to her, supporting her until she reached a chair.

"Kate we can't just take him there because he thinks he heard a voice," Jeddah told her softly wondering how recovered she was.

"He knows what he's doing Radon. I heard the voice too." She confessed, explaining.

Earlier that day as she lay in the infirmary heavily sedated, she saw Simon being wheeled out for surgery. Unable to move, she prayed for God to help Simon. It was then that the voice came. It told her Simon was paralysed; his only hope was for both of them to go to the void. They promised to help him, although there would be a price. Confused, she'd asked if he was God. He'd chuckled, saying no. She then asked why it was so important for them both to go the void. The voice replied that a test was coming, for both them and the Universe.

A look of concerned disbelief crossed their faces.

"He is paralysed, isn't he? How did I know, if the voice was not real? I believe Simon and my future will be determined by the trip to the void, that's why we must go." Kate told them.

"I for one believe her," Jeddah spoke up, before explaining.

When Radon told Gordon he could have Simon's new shield for the portal base, Jeddah had his chief programmer try and install Simon's software, from the Katherine. He said he couldn't even work out the program let alone understand how it worked. He said the program worked on a different principle to everything he'd been taught. In the end, Jeddah had their existing shield, downloaded to the base. They weren't as good as Simon's new one, but far superior to anything the humans had.

"That is why I think we should take him there; in some ways, I think it is his destiny," Jeddah confessed.

"Do you remember when we first asked about the new shield, he'd said the voice told him, we both laughed thinking he was joking?" Radon smiled, remembering.

"Then I say we should do what he asked," Ileana suggested helping Kate back to bed.

The Katherine repaired, rose from the docks, turning south for the portal base. Gordon waited on one of the UN's newly armed subs. Landing the Katherine next to it, Gordon came aboard, going to Simon. His grief was evident when he saw Simon's condition. Wishing him well he quickly left a broken man. Wiping tears from his eyes, he awkwardly said goodbye to Simon's friends.

"If it's the last thing I do, I'll find the ones responsible and bring them to justice." He promised, hugging Kate before departing.

"He's a good man, he'll find them," Kate told the others as the Katherine rose into the air, before entering the portal.

Behind them Gordon cleared the portal base, turning on Simon's shield remotely.

"That I pray stops anyone from ever entering here and interfering with the portal system again." He declared, smashing the remote on the rail, before throwing the remains into the ocean.

On Oregarth, the news of Simon's condition was received with an outpouring of anguish. Many left flowers at the Katherine, fearing the future without their protector. Radon and Jeddah assured them that all was not lost. Simon had laid the groundwork for peace throughout their Galaxy; it was up to them to honour it. Following Simon's wishes, his friends boarded the Katherine again, as the whole population boarded their ships to accompany him.

Three days of travelling through the portal brought the fleet out near its destination. Jeddah being cautious, had them exit a day's journey short of the void. Travelling through the day, Radon on the bridge watched as the boundary with the void grew closer. He still feared this area, wondering if Simon was being misled.

Coming to a stop, Simon was moved to the bridge. Kate sat by his side, as their friend's one at a time said their goodbyes to them both. Radon last, stood beside his friend gripping his hand unable to say a final gesture to him.

I will come with you, my friend." Radon offered, holding Simon's hand.

"No Radon, they said only Kate and I could enter. I ask you to look after our friends until we return." Simon croaked out, Radon nodding speechless moved away. It was an emotional time for them all; it was hard to believe the actual short time they had all spent together, considering what had been achieved. In the end, they all moved to the cargo area, boarding their shuttle.

Kate thanked them all, tears running down her face, as she pressed the door switch, sealing it. Moving to the bridge, she opened the outside door as the shuttle nosed out before engaging its engines.

Ileana and John like everyone else stood watching as the Katherine grew smaller as they docked with Jeddah's command ship. It was only then that Ileana and John noticed Radon wasn't there.

"Where's Radon?" John asked.

"He's on the Katherine with Simon's bodyguards, they refused to leave Simon and Kate alone," Jeddah told them, having promised Radon he wouldn't tell anyone until it was too late.

"The voice said for Simon and Kate to come alone." Ileana pointed out.

"Well as the humans say 'that's tuff luck," Jeddah answered.

"The First as they're called might kill them," Adrian added, wishing he'd known because he would've stayed too.

"I said the same thing to Radon and the ten bodyguards, they all laughed. Radon said they'd all be dead already without Simon so what difference did it make." Jeddah smiled.

"Does Kate know they're aboard?" John inquired.

"No, they'll remain in hiding, only showing themselves if there is trouble," Jeddah replied, wishing he too had stayed.

On board the Katherine, Kate opened the portal letting Jeddah and the fleet leave for Oregarth. Once they'd departed, Kate engaged the engines as the ship moved slowly forward, gathering speed.

"Thank you, Kate for everything." Simon groaned, his voice affected by the compressor.

"I wouldn't have had it any other way my love." She answered kissing him on the lips before moistening his eyes.

"Do you think it was worth it?"

"Yes, Simon of course it was. Look at what you achieved, millions if not billions of people of different races are living in peace thanks to you. And somehow I doubt that it's over, remember you promised me a marriage." Kate smiled holding his hand, as the ship travelled onwards.

On board, the Katherine, Radon and his men set up a place to stay at the rear of the ship. They had secretly hidden food and water to last them for months in this area before they departed.

"Shouldn't we tell Kate we're here? It's too late to do anything about it now." One of the bodyguards suggested.

"No, we might upset her. Better to stay hidden." Radon answered, remembering his last meeting with Jeddah on Oregarth.

Radon, before they left, had called a meeting with Jeddah and all of the ship's Captains, he told them of his plan to stowaway. Jeddah at first had been adamant that he wanted to go too. He had talked him out of it by pointing out he had family while Radon didn't. Of course, the Captains all wanted to go with him as well, causing quite an argument. In the end, he allowed Simon's remaining 5 bodyguards, plus 15 volunteers including two officers, to be drawn by lot. He then asked his senior officer Captain Jaidus to command in his absence. He was surprised when Jaidus nominated Jeddah to command all forces while Radon was gone. Jeddah at first was stunned having thought he and his people would have to soon leave to find a planet of their own or return to the Federation.

"But I'm not Oregarthian," Jeddah answered unsurely.

"We Oregarthians have always seen you as our second in command to Radon. We see no reason why we all can't live here in peace with you in command. It has worked so far, and we trust you to protect our people." Jaidus put forward getting support from the Oregarthians officers and the Flax officers.

"Thank you." Was all Jeddah replied, visibly moved by their faith in him?

Once the meeting was over, Radon had taken Jeddah to examine the portal, Simon had built on Oregarth. This was the replacement one for the one destroyed by the Roax before he built the present one on the Katherine. Jarob explained its abilities to Jeddah who was now in command. It gave him some limited travel options in Simon's absence.

"Well, at least we can travel to Salvation or the Federation that's something." Jeddah pointed out, certain that given time Jarob would add other destinations once their locations were established.

"Thank you for accepting the command Jeddah. I feel safer knowing you're here." Radon confessed as they left the portal base.

Just don't be gone too long, my friend. You know how important you and Simon are to us." Jeddah replied as they walked back to the Katherine.

The sound of footsteps in the corridor, made Radon forget the past. He signalled for everyone to be quiet. Everyone froze, as someone could be heard moving along the corridor getting closer. The footsteps stopped, as a loud bang on the door, resonated through their room. No one said anything, all looked to Radon for guidance.

"Radon!" Kate's voice sounded. "He's not happy with you and your soldiers for coming with us. Are you going to open the door?" Kate demanded, sounding none too happy.

"Shit!" Radon whispered, using an old Earth word that sounded appropriate at this moment, he then walked to the door.

THE END OF BOOK ONE.

PLANET NEW AMERICA
THE YEAR 2999

"Did they see you come here, son?" Johan asked his boy, as he bandaged his bleeding arm.

"No I don't think so dad, but they killed the other boys with me." He moaned, as he fought against the pain that throbbed from the burn mark on his arm and the thought of losing his friends.

"I've warned you before about going out at night looking for food on the plains son. Why didn't you listen to Benjamin?" His father said more in fear than anger.

"Mum's sick and the rest of our small community are starving. We all thought we could find something near the old abandoned naval base."

"Look, son, I know you meant well, but the Overmen have satellites everywhere, you know that."

"We were wearing camouflage suits with infrared jammers, they shouldn't have seen us." Benjamin pointed out. His father stared at his 15-year-old son, not knowing what to say when a thought came to him.

"Did all your friends who planned this raid go?"

"Yes, although Tomas, the son of the foreman at the grain silos became sick. He went home just before we left. He was lucky."

"Yeah, he sure was," Johan admitted, hiding his thoughts, as he remembered the past.

Since the uprising against the government had failed twenty years ago, there'd been no peace, only bloodshed. The Overmen as they were known, enforced the curfews stopping anyone from leaving their homes after dark. Food was in short supply, with many of the grain producing areas devastated, in the reprisals that followed the attempted coup.

Johan himself had fought in the failed coup, to try and bring democracy back from the years of military rule. They'd failed miserably, their whole plan betrayed by a spy planted inside their organisation. The Junta had come down hard. Using their spaceships, they had bombarded the planet, destroying whole countries, in their insane show of force. Cowered by the overwhelming reprisals, Johan like many others had deserted, going home. Now he lived in fear that someone might give him up for a handful of food from the Junta.

Seeing the sun starting to appear over the hills to the north, Johan prayed the Overmen would be happy with the children they'd killed. The sound of an approaching airship made him curse; knowing they'd tracked his son home.

"Hide kids! Get into the bomb shelter!" He yelled. As Benjamin lifted the heavy reinforced door in the lounge room floor, Johan rushed to his bedroom. Picking up his wife from the bed, he carefully carried her to the lounge room, before walking down the stairs into the now open bomb shelter. Placing her on a makeshift bed he told Marline, his daughter, to look after her mum. Returning upstairs, he found Benjamin charging a laser pistol.

"Get downstairs with your mother and sister now!" Johan ordered.

"No dad this is my fault! I'm staying with you." His father made to reply, but the words didn't come. He was proud of his son, for what he'd done. He now stood before him as a man.

"Okay, you watch the rear and don't fire unless I say." He smiled, taking the second pistol. He'd just closed the bomb shelter doors when a mind-numbing roar erupted in front of him. The aircraft had fired a blast twenty paces in front of the house. The explosion ripped the front door off its hinges, sending it cannoning into Johan. He was thrown back across the room, landing heavily on the floor.

Benjamin shaking, fearing the worst, ran from the rear of the house. He found his father lying hurt on the floor near the crumpled front door. Checking his wrist, Benjamin felt a pulse knowing his father was luckily just concussed. He had a savage cut on his right leg and another on his forehead but they in time would heal. As if sensing his son's touch, Johan opened his eyes slowly taking in his surroundings. Outside a voice boomed over the countryside.

"You inside the house come outside and surrender, or we'll burn your home to the ground. You have one minute to comply." Benjamin, looked at his father, trying to find the words, nothing came. Standing, he silently walked to the crumbled remains of the front door.

"Don't go, son! Help me up, I'll go instead." His father cried out. Trying to stand, he grabbed onto a chair for support, before falling backwards, onto the floor.

"I love you dad," Benjamin answered, walking outside. Terrified he hesitantly stepped out into the open, stopping in the middle of the dirt road, which ran past their home. Dropping his pistol, he raised his hands above his head. Looking up at the Overman's ship, Benjamin felt a sense of peace settle over him, as he awaited his fate.

On board the Atlanta, Captain Ryan looked at Benjamin on the ship's screen. The computer using facial recognition software compared him to the image of the youth taken earlier, who'd managed to escape from the old naval base. They'd been clever in evading all the security measures around the base. Their mistake was someone loyal to the Junta had betrayed them.

"It's him, Captain, there can be no doubt," His second in command Hester Dom, confirmed, waiting for the order to fire.

"He's a brave one, that's for sure." the Captain smiled. Ryan personally would have let the kid go. The area's population was starving, what else did the Junta expect people to do, just die? Unfortunately, that wasn't his call and orders were orders. He was just about to tell his bloodthirsty second in command to open fire when the ship's sensors sounded a warning.

"What's going on?" He shouted, as the automatic defence system, deployed their shield.

"A large object is moving towards us at high speed underwater." The operator of the sensor array replied.

"Where did it come from?" The Captain asked.

"It appeared in the area where the portal used to open." The same crewman answered stopping all chatter.

"That area is off limits, no one uses the portal." Lieutenant Dom pointed out.

"It appears someone has Dom. Go to battle stations. Inform High Command we have a breach." The Captain ordered.

Standing below them, Benjamin's quiet moment was interrupted, as out of the ocean to his right, a huge ship broke the surface. With a heart-pounding roar, the ship rose into the sky, moving directly towards Benjamin's village. The ship was massive. Brilliant white in colour, it shone in the first rays of the morning light. Benjamin shading his eyes saw the ship resembled the Star cruisers the Junta used.

He knew from school that the design for these ships had come from a race called the Roax. The remains of this advanced race were now living on a planet called Salvation, colonised by people from Earth. Their home planet New America had once been linked to Salvation, by a Portal device. His own planet's population had passed through Salvation on their way to colonise this planet. Many years ago the portal had been destroyed, meaning space travel by ships was their only means of travelling in space.

Benjamin had once seen a Star cruiser up close. It had stopped at the village, to pick up grain, which was being sent to one of New America's Satellite planets. Looking at this ship now, he realised how unimpressive their ships were, compared to this one. It to him seemed to radiate power. Watching it, he felt the thumping noise in his chest, as its engines reverberated through the very ground he stood on. For some reason, he felt a premonition of coming death from the mystery ship.

As if the Cruiser had finally noticed the other ship, it came to a stop. Turning slightly, it faced the Overman's ship. Standing there in the open, Benjamin couldn't help comparing the Overman's ship to the new arrival. Box-shaped, painted in drab camouflage brown and green colours, the Overman's ship was nothing more than a flying gun platform. Built to keep the population inline, it had the aerodynamics of a flying brick. He'd always thought the Overmen ships massive and unstoppable. Now he saw them as rabid dogs, confronted at last by a lion.

Looking closer, he saw the cruiser had writing on its bow. Studying it, shielding his eyes for a better look, recognition hit him like a hammer. Remembering his history lessons, he dropped to his knees in astonishment and fear.

"The Katherine" he murmured, a smile slowly spreading across his face.